Author Note

I've always loved Westerns, and when I started writing historical romance Western settings were the natural choice. The idea behind *His Mail-Order Bride* is simple: a young woman on the run assumes another woman's identity—an action that lands her in trouble and leads to difficult moral choices.

Charlotte Fairfax is a complex heroine. Born to wealth but then deprived of every security she is accustomed to, she needs to evolve from a naïve, innocent heiress into a resourceful young woman who is able to support herself in the frontier region.

In contrast with Charlotte, Thomas Greenwood is a straightforward hero. He has had a tough life, filled with rejection and hard work. All he wants is a woman of his own. A wife. A companion. Someone to love. Someone to help with the chores.

When the dainty, whimsical Charlotte turns up instead of the sturdy mail-order bride Thomas has been expecting his life turns into chaos—in more ways than one.

In the opening scene of *His Mail-Order Bride* you'll meet Charlotte's sisters: the feisty, daring Miranda and the clever but highly strung Annabel. They deserve their own stories, which have become a trilogy—The Fairfax Brides. And at the end of Annabel's story comes a solution to the family feud that has forced the girls to flee to the West.

I hope you enjoy *His Mail-Order Bride* and will want to go on to read Miranda and Annabel's stories.

HIS MAIL-ORDER BRIDE

Tatiana March

Published in Great Britain 2017
by Mills & Boon, an imprint of HarperCollins*Publishers*
1 London Bridge Street, London, SE1 9GF

© 2017 Tatiana March

ISBN: 978-0-263-92568-5

Our policy is to use papers that are natural, renewable and
recyclable products and made from wood grown in sustainable
forests. The logging and manufacturing processes conform to the
legal environmental regulations of the country of origin.

Printed and bound in Spain
by CPI, Barcelona

Before becoming a novelist **Tatiana March** tried out various occupations, including being an accountant. Now she loves writing Western historical romance. In the course of her research Tatiana has been detained by the US border guards, had a skirmish with the Mexican army and stumbled upon a rattlesnake. This has not diminished her determination to create authentic settings for her stories.

Books by Tatiana March

Mills & Boon Historical Romance

The Fairfax Brides

His Mail-Order Bride

Mills & Boon Historical *Undone!* eBooks

The Virgin's Debt
Submit to the Warrior
Surrender to the Knight
The Drifter's Bride

Visit the Author Profile page at millsandboon.co.uk.

For my sister,
who likes sea shanties.

Chapter One

Boston, Massachusetts, May 1889

Charlotte Fairfax stood on the balcony at Merlin's Leap, her hands clasped around the stone balustrade. Down in the restless ocean, waves crashed against the cliffs with an endless roar. Spray flew up in white columns. A chilly mist hung in the air. In the distance, the lighthouse at Merlin's Point, not yet lit up for the night, silhouetted against the dark bank of clouds.

Morbid thoughts filled Charlotte's mind. A hundred years ago her ancestor, Merlin Fairfax, had leaped to his death from this very spot. Had he been pushed, as his widow claimed? Had his younger brother murdered him? Rumors persisted even today, suggesting that he had.

Did cruel nature pass down through generations?

Was one branch of the Fairfax family tainted with evil?

How far might Cousin Gareth go to get his hands on her inheritance?

A tap on her shoulder made Charlotte jolt and cry out in alarm. She whirled around, fear throbbing through every muscle. Her shoulders sagged with relief when she saw her sister Miranda.

"You scared me." Her words came on a nervous sigh. "I didn't hear you open the door."

"Come inside," Miranda said. "We need to talk."

Charlotte followed her sister into the upstairs parlor that overlooked the ocean. Through the wide bay window, she could see a flock of seagulls dipping and wheeling over the foaming whitecaps, could hear the muffled sounds of their screeching.

Built of gray stone, solid as a fortress, Merlin's Leap stood on a rocky headland just north of Boston. All three Fairfax sisters had been born in the house, had enjoyed a happy childhood there, and had been looking forward to entering adulthood. And then, everything had changed four years ago, when their parents drowned in a boating accident.

The middle sister, Miranda, was the tallest, and the only one who took after their father. Blonde, blue-eyed, she looked elegant and feminine, but she could outrun, outride and outshoot most of the men on the estate.

At twenty-four, Charlotte was the eldest. Small and slender, with curly dark hair and hazel eyes, she was dreamier than her sisters, and less practical. When circumstances called for it, though, the stubborn streak that usually remained hidden behind her gentle facade came out, turning her into a fighter.

Annabel, the youngest, was only eighteen. She shared the same petite frame and dark coloring as Charlotte, but her hair was straight instead of curly. They were alike in personality, too, quieter, not nearly as bold or feisty as Miranda.

In the parlor, the big stone fireplace had been lit in deference to the cool spring day. Annabel stood by the hearth, a wool shawl wrapped around her threadbare gown. The rigid set of Annabel's shoulders and her fraught expression filled Charlotte with alarm.

We need to talk, Miranda had said.

Not sisterly gossip.

But the kind of talk that altered lives.

Her pulse accelerating, Charlotte hurried across the room to her youngest sister. She halted beside Annabel in front of the fire and held her hands out to the flames, fortifying herself.

Miranda tiptoed to the entrance and peeked into the corridor to make sure the housemaids were not spying on them. Then, taking care not to make a sound, she closed the door and returned to her sisters.

Turning to Charlotte, Miranda spoke bluntly. "You have to leave today."

The fear inside Charlotte knotted tighter. "What did you find out?"

"Cousin Gareth has given the servants the day off on Saturday. He has given them money to spend, and offered them the use of the carriage to go into Boston."

"He is getting everyone out of the way," Annabel said. "He'll ravish you, and then you'll have to marry him, and he'll get his dirty paws on Papa's money."

Charlotte flinched. Annabel was too young for such talk, but she had been the one to walk in on them and rescue her a week ago, the first time Cousin Gareth had tried to force his attentions on her. Gareth had been pursuing her since Mama and Papa died, but only recently had he made it clear that he would use any means to achieve his aim.

"At least the two of you are safe from him," Charlotte reminded her sisters. "I don't agree with the old English custom of leaving everything to the firstborn, but Papa did, and that means I'm the only one in danger."

Miranda's elegant features puckered into a

frown. "Papa was a fool not to trust young women to manage their own fortune. You don't get the money until you're twenty-five, but if you marry your husband will get everything at once. Gareth has been gambling. He is in debt and desperately needs funds."

"And he knows that on my next birthday we'll be rid of him." Anger rose in Charlotte. "I'll throw him out of Merlin's Leap. He's been living on Papa's money and keeping us prisoners here. One more year, and then we'll be free of him."

"He knows that," Miranda said bleakly. "That's why he is getting desperate. You'll have to leave at once and find a safe place to hide from him. I stole a gold piece from his pocket this morning. Before the end of the day he'll notice it's gone."

"How can I get away?" Charlotte spread her hands in a futile gesture. "Cousin Gareth has the footmen and the grooms watching every move we make. Even the cook and the housemaids are spying on us."

Miranda leaned closer to her eldest sister and lowered her voice. "Annabel and I will distract the servants, so you can slip out. You must shelter in the forest and walk all the way to Boston. Once you get to the railroad station, you can blend in with the crowd and take a train to someplace where people don't know you."

"But I'll only have ten dollars!"

"Twenty," Miranda said. "The gold piece I stole was a double eagle." She shifted her shoulders in an impatient gesture that brushed aside the obstacle of lack of funds. "You'll have to find a safe place to hide, and come back to Merlin's Leap next year, after your birthday, when you can claim your inheritance."

"You can dress in boy's clothing and—"

Miranda cut off Annabel's excited chatter. "No, she can't. She needs to look like a respectable lady. An educated person who can get a job as a governess or teacher, or a lady's maid."

"I can't…" Charlotte inhaled a deep breath. "I wouldn't know what to do…where to go…how to find a suitable position…"

"You have to," Miranda said. "We can't come with you, as we need to distract the servants so you can escape. If you stay here, Cousin Gareth will force you to marry him. You'll be tied to him for the rest of your life." Her tone hardened. "Of course, you can just let him bully you, and take Papa's money, and anything else he might want."

Like always, Miranda knew how to stir up courage in her sisters. Charlotte fisted her hands into the worn fabric of her ancient wool gown. One of Gareth's petty tyrannies had been not to let them have any money, or buy anything new since their parents died. Up to now, they'd had enough to eat, but Charlotte suspected starvation might be his next weapon.

"All right," she said. "I'll go and pack."

I'll go and pack. Just like that. The end of one life and a leap into the unknown—perhaps not as drastic as a leap from the balcony into the churning ocean below, but equally frightening to Charlotte.

"But what about you…" She swallowed the lump of fear that clogged her throat. "What if Cousin Gareth takes out his fury on you? He might suspect you know where I've gone to and try to beat the information out of you."

"Beat the information out of me?" Miranda's tone held scorn. "I'd like to see him try." She raised a clenched fist. "I haven't forgotten those boxing lessons I got from the Irish stable lad when I was small. If Gareth lays a finger on me, I'll punch him right on the nose."

"I don't think he'll bother us." Annabel spoke slowly, mulling it over. "He is not a violent man, but a scheming one. He'll see no benefit in harming us. He'll leave us alone because he'll be too busy trying to find you."

"I think the same," Miranda said firmly. "He'll rant and rave and then he'll take off to the nearest Pinkerton bureau and hire detectives to track you down. And that means you'll have to be very careful not to leave a trail."

Charlotte suppressed her misgivings. Most likely, Annabel and Miranda were right. Moreover, as the heiress she was responsible for Papa's money. The best way to protect her sisters was to stop Cousin Gareth from getting his hands on their fortune, and that meant she had to leave, go into hiding, just as they had agreed.

Miranda glanced at the grandfather clock ticking in the corner of the room. "You must be ready to slip out exactly at one o'clock. The servants will be sitting down for their lunch. Annabel will create a commotion in the kitchen. I'll set fire to the papers on Gareth's desk in the library. I have a bottle of lamp oil put aside for the purpose. You have less than ten minutes to get out of the house and down the gravel drive and into the shelter of the forest."

Miranda stopped talking. Her arms came around Charlotte in a fierce hug. For a few seconds, they held on to each other. Charlotte inhaled the familiar scent of the lavender soap they all used and drew courage from the feel of her sister's warmth.

Then Miranda released her grip and stepped back.

"Go," she said. "We have no time to waste."

Annabel took her turn to hug Charlotte, clinging tight with trembling arms. The excitement she'd shown only moments ago had dissolved into weeping. The most sensitive of them, Annabel sometimes appeared high-strung, but it might have merely been her youth.

"I'll write to let you know where I am," Charlotte said. She saw Miranda scowl and hurried to reassure her. "I know Cousin Gareth will intercept the mail. I'll find a way to write and let you know I'm safe."

Miranda gave a quick nod, blinking back tears. Charlotte was surprised to remain dry-eyed, but she suspected her calm was far from natural. The terror of what she was about to do had rendered her too numb to feel anything else.

"Emily Bickerstaff," Annabel said through her sobs. "When Mama and Papa insisted you try out that horrible boarding school, Emily Bickerstaff was the nearest you had to a friend. If you write to us under that name, we'll know it's you, and we can read between the lines."

"Excellent suggestion," Miranda said. "Take note of that, Charlotte. Write to us using the name Emily Bickerstaff, or mention her name in the letter."

"I'll remember." Charlotte forced a shaky smile for the benefit of the weeping Annabel. Sometimes they forgot that when their youngest sister managed to control her volatile emotions, she was the cleverest of them all.

Miranda went to the door, eased it open and

glanced down the hall once more to make sure
no one had been listening. Turning to look back,
she signaled with her hand. Charlotte walked out
of the parlor, her heart hammering against her
ribs as she headed along the deserted corridor
toward her bedroom. If things went badly, the
sisters might never see each other again.

Charlotte stood waiting by the tall window in
the hall, hidden behind the thick velvet drapes.
She wore leather half boots, a pale gray blouse,
a green wool skirt and a jacket to match. Her
oldest clothing. Something to blend in with the
crowd. She'd packed a small traveling bag that
contained a pair of kid slippers, two extra sets of
underwear, a nightgown, another blouse, and a
few toilet articles and personal treasures.

The clock chimed to announce the full hour.
One o'clock. Charlotte strained her ears. A few
seconds later, a high-pitched shriek came from
the direction of the kitchens. Then a hysterical
voice yelled something about a mouse. *Well done,
Annabel,* Charlotte thought. A rodent would send
the servants scurrying.

She could hear more voices, this time from
the other end of the house. Masculine shouts.
Then the tinkle of breaking glass and the acrid
smell of smoke. Charlotte took a deep breath and
emerged from behind the curtain. She hurried to

the front door, unlatched the lock and darted out and clattered down the stone steps, speed more important than moving without a sound.

Her running footsteps crunched along the gravel drive. Arrow straight, the drive seemed to stretch ahead endlessly. In the sky the clouds had thickened, and were now shedding a fine drizzle that bathed the landscape in a curtain of mist.

Charlotte veered left, across the lawns, toward the forest. Her heels sank into the soft earth. The wide brim of her bonnet protected her face from the rain, but she could feel the dampness penetrate her clothing. Already, her skirts were heavy and clinging, hampering her speed.

The line of trees ahead formed a green wall that didn't seem to get any nearer as she hurtled along. Her bag bounced against her thighs, a painful slam at every step. She didn't dare to look back over her shoulder to see if anyone was watching. She simply ran, legs pumping, muscles straining, skirts flapping. It seemed an eternity before she reached the thick canopy of the forest and dived into its shelter.

Her heart pounded, partly from fear, partly from the effort of the wild dash. She paused to catch her breath, and finally turned around to survey the house. Mist hovered over the lawns, but there were no signs that anyone had noticed her escape. Through the library windows she could see an orange glow, already fading.

Charlotte turned around, forced her way deeper into the forest. It was less than a mile to a streetcar stop, but she didn't dare to take local transport. People might recognize her, remember her. She'd obey Miranda's instructions and walk all the way to Boston. Four miles. Charlotte gripped her bag tighter in her hand, ducked between branches and set off through the forest, making her way south toward the city.

Twilight was falling when the train pulled in at the railroad station in New York. Charlotte gripped her leather bag in one hand and climbed down the iron steps from the second-class car of the New York and New Haven Railroad Company train. She came to a halt upon the teeming platform and swept a frightened glance around.

So many people. So much noise.

Porters dashed about, pushing through the crowds. Relations welcomed passengers with joyful greetings. Street vendors hawked their wares. Dogs barked. Beggars cried out their pleas. Street urchins raced about, yelling at each other. The cacophony of sounds filled her ears, booming and relentless, like the trumpets of doom.

The journey had taken her two days, even with the trains rushing along at speeds in excess of twenty miles an hour. Who could have imagined that apart from the costly express service there was no direct connection, but a bunch of local railroad companies, half of which seemed to be going bankrupt at any given time? She'd had to change trains three times, and the overnight stop in Hartford had made a further dent in her funds.

"Miss, do ye need a place to stay?"

Startled, Charlotte whirled toward the coarse voice. A man had stopped beside her. Short and stocky, he wore a gaudy brown suit. He whipped his bowler hat down from his head, exposing coils of oily black hair. His dark eyes raked over her in a bold inspection. His lips curled into a suggestive smile.

"New into town, ye'll be," the man said, with a note of satisfaction in his tone. "A pretty girl like you could do well in the right place. I'll show ye where to go."

He reached out to take her traveling bag. Charlotte gave an alarmed squeak and jumped backward. She gripped her bag tighter, spun around and hurried down the platform, away from the man. In her haste, she kept bumping into people. Rough hands groped at her and another man shouted a lewd comment after her.

She increased her pace, panic soaring inside her. She might be innocent, with no exposure to life outside of Merlin's Leap, but she possessed common sense. A young female alone in a big city was easy prey to the worst elements of humanity.

Her hair was disheveled after her flight, her clothing dried into wrinkles from getting soaked in the drizzle, her face a mask of fear and uncertainty. Everything about her revealed that she was down on her luck and therefore an easy target for the predators.

Along the platform, a conductor was yelling instructions to board a departing train. "Train to Chicago and cities and towns west," the dapper little man shouted. "All passengers to Chicago and cities and towns west must board immediately."

Charlotte's gaze fell on the open door of the railroad car. Her steps slowed. She knew she didn't possess enough money for the long-distance fare, but boarding a train without a ticket seemed less terrifying than facing the dangers of New York City after nightfall.

The train blew its whistle. The iron wheels screeched, spinning into motion. Charlotte gripped her bag tighter and sprinted forward. Reaching up, she grasped the handle on the door and climbed up the steps into the railroad car.

The train chugged over the flat prairie with a dull monotony. Charlotte dozed in the hard wooden seat, crammed between a large woman on the way to her sister's funeral and a thin salesman who sold farm equipment. Sunshine streamed in through the windows, making the air hot and stuffy.

All through the night, as the train rolled from town to town, making frequent stops to take in water for the steam engines, she had moved from compartment to compartment, snatching a moment of sleep whenever she could, while at the same time trying to avoid detection by the conductor.

The man beside her shifted in his seat. He fumbled in his coat pockets, his bony elbows butting into her side. Charlotte stirred from her slumber and cast an alarmed glance down the gangway. The conductor in a peaked cap and uniform had entered through the frosted glass door at the far end of the car, and he was inspecting tickets.

With a muttered apology, Charlotte jumped up and hurried in the opposite direction. At the end of the car, she darted through another door and lurched toward the convenience tucked away in the corner. She'd already made it without a ticket most of the way to Chicago, and she had no intention of being caught now.

The lock on the convenience door appeared stuck. In a burst of panic, Charlotte rammed her hip against the peeling timber panel. The door sprang ajar, and then jammed again, meeting some obstacle on the other side. Scuttling backward like a crab, Charlotte squeezed in through the narrow gap. She dropped her bag at her feet, kicked the door shut and turned around to survey her refuge.

A soundless scream caught in her throat.

In front of her, a young woman lay slumped beside the toilet bowl. The folds of her plain brown gown rippled in the draft that blew up from the iron rails below.

Her legs unsteady, Charlotte inched closer. Her breath stalled as she saw the marble white skin and the lifeless look in the open eyes of the woman.

The image of her parents flashed through her mind. Nothing in her twenty-four years had matched the ordeal of visiting the mortuary with her sisters to identify their bodies after they had been recovered from the sea.

Nothing until now.

Nearly swooning, Charlotte lurched forward and clung with both hands to the edge of the porcelain washbasin. In the mirror, her reflection stared back at her. Her face was ghostly pale, her eyes round with fear. Like a black cloak, her hair tumbled past her shoulders, her upsweep fully unraveled.

Scowling at her image, Charlotte struggled to

contain the harsh breaths that tore in and out of her lungs. She couldn't afford to give in to hysteria now. *Dead is dead.* A lifeless body presented no danger, required no rescue.

As her terror ebbed, her attention came to rest on a collection of items on the small metal shelf above the washbasin. A bundle of papers. Next to them, an empty apothecary bottle rattled from side to side, the stopper missing. Charlotte picked up the glass vessel and studied the label, neatly printed in blue ink.

Laudanum.

Pity clenched in her chest. What could have been such a dreadful burden? What had happened to extinguish the lust for life in someone so young? The urge to understand swept aside all hesitation, and Charlotte picked up the bundle of papers. Her fingers trembled as she shuffled through the documents.

Railroad ticket to Gold Crossing, Arizona Territory.

A letter, signed by someone by the name of Thomas Greenwood, referring to arrangements made through an agency. It confirmed that a room had been reserved for Miss Jackson at the Imperial Hotel, where someone would meet her with further instructions.

The last piece of paper had been folded over twice. Charlotte unfolded it.

The single page contained two shakily scribbled words.

"I'm sorry."

Overcome with compassion, Charlotte sank to her knees beside the body and steeled her senses against the putrid odors of the shabby railroad convenience. As she studied the woman's waxen features, desperation whispered its own cruel demands in her mind. Charlotte hesitated, then swept her scruples aside and searched the dead woman's clothing.

"Please forgive me," she muttered, shame burning on her face as she pulled out a small cotton drawstring purse and examined the few coins inside. "You don't need this anymore, and I need it so very much."

Tears of pity and shame stung her eyes as she continued her inspection. She found nothing more, but understanding dawned as her gently probing fingers encountered the contours of a belly swollen in pregnancy.

Poor Miss Jackson.

Charlotte ended her harrowing search and stood. Her hands fisted at her sides as she stared down at the wretched waste of a suicide.

God have mercy.

God have mercy on Miss Jackson. God have mercy on her own desperate flight that took her away from family and home. God have mercy on every young woman whose life had been ruined by a predatory male and on every child who never got the chance to be born.

"I'll pray for your soul," Charlotte said, her throat tight with emotion. She slipped the purse with coins into a pocket on her skirt and gathered her traveling bag from the floor.

Her gaze lingered on the slumped form of Miss Jackson a moment longer. What would they do to her? A suicide couldn't be buried in consecrated ground. Would anyone speak words of understanding and forgiveness over her grave? Or would they only preach about hellfire and damnation?

In a quick motion, Charlotte set her bag down on the floor again. Her hands went to her neck, where a small silver cross hung on a chain. It seemed to take forever before her trembling fingers managed to unfasten the clasp.

Holding the cross in her hands, Charlotte crouched to reach around the slender neck of Miss Jackson and fastened the chain. *Don't you dare anyone steal it from her,* she admonished in her mind.

The piece of jewelry, a birthday gift from her sisters many years ago, was not of great value, which was why Cousin Gareth had allowed her to keep it. Now the cross would be like a blessing for Miss Jackson, and the gesture eased Charlotte's conscience over the money she had taken.

Charlotte finished by throwing the bottle of laudanum down the toilet chute and stuffing the suicide note in her pocket. *There*, she thought as she straightened and surveyed the scene. The cause of death might have been an attack from an illness, which might make all the difference in how they buried her.

Picking up her bag once more, Charlotte clutched the railroad ticket and the letter from Thomas Greenwood in her hand. She pulled the door ajar and peeked in both directions to make sure the corridor was empty before she slipped out.

A plan was forming in her mind, born as much of lack of alternatives as opportunity and impulse. Charlotte Fairfax needed to disappear until her twenty-fifth birthday. If she could become someone else for a year, she would be safe from the Pinkerton agents Cousin Gareth was bound to send after her. Too much money was at stake for him to simply let her run away.

Making her way down the corridor, moving up from third to second class, Charlotte strode along until she spotted a vacant seat. The compartment was occupied by a family. The parents sat on one side, feeding breakfast to a pair of sleepy children perched on the opposite bench.

"Excuse me," Charlotte said, in a voice loud enough to capture their attention over the churning of the train. "Would you be kind enough to allow me to join you?"

"Don't you have a seat in another compartment?" the woman asked. In her thirties, with delicate features and wispy brown hair hidden by a bonnet, she was pretty in a tired, worn-out way.

Charlotte fiddled with the clasp of her leather bag and lowered her gaze, pretending to be embarrassed. "I would prefer to move. Sometimes gentlemen act too familiar. It makes a lady traveling without a chaperone feel uncomfortable."

The woman leaned across to wipe the mouth of the little girl in pigtails and glanced at her husband. A lean, bearded man in a wide-brimmed felt hat and a tightly buttoned black coat, he gave a silent nod of approval.

"You're welcome to join us," the woman said.

"Thank you." Charlotte managed a strained smile as she settled next to the children. "I'm Miss Jackson," she said. "I'm traveling to take up a position in the Arizona Territory."

Afternoon sun scorched the dusty earth as Charlotte made her way from the railroad station along the single thoroughfare that ran through Gold Crossing. She lugged her leather bag with both hands. Sweat beaded on her brow and ran in rivulets down her back and between her breasts. In the Arizona heat the green wool skirt and jacket suitable for spring weather in Boston baked her body like an oven.

She had spent ten days traveling, sleeping rough on trains and railroad stations, exhausting her funds with the cheapest meals she could buy.

Each time she had to change trains, the town had been a little smaller, the passengers a little rougher, the train a little shabbier. The last legs of her journey had been westward from Tucson to Phoenix Junction with the Southern Pacific Railroad, and then a spur line north that terminated in Gold Crossing.

Only two other passengers had alighted at the platform where the train still stood huffing and puffing. The pair of grizzly men had stared at her, the way a hungry dog might stare at a juicy bone. Charlotte had hurried on her way, without giving them an opportunity to offer their assistance.

Imperial Hotel. She squinted down the street where a few equally rough men seemed to have frozen on their feet, like pillars of salt, ogling at her. Could this really be her destination? The town was no more than a collection of ramshackle buildings facing each other across the twin lines of dusty wagon ruts. Most of the windows were boarded up. It puzzled her how such a miserable place had merited a railroad spur.

A faded sign hung on a two-story building

painted in peeling pink. On the balcony that formed a canopy over the porch a teenage boy stood watching her.

Summoning up the last of her energy, Charlotte closed the distance. The boardwalk echoed under her half boots as she climbed up the steps and swung the door open. A gangly man standing behind a polished wood counter looked up from his game of solitaire.

"Can I help you?" he asked. Perhaps forty, he had sallow skin and faded blue eyes that seemed to survey the world with wry amusement.

"Yes." Charlotte dropped her bag to the floor with a thud. "I have a reservation. Miss Jackson."

The man adjusted the collar of his white shirt beneath the black waistcoat and gave her a measuring look.

"You're late," he said. "You were expected a week ago."

"I'm here now." She approached the counter. "I was told someone would meet me here with instructions. I have a letter from Mr. Thomas Greenwood."

"Greenwood's gone."

Charlotte lifted her chin. "When will he be back?"

The man studied her, a sly smile hovering around his mouth. "He'll hurry back like a bullet from a rifle once he hears you've arrived. I'll send a message out to him. He'll be here tomorrow morning."

"Good." Charlotte exhaled a sigh of relief. "I'll go and rest. If you could be so kind and send dinner up to my room as soon as possible." She hesitated, decided to find out rather than live in hopeful ignorance. "Has Mr. Greenwood arranged to cover my expenses?"

"Yes." The man swept her up and down with bold eyes. "He'll pay, all right."

"Good." Despite the man's intrusive inspection, Charlotte's sagging spirits lifted. "Will there be hot water to wash in the room?"

The innkeeper reached behind him to take a key from a row of hooks on the wall. "Room Four. The last one at the end of the corridor." He handed the key to her and gestured toward the staircase on the far side of the deserted lounge.

"And water?" she prompted.

"I'll fetch a bucket of hot water for you."

"Thank you." Charlotte picked up her bag and set off up the stairs.

She had assumed that no one in Gold Crossing knew what Miss Jackson looked like, but she hadn't been certain. Now relief eased her frayed nerves. She was going to get away with it. New name, new life, until she no longer needed to hide. If Cousin Gareth came after her, he would never find her now.

Charlotte slotted the key into the lock and pushed the door open. Despite the musty scent that greeted her, hope flooded through her as she stood on the threshold. A coverlet in white lace topped the big brass bed. On the floor, a patterned wool rug softened the timber boards. A solid oak armoire stood along the wall.

Not the luxury she had grown accustomed to in Merlin's Leap, but a paradise compared to the days and nights of sleeping rough on trains and in railroad stations.

She was safe.

As long as she could keep up the pretense of being Miss Jackson.

Chapter Two

Thomas Greenwood drove his horse and cart across the plateau, impatience throbbing through his veins. She had arrived.

Last week, when Miss Jackson had failed to appear as arranged, bitterness and disappointment had blotted out his hopes for a better future. He'd assumed he'd been swindled by some unscrupulous female who had taken his money and cashed in the railroad ticket he'd sent for her.

But now she was here.

His jaw tingled from the close shave and his fingertips smarted where he had scrubbed out the dirt beneath his nails. The Sunday suit strained across his wide shoulders. Thomas sighed as he considered the six years of heavy toil that had hardened his muscles into coils of steel.

It would be different now.

A woman in his life. A soft voice to ring in his

parlor, the pleasure of a willing companion in his bed. A loving heart to beat in harmony with his.

That was the most important requirement for Thomas.

A loving heart.

Someone who would see him as he was. Not just a giant of a man with big hands and feet, and a chest so wide he had to slip sideways through narrow doors, but a man with a gentle soul and a keen mind, even though he lacked formal education.

He had no wish for a beauty. A beautiful woman would put on airs and graces, expect to be waited upon. He needed a woman who could do her share of the chores. Of course, he'd be willing to pamper her, when it seemed fitting. He took pride in being a protector of the weak, but even a female needed to be competent.

That's why he'd asked for a plain woman. And of all the plain women the agency had put forward to him, he'd chosen Miss Jackson, for she had the greatest reason to be grateful for a man's protection. He hoped her situation might help her to accept the hardships that went with living on an isolated homestead.

When Thomas reached the cluster of buildings that formed Gold Crossing, he could barely summon up the patience to alight in an orderly manner from the cart and secure his horse. He thundered across the wooden sidewalk and burst in through the doors of the Imperial Hotel.

"Where is she?" he called out to Art Langley at the reception.

"Room Four." Langley gave him a sly grin, jerked his thumb toward the staircase and resumed flicking over the playing cards lined up on the counter in front of him.

Thomas hesitated. It wasn't proper for him to barge up into her room, but soon the right to see her even in the most private of circumstances would be his. What difference did a few hours make? Surely, Miss Jackson would not be offended if, in his eagerness to meet her, he brushed aside formal manners?

He set off up the stairs, the heels of his boots ringing with an urgency that matched the pounding of his heart. Room Four was at the end of the dimly lit corridor. He knocked on the door and snatched his hat down from his head, cursing the haste that had made him forget to stop in front of the mirror to tidy up his appearance.

He raised one hand to smooth down his unruly hair, as straight as straw and in the same golden color. Dust from the desert trail itched on his skin but he hoped the suntan from long days out in the fields would cover up any dirt on his face.

The key rattled in the lock. The door before him sprung open.

Thomas could only stare. Disbelief knocked the air out of his lungs.

In front of him stood a small woman, clad in a pale gray blouse and a frothing white skirt that looked more like a petticoat. Glossy black curls streamed down past her shoulders. Red lips, like strawberries ready for the picking, made a vivid contrast against the paleness of her skin.

"Miss Jackson?" he ventured.

"Yes?" She took a step away from him and measured him with a pair of wary hazel eyes.

Thomas felt his arm twitch as he fought the impulse to reach out and touch her, the way one might touch the petals on a bloom, or the carving of an angel in a church, or some other thing of beauty.

She was the loveliest woman he'd ever seen. And she would be his wife. She would share his bed. At that last thought, an altogether more earthly sensation surged through the lower parts of him, as forceful as a kick from a stubborn mule.

But will she cook for you, clean for you, nurse you in sickness, tend to the chickens, help with the farm work? whispered a voice at the back of his mind, but Thomas refused to pay any attention to it.

"Have you been sent by Mr. Thomas Greenwood?" the woman asked as he simply stood there, observing her in stunned silence.

"I am Greenwood."

Miss Jackson appeared to hesitate. Her gaze flickered down to her clothing, then back up to him. She whirled on her dainty feet and darted back into the room, where she tugged at the rumpled bedspread, as if to remove it from the bed. Then she gave up the effort, let out a small huff of frustration and hurried back to him.

"You may come inside, Mr. Greenwood. We shall conduct our meeting here. I shall leave the door open." She stepped aside and waved him through. Crouching in a graceful motion, she picked up a wooden wedge provided for the purpose on the floor and jammed it beneath the door.

Thomas nodded his approval at the precaution to protect her reputation. It had been the right idea to send for a woman from the East, instead of seeking a saloon girl who might wish to turn her life around. He wanted an educated companion. Poetry instead of ditties. Shakespeare instead of rowdy tales.

"Perhaps you could tell me a little more about the employment," Miss Jackson said. She was clasping her hands together in front of her. Thomas got the impression she did it to stop them from shaking. He hunched his shoulders, trying to appear smaller, in case it was his size that intimidated her.

"Employment. Is that how you think of it?" He pondered the idea. "I guess it's not far wrong. You'll certainly be busy with the chores. Cooking and cleaning and such. It's not a big place. There are no hired hands, so it will be just the two of us, until the little one comes along."

Thomas lowered his gaze to the frills on her white cotton skirt and frowned, puzzled by the slenderness of her waist. He let his attention drift back up to her face and saw her eyes snap wide. Her pale skin had turned chalky white.

"A wife," she breathed. "You are expecting me to be your wife."

A nagging doubt, like the persistent buzzing of a bee, broke out in Thomas's head, but his overflowing emotions and his aroused body brushed aside all questions. In his pocket, the letter from the agency spoke of a plain woman, sturdy, well suited to life on an isolated farm. In front of him, a delicate beauty stared up at his face, confusion battling with terror in her huge hazel eyes.

Thomas nodded. "Wife. That's what you've contracted for."

"I..." She made a flicker of impatience with her hand, a totally feminine gesture that held Thomas enthralled. "I believe there has been a misunderstanding," she informed him, her chin rising in a haughty angle. "Perhaps you might explain how I can extricate myself from this contract."

Six lonely years of scrimping and saving to send for a woman of his own, six lonely years of building up the homestead, hacking out a living from soil never tilled before, working until his fingers bled and his muscles cramped with fatigue, crashed over Thomas like a spring flood.

He'd paid for a wife, and he'd have one. This particular one.

"I've paid two hundred dollars to bring you here," he said in a voice that was low and tight. "If you wish to break the contract and marry someone else, I'll have my money back."

His hands clenched into fists. Thomas hid them behind his hat, but he knew his anger showed, on his face and in his rigid posture. From the woman's terrified expression and from the strangled gasp that left her throat he understood how much his tightly controlled outburst must have frightened her.

"I'll wait downstairs," he said, trying to appear calm. "You have one hour to think it over. Either you'll find a way to pay back the cost of your journey, or you'll marry me, just as you've contracted." Thomas turned to go but paused to glance back at her over his shoulder. "Wear something else for the wedding," he told her. "That skirt looks like a petticoat."

He shoved his hat on top of his head and strode off.

* * *

Charlotte stared at the empty doorway and listened to the clatter of footsteps as her visitor stomped away in anger. "It *is* a petticoat," she whispered to herself.

In her anxiety she'd forgotten to pay attention to her clothing, and her state of undress had only dawned on her when she felt Mr. Greenwood's intense gaze on her.

She'd considered covering up with the bedspread, but it occurred to her that an unmade bed might appear even worse. And the towel hanging from the bedpost had been too small to be of any use. So she had chosen to brazen it out. A lady did not draw attention to her faux pas.

Charlotte cast aside the lingering embarrassment over parading in front of the man in her undergarments and gave in to the panicked thoughts that crashed around in her head.

Miss Jackson was a mail-order bride.

She was a mail-order bride.

The image of Thomas Greenwood formed before her eyes. He was a giant of a man, taller even than Papa, and broad in the shoulder. The wide checkbones gave him something of an Indian look, but he had fair hair and pale eyes. And in those pale eyes lurked the steely edge of an implacable will. Not even a storm would make him yield, Charlotte suspected. Against him she had the power of a gnat.

She *would* have to marry him, unless she found a way to come up with two hundred dollars. Which she couldn't, of course. She hardly had any money at all, and Thomas Greenwood knew it. *Wear something else for the wedding.* She huffed as she recalled the male arrogance in his tone as he issued the command.

What could she do? Should she make a confession? Explain her plight and ask for his help? *No.* Charlotte discarded the idea at once. The man wouldn't believe her. He would think it a lie, an attempt to break the contract without reimbursing him the money he'd spent on her passage.

She pinched her eyes shut. The fear she'd hoped to have left behind tightened like a snare around her once more. She could feel Cousin Gareth's greedy hands groping at her breasts, could feel his whiskey-soaked breath on her lips.

Once I bed you, you'll have to marry me, and your money will be mine.

It had been drunken talk, but for once in his life Gareth had told the truth.

She had no money, no means to support herself, and she couldn't risk being found. Her thoughts returned to the fair-haired giant waiting downstairs. Despite his formidable physique and blatant masculinity, there was something gentle about him, something kind and patient.

She imagined being married to him, facing him across the breakfast table in the mornings, sleeping curled up in bed against him at night. The idea filled her with a sense of relief, as if she had sailed into a safe harbor. It might work…it might be just the solution…if she managed to keep it a marriage in name only…

Charlotte squared her shoulders, as if to balance the heavy weight of responsibility that rested over them. She had no choice. She needed to protect her inheritance, both for her own sake, and for that of her sisters.

She would have to marry Thomas Greenwood and find a way to keep him from claiming his husbandly rights for a year. Then, once she turned twenty-five and gained access to her inheritance, she could get the marriage declared invalid and return home to Merlin's Leap.

Charlotte clomped down the stairs, kicking up a racket with the heels of her leather boots. Thomas Greenwood might be in a position to order her about, but if she wanted to retain some control of the situation, she would have to make it clear right from the start that obedience wouldn't be part of her wedding vows.

She found him sitting at the table nearest to the

exit, sipping coffee from a china cup that looked like a doll's service in his hand. It occurred to her that he had positioned himself where he would have the best chance of intercepting her, should she attempt to make a run for it.

"I am ready for the wedding," Charlotte informed him. She tried to make her comment tart but the tremor in her voice emphasized her failure.

The man took in her clothing, nodded with approval at the green skirt she had put on. As a concession to the heat, she'd left off the matching jacket, and only wore the pale gray blouse he'd already seen upstairs.

As she felt his gaze on her, her breath stalled. He was a handsome man, around thirty, and Charlotte had little experience in being the subject of a bold masculine inspection. It made her tingle in an odd way, in intimate places, stirring up a new kind of unease that had nothing to do with fear.

"Have you packed?" her bridegroom asked.

"No. I thought we'd be staying here for the night."

The night. Their wedding night. The idea made a blush flare up on her skin, adding to the heat of the room. She fixed her attention on the toes of her half boots, refusing to look up, but she could hear the scrape of the chair against the floorboards as Thomas Greenwood hoisted his muscular frame out of the seat.

"We'll leave immediately after the ceremony," he told her. "I'll settle the account while you pack."

Charlotte sneaked a peek at him as he strode over to the counter and reached into a pocket on his black suit. The care with which Thomas Greenwood counted out the coins into the open palm of the innkeeper suggested that his financial situation was scarcely better than her own.

A somersault of guilt pitched in her stomach. He must have spent all his savings on a wife. Instead of the sturdy helpmate of his dreams, fate had saddled him with a woman who knew nothing about farming. Her domestic skills didn't extend beyond embroidering undergarments or composing weekly menus with the cook.

And she wouldn't even be able to make up for those shortcomings by showing willingness in the marital bed, Charlotte thought with dismay, another fiery blush flaring up to her cheeks. All in all, Mr. Greenwood might end up feeling that from his point of view the marriage was a very bad bargain indeed.

He turned around. "Go on now," he said. "Get your things."

There was kindness in his tone, kindness and patience. It might be possible for her to navigate the storms that lay ahead, Charlotte told herself as she took the stairs back up to her room. A sense of honor stirred in her. Thomas Greenwood was providing her with a sanctuary at a time of distress. During the year she remained in his custody, she would have to treat him with the respect and courtesy he deserved.

The decision eased her tension and she flitted about the room, gathering up her meager possessions. Two sets of cotton drawers and shifts hung on the back of a chair, where she had spread them out to dry after washing them last night. She folded the flimsy garments, smoothing her hands over the wrinkled fabric.

As she bent to retrieve her leather traveling bag from the floor, her eyes fell on a shadow in the open doorway. Thomas Greenwood stood watching her, arms crossed over his chest, one shoulder propped against the door frame. A dark flush tinged his suntanned cheeks.

Charlotte swallowed the lump of nerves that clogged her throat at the possessive glint in his eyes. She jerked her attention back to the task of packing her belongings. A fiery blush surged all the way from her neck to the roots of her hair at the realization that he had witnessed her handling her intimate clothing. More than likely, he'd imagined her dressed in nothing else.

Her mind scattered. She tossed the bundle of

undergarments into her bag, cramming them on top of the things already there—a book, a box of personal treasures, a nightgown, a pair of kid slippers and a white blouse. She added the silver-backed mirror and hairbrush from the top of the dresser and snapped the jaws of the bag shut.

"I'm ready," she said, even though his heated gaze rooted her to the floor.

He cleared his throat and edged inside the room. "Is this all you have?"

"Yes." Charlotte took a deep breath to ease her constricted lungs. "I only brought what I could carry, to make traveling on the train easier."

"Did you send the rest as freight?"

"This is all I have." She didn't elaborate, merely grabbed the bag by the handle and set off marching toward the door.

"Let me." He circled the bed in a few long strides and reached for her bag. His hand curled over hers, strong and warm. A shiver rippled along her skin. The reality she'd tried to push aside broke through her senses, and the truth of the situation turned her knees to water.

She'd be married to this man before the sun finished its journey across the sky. He'd be her husband, with the rights and expectations that went with the position. She intended to keep him from consummating the marriage, but how could she make sure? Despite the honor and decency she sensed about him, Thomas Greenwood might not have the patience to wait. He might simply take what he justly believed to be his.

When they got downstairs, Charlotte followed Thomas Greenwood out through the double doors, onto the wide porch of the Imperial Hotel. At the far end of the rutted street, she could see a small church gleaming white in the sun. She stared at the cross on the roof. It seemed to be pointing up to the heavens, like the finger of God lifted in fury to warn her against the sin she was about to commit.

In her anxiety she failed to notice that her bridegroom had come to a halt at the top of the porch steps. She kept on walking and slammed smack into his broad back. He didn't even flinch at the impact, merely reached around with one powerful arm to propel her forward, until she was positioned beside him.

In front of them, an old man with pure white hair and wrinkled features stood clutching a prayer book between his hands. He wore an odd mix of clothing, a formal black coat with dirty denim trousers. He smiled at Charlotte, a benign, absent smile as he studied her through the thick lenses of his spectacles.

"The preacher will wed us here," Greenwood said. He wrapped his fingers around hers in a steely grip, as though to quash any lingering thoughts of an escape.

Married. They were about to be married.

The realization broke through Charlotte's panic, like the sound of a ship's horn breaks through a fog. She'd dreamed of marriage, of course she had, every girl, every woman did. At twenty, she'd been getting ready to start searching for a husband, and then Mama and Papa had died...

She slanted another glance at the man standing beside her. Even leaving out his imposing physique, he was attractive, with healthy skin and an even row of white teeth. The prominent cheekbones gave him a stern look, but the sensitive curve of his wide mouth softened it.

If they had met in Boston, if they had courted and fallen in love, she'd be proud to be standing beside such a man in a church, family and friends sitting in the pews behind them, the organ playing a wedding march.

But now, she stood beside a stranger, on a ramshackle hotel porch, in front of a geriatric preacher who contemplated her with a pair of myopic eyes. Evidently, her husband-to-be didn't consider it worth the trouble to walk over to the church. She embraced the gift, not pausing to question his motives. Telling lies on the porch of the Imperial Hotel didn't seem nearly as great a sin as voicing the same untruths in a temple of God.

"Get on with it," Greenwood told the preacher. "And make it quick."

With an annoyed frown, the old man closed the prayer book he'd opened, and lowered it in his hands. He took out a small card from his coat pocket and read from it. "Do you, Thomas Greenwood, take this woman, Maude Jackson, to be your lawfully wedded wife?"

"I do." The reply resonated clear and firm.

Charlotte swayed on her feet as she realized how close she'd come to being exposed. She hadn't known the first name of Miss Jackson. If her bridegroom hadn't furnished the preacher with the information in advance, she might have been caught in a lie before the marriage ceremony was even finished.

Behind them, the porch timbers creaked with heavy footsteps. Charlotte glanced back over her shoulder. A squat man in a long canvas duster had arrived. Another man climbed up after him, a battered hat clasped in his hands. Then a third appeared, a dark-complexioned man with a patch over one eye and a neatly trimmed beard.

"How much?" the first man grunted.

"Get it done," Greenwood said to the preacher.

"Two hundred." The reply came in an insolent voice Charlotte recognized. She whirled around and saw the lanky innkeeper lounging against the door frame. An amused expression brightened his narrow features.

"Three hundred," said the man in a long canvas duster.

"Four," one of the others called out.

Greenwood took a step toward the preacher, tugging Charlotte along with him. He scowled at the ancient reverend. "If you don't finish it quick, there'll be trouble."

The preacher squinted past Charlotte at the gathered crowd of men, nodded and speeded up his words. "Will you, Maude Jackson, take this man, Thomas Greenwood, to be your lawfully wedded husband?"

Charlotte stole another glance behind her. The number of men had grown, and the amounts they were shouting had escalated to a thousand. She couldn't understand the cause of the fracas, but she was left in no doubt about the urgency with which her bridegroom wanted the ceremony completed.

Instinct told her to stall.

"Excuse me." She raised her chin and addressed her words to the preacher. "Is it really appropriate to ask him first?" Her eyes flickered to Greenwood, who stood by her side, bristling with impatience. "Shouldn't you ask me first?"

"What does it matter?" The words rumbled

out of her bridegroom in a harsh growl, as if they were his heart and guts yanked out. "The end result will be just the same."

A solitary burst of laughter vibrated along the porch. Charlotte turned around and spotted the innkeeper chuckling on the doorstep. "What exactly about my situation do you find so amusing?" she asked, irritation overcoming her anxiety.

The man jerked his chin to take in the crowd of spectators. "You don't get it, do you?"

She frowned at him. "Get what?"

"They are bidding for you." He shook his head in wry amusement. "It's like a cattle auction, and you are the cow on the auction block. Greenwood could sell your marriage contract to the highest bidder. If he had any sense at all, he'd make a profit on you and order another bride for himself."

Charlotte spun to her bridegroom and tipped back her head to look up at his face. "Is it true?" she demanded..

His fingers tightened around hers. "Say your vows now, before I have a chance to consider what a thousand dollars might mean to me."

Alarm soared inside Charlotte. She surveyed the group of men gathered on the porch and recognized the pair who had alighted from the train with her. One sent her a bold grin, his grimy fingers fondling the moustache that decorated his upper lip.

She spun back to the preacher and blurted, "I do."

"With the powers vested in me by the Territory of Arizona, I declare you man and wife." The preacher completed the ceremony in haste and invited two of the spectators to act as witnesses. Charlotte watched the strangers scratch their names on the piece of paper, and shivered with the knowledge that she had now become the property of Thomas Greenwood.

Another ripple of laughter came from the porch.

Charlotte darted a sour glance at the innkeeper. "What is it now?" she asked him tartly.

"Of course, if you'd had your wits about you, you could have taken charge of the auction yourself. You could have accepted a thousand, paid Greenwood back his two hundred and kept the rest. You could have taken your pick, married any one of these men."

Charlotte swung her attention back to her new husband.

Greenwood finished passing a handful of silver to the preacher. "Let's get going," he said and turned toward her, but he was refusing to meet her eyes. From his reaction Charlotte understood the innkeeper had been telling the truth.

Thomas Greenwood had tricked her.

It occurred to her it was not out of laziness that he had chosen to have the wedding performed on the hotel porch, but that he had wanted to get it over with quickly, to minimize the time she would be bombarded with competitive offers.

Resentment unfurled in her belly at being treated like a fool, but another thought broke through her anger. Could it be that her new husband lacked the understanding of his own worth? Could he not see that she would have chosen to marry him a thousand times before any of the other men clustered on the porch of the Imperial Hotel? And if that was the case, should she enlighten him?

Unable to make sense of his turbulent feelings, Thomas tugged his dainty bride down the porch steps behind him. She was totally wrong. Small hands, delicate frame and a face that could make a man lose his sanity.

Considering she was wholly unsuitable, why had he been in such a hurry to marry her, instead of making a profit on the transaction? He could have accepted a thousand dollars for her and sent for another bride, someone better equipped for life on his isolated homestead. A plain woman would tolerate poverty more easily, would be grateful for the love and protection he could offer her.

A plain woman. The tintype photograph he carried in his coat pocket weighed on his mind. He'd taken the picture out for a good look while he drank his coffee in the lounge of the Imperial Hotel, waiting for his bride to come downstairs.

He'd turned the image this way and that, studying it close and squinting at it from afar, but however hard he'd tried, he hadn't been able to reconcile the homely woman in the picture with the enchanting creature in a frothing white petticoat.

And what about the baby on the way? Even now, with the heavy wool skirts padding out her waist, his bride was slender, but Miss Jackson *had* to be with child. Why otherwise would a woman like her consent to marry a stranger? Without the disgrace of an unwed pregnancy she'd be fighting off suitors.

Thomas halted by the cart where the chestnut gelding whinnied and beat its hooves against the dusty ground, eager to start for home. He lifted his wife's bag over the side of the cart and turned to her. "If you like, you can lie down on the wagon bed, instead of sitting up on the bench. I've made a bed with straw."

She craned up on tiptoe to inspect the canvas-covered mound of straw in the roughly constructed wooden conveyance. "Why would I want to do that?" she asked, with a quick glance at him. "If I lie down I won't be able to see where we are going."

"I thought it might be better for the baby. Allow you to rest, instead of bouncing up and down on the hard bench."

"The baby?"

"It's all right," Thomas said. Gingerly, he touched the back of his fingers to her cheek. The feel of her soft skin filled him with wonder. "I know you're with child," he said quietly. "The agency told me. I asked them not to put it in the marriage contract. I didn't want any record that the baby isn't mine, in case you didn't want the child to know."

He saw her eyes grow wide, and he noticed their exact color, a rich hazel that glowed like dark gold against the long lashes. She hesitated a moment, then spoke in a low voice. "Why would you be willing to marry a woman carrying another man's child?"

Thomas turned to soothe the horse, which had grown nervous by the wait. What could he say? *To save you from shame and destitution. To make sure this child does not have to grow up as I did, unwanted and unloved.* He gritted his teeth and kept silent. Some things were too personal to reveal, too painful to discuss.

"Why did you pick me as your wife despite the child?" she pressed.

Thomas cleared his throat. "The child deserves a home. He's done nothing wrong. You might have made a mistake, but I can't see why you should spend the rest of your life paying for it, and the child should not pay for it at all."

Thomas finished untying the horse and faced his wife. He wondered if his breath would ever stop catching in his throat when he looked at her. She stared up at him, an odd, stricken expression on her exquisite face. Regret rippled through Thomas at the thought that she might be comparing him with the man who had fathered her child.

"Let's get going," he said gruffly. "Do you want to sit on the bench, or lie down in the cart?"

"I'll sit with you." She eyed the high bench. "Provided I can find a way of getting up there."

Thunderstruck, Thomas froze before her. His heart kicked into a gallop. He curled his hands around her narrow waist, wondering once again how she could remain so small with the baby growing inside her. Holding her carefully, the way one might handle a precious ornament, he lifted her up to the bench of the cart.

"Are you sure you're going to be all right?" he asked as he noticed the beads of perspiration glinting on her brow. She had strapped on a green bonnet, and the sunshine filtering through the fabric gave her pale complexion a sickly hue.

"I'm fine," she replied with a strained smile.

For the first time, Thomas saw the dimples that decorated her cheeks. He could do nothing but stare. After a moment, he shook himself awake and climbed up beside her. Conscious of her pregnant state, he kept the horse to a slow walk.

As they left Gold Crossing behind and turned onto the desert trail, Thomas could feel his body tingling at her nearness. How had it happened? He had chosen a plain wife, abandoned by another man. But instead, he had gained a wife who could start a riot in any gathering of males, and the feelings she stirred up in him alarmed as much as fascinated him.

Charlotte bounced on the rattling bench. The sun beat down on her. Her skin itched inside the thick wool skirt. Dust clogged her nostrils. Her thoughts churned round and round in her head. Beside her, her husband sat in silence, controlling the cart horse with practiced ease. Every now and then, he slanted a hungry glance at her.

Each time, her breath stalled and her body tensed.

He thought she was with child.

Charlotte bit her lip as she recalled the lifeless

body of poor Miss Jackson. If Thomas Green-wood had accepted the pregnancy, what had caused the young woman to sacrifice her life and that of her unborn child? Had she been unable to overcome the shame of being abandoned by the suitor who had ruined her? Or could it be that she had loved him so much that she could not toler-ate the thought of becoming someone else's wife?

With a sigh, Charlotte pushed Miss Jackson out of her thoughts. It was unlikely she would ever find out the answer, or hear anything of Miss Jackson again.

She slanted another look at Thomas Green-wood from the corner of her eye. He sat lean-ing forward, forearms resting on his knees, dust painting streaks of brown on his black suit. A jolt of guilt struck her as she remembered the denim trousers and flannel shirts she'd seen most of the men in Gold Crossing wear.

Her husband had dressed up for her, had done his best to celebrate their wedding. Getting a wife must be important to him. When the time came for her to make her confession, she would ex-plain, beg for his forgiveness. Perhaps he would understand. And she would offer him ample fi-nancial compensation for the inconvenience of having to find another wife.

"Did the agency tell you how far gone the baby is?" she asked.

Thomas arched his brows and cupped one hand behind his ear, to indicate he hadn't been able to hear her words. She repeated her question, raising her voice to carry over the clatter of the horse's hooves and the grinding of the wagon wheels.

"Five months," he replied. "I've arranged to take a job at the copper mine in Jerome to earn enough to pay for the doctor when the baby is due in September."

Five months. By the end of the summer, he'd expect her to waddle about. Experimentally, Charlotte puffed out her stomach, until her muscles strained against the waistband of her green wool skirt. It was no good. She couldn't fake a belly ballooned in pregnancy, even if she gorged to gain weight.

And, judging by her husband's comments about scraping the money together to cover the medical expenses of childbirth, overeating wouldn't be a solution, even in the short term, for food would be too scarce. Charlotte gritted her teeth. She had a month. Two at best. Then she would have to either make her confession or escape.

Chapter Three

The bouncing of the cart made her stomach twist with nausea. Charlotte swallowed hard to keep down the bile rising in her throat. If she retched up the remains of last night's beef stew perhaps she should blame it on the plight of a pregnant woman instead of motion sickness.

"How long before we get there?" she asked.

They had been traveling at least an hour. After the first few miles, they'd left behind the sandy plateau and were now weaving between rolling hills covered with desert scrub. It seemed impossible fertile farmland could be located anywhere nearby.

Her husband turned to her, his gray eyes flickering over her with concern. "Are you all right?"

"Just a little tired." Charlotte tugged at the stifling fabric of her wool skirt. "And hot."

"You ought to have changed into something cooler."

She gestured at her leather bag that rocked up and down in the cart behind them. "Do you think I carry an entire wardrobe in there? All I have is another blouse, the undergarments you've already seen and the petticoats you complained about."

His brow furrowed. "You should have told me. We could have stopped at the mercantile to get you a plain cotton dress."

A plain cotton dress. Charlotte pursed her lips. She'd never owned such a garment in her life. Seeking to blend in with the crowd when she escaped from Merlin's Leap, she'd worn her oldest clothing, but she hadn't expected to end up in a hot climate.

"Dresses cost money," she commented.

Thomas stiffened by her side. "I can provide what you need, and what the baby needs, even if it means selling my land and working for others."

"Don't say that!" Charlotte sat bolt upright on the bench, twisting around to stare at him. A gust of wind caught the brim of her bonnet, and she raised both hands to hold it secure.

Their eyes locked, and the naked longing in his gaze slammed into her heart like a blow. In that single look, all his dreams, all his hopes poured over her.

Every thought scattered from Charlotte's mind

as the strength of her new husband's emotions flooded out to her. Without thinking, she released her grip on the bonnet and reached out to brush one fingertip along the curve of his cheekbone.

A strangled sound tore from Thomas Greenwood's throat. His hand came up to capture her wrist and he pressed his cheek into her palm. His eyes closed, as if he wanted all his senses to focus on that simple touch.

Charlotte couldn't breathe. An alien tension tugged deep in her belly.

She'd hated it when Cousin Gareth touched her, but this was different. She fought the temptation to slide her fingers into the golden hair of Thomas Greenwood, so she could hear him make that sound of longing again.

The cart sank into a rut and bounced into sudden lurch that jolted them on the bench. Greenwood released his fingers from her wrist and turned to study the trail ahead, controlling the reins with both hands.

Charlotte gripped the edge of the wooden platform and clung on tight. As she slowly regained her mental balance, her imagination rushed ahead.

She saw the coming year unfold. They would forge a companionship, a life together, with shared domestic routines and moments of leisure. And, even though she had to find a way to keep

Thomas from consummating the marriage, some level of intimacy might develop between them. And then, when it became safe for her to return to Merlin's Leap, it would all come to an end.

A premonition added to her guilty conscience.

She would end up breaking Thomas Greenwood's heart.

The journey over the rolling scrubland lulled Charlotte into a fatigue that bordered upon sleep. After those few tense moments of staring at each other, with the hot desert air between them sizzling with unspoken emotion, they had retreated behind neutral manners, conversing in awkward snatches.

Thomas Greenwood was what she'd heard the people on the train call a sodbuster. He grew wheat and corn and vegetables. Because of his isolated location, he didn't get caught in the feuds that raged between cattlemen, who demanded open range, and farmers, who sought to fence their fields to protect their crops.

"It's after the next turn," he told her, pride evident in his tone.

Charlotte sat bolt upright on the hard bench and surveyed the hillside ahead. The trail snaked in twists and turns between clumps of cacti. Greenwood took a sharp turn left and urged the horse into a canter to clear the steep rise of the hill.

As they crested the ridge, a small fertile valley spread before them. Speechless, Charlotte stared at the creek that cut a sparkling ribbon through the middle. Beyond the tall trees that shimmered with silvery leaves, she caught sight of the blue glints of a lake.

"Water?" She turned to Thomas. "You live by a lake?"

"A reservoir." A satisfied smile curved his lips. "The beavers built the dam. I merely improved their design."

"Beavers?"

His smile broadened into a grin. "That's right. But don't get any ideas about a fur coat. They are my friends and neighbors." He jumped down from the bench, circled the cart to her side and reached up with both arms.

"Welcome home, Mrs. Greenwood."

Charlotte braced her hands on his shoulders as he lifted her down. Thomas set her on her feet, but instead of stepping away, he bent toward her. Pausing to snatch off his hat, he lowered his head and brushed a kiss on her lips.

It was over in a heartbeat, but the tingling sensation clung to Charlotte's lips, even after Thomas had drawn back to his full height.

She'd never been kissed by a man before, and it seemed to her there should be more to it. She stole a glance at Thomas. He was scowling, as if something had annoyed him.

"I'll show you the house," he told her in a voice that sounded rough and impatient. With an abrupt turn on one worn boot heel, he strode away, across the small clearing and along the path between trees with their silvery leaves.

Charlotte hurried after him, her heart pounding. Why had he suddenly grown so terse? Had he felt the flatness of her belly when he lifted her down? Was he suspecting something?

Panic unfurled in her chest when she considered the hurdles she would have to navigate as part of her deception. She could do nothing but go on living as she had lived in the past ten days, since she fled out into the cold spring afternoon at Merlin's Leap—by her wits, one minute at a time.

Thomas strode down the path to the front door, his boots thudding in an angry beat against the hard-baked earth. He needed to get ahold of himself. After just one tiny kiss, lust flamed like a brushfire through him, and it was scaring him witless.

He must let his bride get used to him first, to his strength and size, to his constant presence. The best strategy was to win her over gradually. Allowing greedy passions to rule his mind could ruin any hope of a happy marriage.

Thomas believed in creation. God had given men the capacity to enjoy the intimacy necessary for the survival of mankind and, being equitable in His creation, God must have given women the same capacity. But it was the man's duty to make it so. Be gentle and patient. He would weave a web of temptation around his wife, until her own senses guided her into his arms.

Behind him came the rustle of light footsteps, and he knew she had hurried after him. Satisfied that he had his urges under control, Thomas turned to face his wife. She peered up at him, alarm stamped on her lovely features. He wanted to kick himself for having kissed her too soon. He lowered his voice, as if she were a frightened doe he sought to tame.

"Ready to take a look at the house?"

She nodded but did not speak.

He kept up a steady stream of talk as he climbed up the front steps, pushed the door open and waved her inside. "The house is built with split logs. I couldn't dress the lumber properly on my own. You need two men to operate a whipsaw. I had plenty of timber, so I just sliced the logs down the middle."

"You built this house yourself?"

"Every single groove and joint."

He watched her as she surveyed the big central room. Light flooded in through the open door-

way and from the wide window on the opposite
wall. Slowly, she untied the laces of her green
bonnet and removed it from her head. His stomach tightened at the way the slanting sun picked
out coppery glints in her black hair and painted
dappled shadows over her slim frame, as if nature
itself wanted to touch her, just as badly as he did.

She drifted around the room, in front of the
window, past the row of kitchen cabinets, to the
long table flanked with two benches.

"If you don't like the benches, I can make
chairs," Thomas told her.

She glanced at him, crossed the room to the
pair of carved wooden love seats that faced each
other in front of the massive stone chimney. She
ran her fingers along the scalloped back of one
of them.

"Did you make these?"

"Yes."

"It must have taken a long time."

"The winter evenings offered me plenty."

He wondered if she understood the skill that
went into carving wood, or appreciated the financial outlay he'd incurred for the new cookstove.
He'd ordered it all the way from Flagstaff, right
after Miss Jackson had agreed to marry him if
he sent the funds for her passage.

His bride gestured at the doors on either side
of the fireplace. "What's in there?"

"That's the bedroom." His body tightened as he strode across the floor and flung the door open. The wide room had windows on both sides. A tapestry depicting a winter woodland scene hung on the wall above the bedstead.

"Did you make the bed too?" she asked.

"Yes, and the pair of nightstands, and the blanket box, and the two chairs, and the chests of drawers beneath the windows. The bed is in the shape of a sled. Reminds me of the snow in Michigan."

"Is that where you are from?"

He nodded, keeping his face empty of expression.

"Why did you leave?"

"I had four older brothers. The farm wasn't big enough for all of us, and land was too expensive to buy." The explanation held some truth in it, and Thomas quickly closed his mind to the rest of the memories.

He watched his wife standing beside the bed and tried to keep his imagination under control. "Did you see the cookstove?" he asked, as much to distract himself as to keep her talking.

She threw him a questioning look. He pointed back to the living room. She returned to the parlor and studied the appliance. Thomas realized he had no idea of her competence as a housekeeper. They hadn't corresponded. He didn't know much about her beyond her name, her age, and that she had been abandoned by her lover and her pregnancy had caused her to be dismissed from her position as a maid in some rich man's household.

Suddenly the room closed in around Thomas. He needed to soothe his mind, needed to see the sky soaring above him and hear the trees whispering in the wind. He turned and headed out to the porch.

"I'll go and put the horse in the paddock."

"Why is the house not by the water?" his bride called after him when he was already halfway out the door.

"The creek floods after heavy rain and the soil is firmer here."

"Do you bathe in the lake?"

"Sometimes." He raked his gaze over her, his imagination running riot. He forced his mind to focus on practical thoughts. "You must not drink from the creek. There's a well behind the house for clean water."

Thomas turned his back on her again and clattered down the steps, as if Lucifer himself was chasing on his heels. Whatever happened between him and his wife—even if she only spent one week on his isolated homestead and left because she could not face a future in such a lonely place—one thing was certain: his life would never be the same again.

* * *

Charlotte sank down to the wooden love seat. Disaster screamed at her from every carefully crafted corner of the rustic cabin. She closed her eyes and let Thomas Greenwood's words, full of pride, echo through her mind.

Did you see the cookstove? A sigh of regret rustled out of her chest. She wouldn't have known if the stove had been slotted upside down between the cabinets.

Grim determination surged inside Charlotte. Her hands fisted so hard her nails dug into her palms. She'd be the perfect wife. While she remained with Thomas Greenwood, she'd ease the harshness of his life. She'd work until her muscles ached and her fingers bled. And before she left, she would make sure the cabin had become a more comfortable home for him.

Jumping up, Charlotte rushed to the cookstove, an iron monster made pretty by a coat of pale green enamel on the front. "I'm going to call you Vertie," she said and gave the top a friendly pat. "It comes from *vert*, the French word for green. And now you'll have to help me make coffee."

She found a tin of coffee on the open shelves, the beans already ground. A big copper pot hung from a peg on the wall. Two steel buckets stood on the counter, one empty, one half full. Rather than risk a musty flavor, Charlotte picked up the empty bucket and set off in search of the well.

Outside, the sun had dipped below the ridge of the hills and the air was turning cool. Clouds of tiny flies swarmed in the twilight. A pair of blue jays quarreled on the ground, screeching and flapping their wings. Rodents rustled in the undergrowth. It appeared the evening was the rush hour in nature.

The path rounded the side of the house and led to a stone circle rising from the ground. A crank handle and a spout protruded on the right. Charlotte hung the bucket on a hook under the spout and tentatively yanked the handle. A gurgling noise came from deep within the earth.

Encouraged, she attacked the pump with vigor. After a moment, a loud rumble erupted, and a jet of water exploded into the bucket with so much force it bounced up, drenching her face and chest.

A startled cry left her lungs, shattering the evening calm. Charlotte blinked away the droplets clinging to her lashes and mopped her face with her sleeve.

Down the path, she heard the heavy thud of footsteps heading in her direction. Twigs snapped and birds scattered in fright. She looked up and saw Thomas hurtling through the trees. When he reached her, he gripped her shoulders and towered over her. His eyes roamed her features in a frantic inspection.

"Are you hurt?" he demanded to know.

"No." Laughter rose in her chest. "Only wet. And feeling stupid."

"You shouldn't be doing that." He released his hold on her and stepped past her to the pump.

"Yes, I should." She shoved him out of the way, her hip butting against his rock-hard thigh.

With a grunt of surprise, Thomas yielded and moved aside.

"I'm not made of glass, and I'm not made of sugar." Charlotte cranked the pump handle, taking care to keep her movements slow and measured. When water started spurting out of the pipe, she ducked to avoid the spray from the bucket. "I won't break if I fall, and I don't melt if I get wet."

She glanced over at Thomas to see if he'd understood her meaning. He hadn't. She doubted he'd even heard her. His gaze was riveted on her breasts, which heaved up and down with the rhythmic motion as she operated the pump. She had discarded her corsets before setting off on the train journey, and the soaking wet blouse clung to her body, like lichen on a wood nymph.

Charlotte couldn't think. She ceased cranking the pump handle. Suddenly, she felt a great surge of heat on her skin, so great it surprised her not to see steam vapors rising from her drenched garments.

A sense of inevitability filled her. Whatever her misgivings, whatever her desires, whatever her plans, the needs and wants of Thomas Greenwood might be more potent than hers. It might turn out that her married life would be a much harder ocean to navigate than she had allowed for.

"You'll catch a chill." Thomas spoke in a husky rumble. "You should change out of those wet clothes into something dry."

She had to clear her throat before the words came. "I don't have anything to change into, apart from a nightgown."

"Are you hungry?" Thomas asked. "Do you want any supper?"

Charlotte shook her head, unable to speak.

"I'd like to see you in your nightgown." He reached for the overflowing bucket and effortlessly lifted it down from the hook beneath the spout. "Why don't you go inside and get out of those wet clothes. I'll heat up water for you to wash."

Thomas waited for her to move away but she stood rooted on the spot. His expression softened. "Go on now, Maude," he said gently. "You can undress in the bedroom, in privacy."

The name broke the spell between them. "Call me Charlotte," she said, her voice rising with a touch of despair at how little control she seemed to possess over her situation. "I dislike the name Maude. I want you to call me Charlotte."

"Charlotte?" Confusion flickered across his features. Then his frown eased and he gave a slow nod, his eyes steady on her. "I like that." He lowered his voice and added in a low murmur, "More syllables for a man to whisper in the throes of passion."

Charlotte gave a shocked gasp and fled inside.

Chapter Four

Thomas sat on the porch steps and watched the twilight thicken over the valley. A chorus of frogs croaked in the muddy pond near his irrigation station. In the creek, a beaver splashed its tail. A hawk soared overhead. The scent of blossoms from the pomegranate orchard by the lake floated on the breeze.

Sundown was his favorite part of the day. The chores were done. Horses were safe in their stalls, the milk cow in its pen and chickens in their coop. It was the time to relax, time to allow his aching muscles a moment of rest. Time to look forward to supper, and then to sitting down by the fire to work on a piece of furniture, or to read a book by lamplight.

Ever since he'd finished building the house in his second year on the farm, Thomas had sat on the porch steps in the evenings. And every night, he'd wondered what it might feel like, to have someone inside waiting for him.

All his life, he'd longed for that.

To enter a room and feel welcome.

Would he achieve it now? Would his wife smile at him, her face bright with pleasure as he stepped across the threshold? Or would it forever be his fate to live with the silent hostility that had ruined his childhood and youth, until he could no longer take it and had chosen to leave his Michigan home.

There was a risk in marrying an unknown woman.

It was a risk he'd felt compelled to take.

For not trying at all would have been cowardice.

Thomas pushed up to his feet, slapped the dust from his knees. He should have changed into work clothes instead of taking care of the animals in his Sunday suit.

One corner of his mouth tugged up in a wry smile. Didn't matter. He'd not wear the suit again until someone died. His smile deepened. Or perhaps for the christening of his child. Their child. For, according to the law, any child born to his wedded wife would be his, even if another man might have planted the seed.

"Charlotte." He tasted her name on his tongue.

"My wife," he whispered into the silence, enjoying the sound of it.

He raked one more satisfied glance over his valley, now shrouded in deep shadows, and then he walked up the porch steps into the house.

The parlor was empty, the lamps unlit. Thomas turned toward the bedroom. The doors were closed. He didn't know what to make of it. He understood it was common for women to fear their wedding night. It made sense. Most women had little idea what to expect, and it was human nature to fear the unknown, but that should not be the case with Charlotte. The proof of her experience was growing in her belly.

With hesitant steps, Thomas set off across the floor. Before he reached the bedroom door to the left of the fireplace, the door on the right side opened. His wife stood in the opening. The last glimmer of daylight from the window behind her silhouetted her, rendering her thin white nightgown transparent.

Thomas felt his mouth go dry. His heart hammered in the confines of his ribs. He wanted to rush up to her, rake his hands down the dark curls that cascaded past her shoulders. He wanted to frame her face between his palms, tilt it up toward him and kiss her until his body hummed with joy.

She moved.

A step toward him.

Not away from him.

And then she laughed—a tingling, feminine laughter that crawled up his spine and fanned the needs he had just spent an hour trying to bank down.

"Why do you have two doors to the bedroom?" she asked. "I can see us going round and round, looking for each other, one of us going in through one door while the other one is coming out through the other door."

Thomas had trouble speaking. He had to clear his throat before the words came. "It is so that the bedroom can be divided into two later, creating a separate bedroom for the children. That's why I put in a window on both sides, rather than one big window at the end."

She spun around to survey the bedroom. The transparent nightgown gave him a view of her back, different, but just as fascinating.

"I see," she said. "What a clever idea."

Thomas smiled. Tomorrow, he would show her his irrigation station, and some other inventions he'd made to ease the burden of farm chores. She might be surprised to discover that despite his lack of formal education he possessed as much knowledge of mechanics as a trained engineer.

"I'm hungry," he told her. "Will you eat supper with me?"

She whirled back around to face him and edged closer. Either she lacked modesty, or she had no idea how much the flimsy nightgown revealed. Thomas would have bet his life on the latter. When she was only two steps away, she clasped her hands together in front of her in a manner that was becoming familiar to him.

"I haven't cooked supper for you," she said, her expression crestfallen.

Another wave of warmth spread in his chest. This was exactly what he had hoped for. A woman to help with the chores. "It's all right," he reassured her. "I didn't expect you to cook anything. Not on your first night. I was just going to have some bread and cheese."

She pressed the flat of her palm against her belly and held it there. Thomas guessed a pregnant woman might like to do that, to feel the new life growing inside her. His eyes lingered at her waistline. Five months. Shouldn't she be bigger? Without thinking, he blurted out his thoughts.

"You look too thin. Is there something wrong with the baby?"

"No," she said. "There's nothing wrong."

"Are you sure? Have you seen a doctor?"

She shook her head in silent reply.

"Not at all?" he pressed. "Not even in the beginning?"

"No." She came closer to him, touched the back

of his hand in a gesture of reassurance. "Don't worry," she said. "There's nothing wrong with the baby. Nothing at all. I'm just small, that's all. Some women don't show until they go into labor."

He studied her guarded expression for a second, then nodded. He couldn't help the niggling feeling that something was wrong. Maybe earlier Miss Jackson had tried to get rid of the baby. Maybe she had taken some potion and it had harmed the development of the child, stunting the growth in the womb.

Miss Jackson. Thomas frowned. Strange, how it seemed to him as if that person, the person in the tintype photograph he had filed away, was someone else altogether, and not his wife, the woman who had asked him to call her Charlotte.

Turning to the kitchen cupboard, Thomas took out a loaf of bread from a stone jar and a wedge of cheese from the milk safe. "If you keep the burlap cloth moist at all times, it will keep the milk and cheese fresh an extra day, even in the summer heat," he told her, looking back over his shoulder.

Charlotte remained on her feet, hugging her arms around her body.

"Why don't you put your coat on?" he asked.

She rubbed her arms, shivering. "The wool fabric is itchy."

Thomas paused. He glanced back toward the

bedroom. He'd intended to save his bridal gift for when he knew for certain she would stay with him, but it didn't matter. Today was the proper day for giving marriage gifts.

"Wait here," he said, and strode off into the bedroom.

He knelt by the linen chest at the foot of the bed, lifted the lid and searched inside. He pulled out the crocheted shawl and paused for a moment, smoothing his fingers over the soft texture of the fine wool. It was the only token of love he'd ever received, not counting the fact that he had been born. On the morning he'd said goodbye and walked out of the house that final time, his mother had hurried after him.

"Take this," she had whispered. "I made one for you too, like I did for your brothers. For your bride." She'd cast a fearful glance back at the house, where her husband's shadow fell across the window.

"He doesn't know I made it." She'd drawn a breath, and Thomas had heard a sob in her voice. "I wish I could have been...stronger...that I could have defied him...but I couldn't...not even for you." She had looked up with a plea in her eyes. "You understand, don't you?"

Thomas had taken the shawl, slipped it into his bag. Not a saddlebag, for they wouldn't even let him have a horse to see him on his way.

His mother had clung to his arm. "Tell me you understand," she'd begged. "Tell me you forgive me."

Thomas had looked down at her from his height. Small and dark, like everyone else in the family, she'd stared up at him with tear-bright eyes. He would never understand, and he didn't have it in his heart to forgive his mother for not loving him. Perhaps the man he'd grown into might possess the strength to forgive, but the child he'd once been and whom he still carried inside him clung to the hurt.

But he'd said it anyway, even though it was not true.

One final act of love for the mother who had never loved him.

"I forgive you," he said, and asked God to absolve him for the lie.

Kneeling by the linen chest, Thomas lifted the shawl to his face. In the first two years, the scent of the rose water his mother used had clung to the wool. Then he'd made the chest and the spicy scent of cedar wood had replaced the scent of roses.

He pushed up to his feet and went back into the parlor. He shook out the shawl. It was patterned in earthy colors, rust and moss green and the rich red hues of maple leaves in the fall. He moved to stand behind Charlotte and spread the shawl over her shoulders. His arms circled her for a second before he pulled away.

"What is this?" she asked.

"It's a wedding gift for my bride. My mother made it." As Thomas spoke the words, a tiny edge of the old pain chipped away. Perhaps one day forgiveness would come.

"The custom is that I should give it to you in the morning after our wedding night, but I can see that you are cold, and our marriage isn't a traditional one anyway."

Charlotte fingered the soft wool, not meeting his eyes. "It's lovely," she said. "And very warm." She glanced up at him. "Thank you."

Thomas nodded. They needed to talk about it. Their wedding night. And all the nights that came after. But such a conversation might be easier for both of them if he waited until the darkness let them hide their thoughts from each other.

Charlotte clutched the shawl tighter around her. Night was falling, but she didn't feel ready to meet the challenges the darkness might bring. The longer they remained in the parlor, talking, the longer she could postpone facing those challenges.

"I believe I'm hungry after all," she said, and recalled the task that had sent her out to the well earlier that evening. "I was going to make coffee."

She darted over to the kitchen counter, her bare feet soundless on the timber floor. The pail was full of water. An iron pot filled to the brim sat on the stovetop. Thomas came to stand beside her, nodded at the pot. "That's water for washing. I didn't light the fire yet. I stopped to sit on the porch steps for a moment."

"Let me do it." She nudged him aside with her elbow.

Obediently, he eased back, but instead of sitting down at the table, he settled a hip against the edge of the tabletop and leaned back, arms folded across his chest. Watching her. As if to inspect her household skills and pass judgment on them.

Charlotte glanced down at the pile of firewood and pursed her lips. The front of the stove had three hatches, one big, two small. She bent down, opened the biggest hatch and threw a few bits of firewood inside.

"That's the oven," Thomas said. "The wood goes into the smaller compartment on the left."

Charlotte swallowed hard, nodded, removed the bits of firewood and placed them in the smaller compartment on the left, just as he had told her. She could see a round pit in the metal bottom of the compartment and guessed that the firewood, as it burned, would collapse into the third compartment beneath. That must be where a low fire burned for baking and where the ashes gathered for removal.

"How are you going to get the fire started?" Thomas asked.

She looked at him over her shoulder. He pointed at the small pieces of bark gathered in a metal bucket beside the firewood. "Kindling."

Charlotte nodded, rebuilt her pile of firewood with kindling at the bottom and glanced once more over her shoulder, her eyebrows arched in question.

"You need to stack the wood loosely, to allow air to circulate in between. Wood stacked in a tight pile won't catch flame."

She nodded, did it all over again.

Thomas pointed. "Matches are on the shelf."

Rising on her toes, Charlotte searched the shelf, found the small metal tin and clipped it open. Her eyes narrowed in victory. Something familiar. Papa had used matches to light his pipe, and she'd used them for candles. She snapped a match free from the row, looked around for a piece of sandpaper to strike it against but saw none.

Any abrasive surface would do. Her eyes darted from object to object, settled on a heavy cast iron frying pan sitting on the counter. Eager to demonstrate her competence, Charlotte shot one arm out and drew the match across the belly of the frying pan.

"No," Thomas shouted, but it was too late.

The flame sparked, and blew up from the frying pan like a dragon's breath. Charlotte screamed and jumped back. Strong arms closed around her, lifting her off her feet. Keeping one arm wrapped around her waist, Thomas inspected her hands.

"Did you burn your fingers? Show me! Show me!"

Tears stung at the back of her eyes, but they were tears of misery and frustration and helplessness, not tears of pain. Charlotte clenched her hands into fists to keep away his probing fingers. "I'm fine," she muttered.

It took a moment before the intimacy of their position registered in her mind. She was dangling in the air, anchored against his chest. A thick forearm cut like a band of steel across her waist. Thomas was looking down over her shoulder, his head bent next to hers. She could feel the rough stubble on his jaw rubbing against her cheek.

And yet, despite the hold that emphasized his superior strength, his touch was gentle. It was clear that he could subdue her without effort, but something in his manner told her he would never hurt a woman. She need not fear that he might take her by force. The realization eased her terror, but a new kind of tension crept in its place.

Slowly, Thomas released her, settling her on her feet.

"I never wash the frying pan," he explained. "I just wipe it with a cloth, which leaves a layer of grease on the bottom. It keeps food from sticking to the metal." He took another match from the tin, squatted in front of the stove, rearranged the wood, struck the match against his thumbnail and lit the fire. He spoke with his back to her, his eyes on the catching flames. "The coffee is on the shelf."

Her nerves jumped and thrummed. Coffee. Coffee. She'd seen it before. She found the round metal tin on the shelf, took it down and struggled with the lid. Her hands were shaking. The tin slipped from her fingers, fell to the floor with a clang, burst open and rolled along. Coffee granules scattered in a spray over the timber planks.

With a squeal of horror, Charlotte rushed toward the counter for a cloth to contain the mess. Her elbow butted against the pail of water, dislodging the dipper hanging by its hooked end inside the pail. The dipper flung up in the air and sent a spray of droplets across the floor, where they landed over the spilled coffee granules.

Aghast, Charlotte stared at the sticky mess by her feet. She froze. Thomas didn't say anything.

Would he be angry at the waste? Coffee was expensive and she understood he had very little money. Would he scold her, maybe even shout and yell at her?

When the silence cut too deep into her frazzled nerves, she slowly turned around to look at him. Thomas had straightened on his feet. He was biting his lip. His whole body was quivering, and his face was red, as if he had been holding his breath.

He was about to explode.

Ready to meet the assault of his rage, Charlotte drew her shoulders into a hunch, like a turtle hiding in its shell. She'd never been hit in her life, had never tasted the sharp edge of violence before Cousin Gareth's ugly groping.

Startled, she watched, as Thomas bent over, slammed his hands against his knees and dissolved into laughter. Charlotte stared. Her shoulders fell from their protective hunch. Her spine straightened. Humor unfurled in her belly, light at first, like the soft tickle of a cat's tail. Then it took hold, and she burst into an irrepressible fit of giggles.

"People in New York sure have funny habits," Thomas managed between bursts of mirth. "Here in the West, we make the coffee in a pot." He reached to the counter, picked up a rag and handed it to her. "You clean. I make coffee."

* * *

Thomas sat across the table from his bride. She had finally relaxed, even got some color in her cheeks. If anyone had told him he would find clumsiness and incompetence endearing qualities in a wife, he would have told them they had lost their mind.

She had done her best to follow his instructions. And she possessed the ability to laugh at herself. Good humor and willingness to learn were more important qualities in a wife than expertise, Thomas decided.

He cut another piece of cheese, another slice of bread and passed them onto her plate.

"Eat a bit more," he urged her. "It's good for the baby."

"No." She slid the plate over to him. "I've had enough."

They had eaten in silence, both discovering they were famished. Now Charlotte patted her belly and sighed with contentment. Thomas transferred the bread and cheese onto his own plate. He'd learned not to waste a morsel of food.

"How did you end up here?" Charlotte asked. "It's a long way from Michigan."

"How did you end up here?" he countered. "It's a long way from New York City."

Something flickered in her eyes, like a shadow of painful memories. Thomas told himself it might have just been the lamplight. Tonight, he'd lit up two lamps instead of one. An extravagance, for certain, but he wanted to see her clearly.

With his bride in mind, he'd bought lamp oil instead of kerosene—another additional expense, but he didn't want her to suffer from the sting of smoke in her eyes.

And now those eyes were laughing at him, dark and mischievous. "Are you telling me that you came here because some woman sent for you as a mail-order husband?"

"No." He took a sip of coffee and swallowed, using the time to select his words. "I wanted to come south, away from the harsh winters. There's good farming around Phoenix, with irrigation systems. I spent a few months there to see how it's done. Then gold was found up here. I joined the crowd of prospectors, hoping to strike it rich."

She frowned at him. "Gold Crossing is a mining town?"

Thomas grinned. "Not much of a town, huh?"

Her lips pursed into a circle of disapproval, perhaps even of disgust. "It's the scruffiest, most miserable, run-down excuse for a town I've ever seen."

Thomas laughed. "I hope that kind of blunt talking means you'll always be honest with me."

Charlotte didn't reply. Again, he could see that flicker of worry in her eyes.

She had secrets. The knowledge hardened inside Thomas. *Of course she has secrets,* he told himself. Without the offer of a marriage she would have been an unwed mother, an outcast in polite society, a sinner according to many folks.

He leaned across the table to adjust the flame on the lamp. "People flooded to Gold Crossing after Art Langley found gold and recorded his claim. Eight years ago there were almost a thousand people there, living in a tent town that sprung up virtually overnight."

"A thousand people!"

"Hard to believe, isn't it?" He shifted one shoulder in a careless shrug. "The seam of gold petered out quickly, and no one ever found another lode of quartz. By the time they'd finished the railroad spur to take out the ore, the mine had just about played out. People hadn't even had enough time to build proper houses before they moved on to the next boomtown. Most were still living in tents. That's why there aren't streets full of abandoned buildings in Gold Crossing, like there'll be in Jerome in a few years when the copper mine plays out."

"But you stayed on in the area?"

Thomas nodded. "The man who owned this sheltered valley had planned to develop an orchard. He'd planted pomegranate trees. But the town died before the trees had matured to bear fruit. I was able to buy the place cheap." He drank the last of the coffee in his mug. "I have ten cultivated acres. Four each of wheat and corn, and two of vegetables. The valley has about twenty fertile acres in all, but ten is the most I can irrigate in the summer on my own."

Her brows furrowed. "You irrigate the fields?"

"On hot days, I need to pump water from the lake. I have a hose and a sprinkler. I'll show you tomorrow how it works."

"Yes," she said. "I'll learn how it's done, and I'll help you."

Thomas nodded, to confirm that he was indeed counting on her help.

He got to his feet. "Time for bed."

Charlotte rose. She hovered by the table, her nightgown reflecting the lamplight, her dark curls like a snare designed to trap a man's heart. Her frightened eyes darted from him to the bedroom door and back again. If Thomas wasn't mistaken, her long white nightgown was fluttering, not from the draft but from the way her slender body was trembling.

"Go on now, Charlotte," he said softly. "You have nothing to worry about. Here, take the light." He slid one of the lamps across the tabletop toward her. When she picked it up, the glass dome rattled, an indication of how hard her hands were shaking.

"You have nothing to worry about," he reassured her again. "Get into bed. I'll go and check on the animals, and then I'll come back inside and join you."

He watched her spin around and dart into the bedroom, scurrying with hasty footsteps, like some tiny animal seeking a refuge. They'd have to talk about the physical side of their marriage, before she drove herself into a state of agitation.

Chapter Five

When Thomas returned inside, he slid the bolt on the front door and turned down the wick on the lamp he'd used to illuminate his way to the barn and back. For a moment he hesitated. Should he undress in the parlor? Would it offend Charlotte's sensibilities if he removed his clothing in front of her?

He could see a shaft of light shining from the bedroom door that stood ajar. She'd left a lamp on. Was it a sign that she was expecting him? His mouth tightened with uncertainty and nerves.

Go on, he told himself. *You'd best start as you mean to continue.*

He blew out the lamp he'd used outside and marched into the bedroom, letting his footsteps sound boldly on the floorboards. Charlotte lay curled up on her side on the far edge of the thick feather mattress, huddled beneath the covers, her back facing him. On the small bedside chest on the empty side of the bed, the lamp she had carried in from the parlor burned with a low flame.

His side.

Thomas felt his chest constrict with emotion.

The first step of sharing his life with someone else.

His wife had chosen which side of the bed she would sleep on.

He sank into the plain oak chair beside the wall, pulled off one boot, let it drop to the floor with a thud. The second boot. Another thud. Beneath the covers Charlotte didn't stir.

Thomas could tell she wasn't sleeping. Her shoulders didn't rise and fall in the gentle rhythm of even breathing and there was an unnatural stillness about her. She might not realize it, but by her chin, one small fist was clenched tight, the fingers curled in a death grip over the edge of the quilt.

Thomas got to his feet and began to unbutton his trousers. He spoke slowly, keeping his voice to a soothing rumble. "I don't sleep in a nightgown."

The narrow shoulders beneath the covers flinched.

"When the mine played out six years ago, two of the general stores in Gold Crossing shut down and sold off everything at knock-down prices. I stocked up with clothing, bought several union suits for the winters. I also got that feather mattress for the bed. Before, I only had a straw mattress. And I bought the wall hanging, and the pots and pans for the kitchen."

The covers rippled and Thomas knew Charlotte had moved. He wondered if she had done it on purpose, to show him that she was awake and listening.

"I hadn't expected that at twenty-two I might still be growing," Thomas went on. "But it turned out that the hard work of building the homestead padded out my muscles, and the union suits became too tight at the chest and shoulders. So, Mrs. Timmerman—that's the doc's wife—cut the suits of underwear in two across the waist for me. For the bottom half, she fixed a draw cord at the waist. That's what I wear to sleep at night. The bottom halves of my old union suits."

His wife made no comment.

Thomas pushed his trousers down his legs and changed into his makeshift pajama bottoms. Instinct had made him turn his back for the brief seconds it took to complete the task. Now he pivoted on his feet and faced the bed again.

Charlotte had not moved.

Thomas set to work with his shirt buttons. Tonight, his fingers didn't seem capable of the job. "I don't wear anything on my top half," he said, looking down to guide his fumbling fingers. "But if that offends you, I can find an old shirt to put on."

"It's all right." He could hardly hear the thin, brittle voice.

"Good." He pushed the shirt down his shoulders, pulled his arms out of the sleeves and draped the worn garment over the back of the chair, on top of the rest of the clothing he'd already hung there.

Then he eased his way to the bedside, lifted up the worn patchwork quilt and slipped beneath. Taut with nerves, he lay on his back, making sure his body didn't touch hers. He carried on talking in the soft, calming tone.

"It will be four more months before the baby comes, and then it's my understanding that a woman needs time to recover from childbirth. Let's say another two months. That will give us six months to get used to each other before we start the physical side of our marriage."

Thomas rolled onto his side and spoke to the nape of her neck. She'd braided her hair for the night, and between her hairline and the collar of her nightgown he could see a bit of pale, delicate skin and a few wispy curls.

"Does that suit you?" he prompted. "Six months?"

"A year."

"A year?" He forgot all about a soft, calming tone. His roar almost took off the cabin roof.

"One year," she replied, firmer now.

"No," Thomas said. "Six months."

"Nine months."

"Six months."

"Eight."

"Six."

"Seven."

"Six." His tone gained an implacable edge. He was the head of the household. If he agreed to this…this *unreasonable* demand…he'd never win a single argument between them. And he'd die of thwarted desire.

"Six," Charlotte replied in a resigned mutter.

Thomas sighed in relief and smiled at the nape of her neck. Their first marital argument. *Discussion*, he amended himself, or *debate*. Their first marital debate and he'd won. Encouraged by his success, he eased closer to her and braced his weight on one elbow. Leaning over her, his mouth by her ear, he lowered his voice to a rustling whisper.

"I have a bundle board for the bed. It's a piece of timber that slots into the frame, like a small fence to separate the bed into two halves. If it makes you more comfortable, we can use it for the first six months. But tonight I'd like to hold you, cradle you against my chest. It is our wedding night, after all. I'd like a memory of it. Something to look back on."

She didn't say anything. Thomas pulled back, his breath caught, his heart racing in his chest. In this argument...*debate*...he wouldn't dare to push for victory. He'd almost given up any hope that she might consent when he felt a tug of the covers and the slight dip of the mattress. His wife wriggled her rump and scooted backward toward him, edging closer until her buttocks bumped against his arousal.

Thomas froze. He waited. She didn't move away in disgust. Instead, she gave another wriggle to fit herself more snugly into the curve of his body. Slowly, he lifted one arm and slid it across her waist, anchoring her even closer to him.

He didn't dare to breathe. It flashed across his mind that by morning he might be dead from the lack of air, or perhaps his heart would simply burst with emotion. He didn't care if he never saw another dawn. It would be worth it, for a night of this wonderful pleasure of having someone to hold, someone to call his own.

Thomas shut his eyes and slowly exhaled the air trapped in his lungs. With every nerve in his body, he savored the feel of the woman he held in his embrace. Small and slight, she tucked neatly against him. His body enveloped hers, keeping her safe and warm. Her back pressed to his chest. Beneath his forearm he could feel the rapid rise and fall of her chest as she took quick, frightened breaths.

Never in his life had he felt another person so close. Perhaps when he was a baby his mother had suckled him at her breast. He couldn't remember. By the time his earliest memories started, she'd already rejected him, making him into an outcast in his own family, as well as in the community around them.

In his mind, he saw a lifetime of nights like this. Nights like this and, when the waiting was over at the end of the six months, even more magical nights. Filled with emotion, Thomas opened his eyes again and ran his gaze over what he could see of his wife—the crown of the dark head tucked beneath his chin, the edge of a slender shoulder, a tiny bit of bare skin at her neck.

He was no longer alone in the world.

"Go to sleep now," he murmured.

But he knew he'd keep awake all night.

Holding her was too precious to waste on sleep.

Six months. Six months. Charlotte repeated it to herself like a magic spell as she lay in Thomas Greenwood's arms, trying to remember to keep her stomach muscles puffed out to create an illusion of a belly rounded in pregnancy.

Of course, the true reprieve would be much

shorter. In another month, perhaps two, he would discover there was no child. She would have to confess, or make her escape before then.

Her immediate fears calmed, the tensions of the day melted away and her senses became attuned to the man next to her. His arm spanned across her waist and his big body curled around hers, as if designed to protect her, to keep her snug and warm.

Of course, that was how it was meant to be. Man and woman, husband and wife, were God's creations. It made sense they had been designed to fit together, to offer each other warmth and comfort while they slept. The toils of the day were over, the next day yet to dawn. Companionship during the night offered a chance to recuperate and build up strength to meet the challenges the dawn would bring.

Charlotte sighed in the darkness.

And those challenges would be great in number.

She cast her mind back to her abysmal efforts with the cookstove and making coffee. She'd learn. She might end up letting Thomas down in so many ways, but she wouldn't let him down as a housekeeper. Brimming with resolve, she emitted a small huffing sound of determination.

"Can't you sleep?" The question came in a low rumble behind her.

Charlotte hesitated. It would be easy to pretend to be asleep, but she didn't want to deceive him any more than she had to.

"No," she said. "My mind is too busy for sleep."

"Don't worry. It will be all right. Your life has changed in so many ways. New home. New husband. A baby on the way. It will take time to adjust to everything."

Now, Charlotte told herself. *This is the opportunity to tell him the truth and spare him from hurt.* She closed her eyes and remembered the feel of Cousin Gareth's cruel hands on her, the smell of liquor on his breath. She could hear his ugly whispers, and then she could hear Miranda's voice.

Or you can just let him take Papa's money and anything else he might want.

It was not just her future. As the firstborn, the responsibility fell on her to safeguard the family fortune. She owed it to Miranda and Annabel to protect their inheritance. It might be callous, but the welfare of her sisters ranked higher than the welfare of a stranger. And Thomas was a strong, capable man. She could pay him ample compensation for his help. He could rebuild his life after she was gone.

"I understand," Thomas said. "It doesn't matter."

"What?" Charlotte realized he had said something, asked something, but she had been too pre-occupied with her thoughts to listen. "Sorry... I wasn't listening... I was thinking of home..."

The arm across her waist tightened. Once again, Charlotte tensed her stomach muscles, pushing them out.

"I was asking about the man who is the father of your child. I'd like to know something about him. Whatever you feel comfortable telling me."

What could she tell him? She could think of no imaginary man. Part of the truth would serve best. She gave him Cousin Gareth. "My parents died four years ago. I was twenty. I know a lot of women are married by that age, but my father, although he was old-fashioned in many ways, did not wish to hurry us into marriage. I have two sisters. Miranda is twenty-two and Anna-bel is eighteen."

She felt a soft, soothing touch on her temple. A big hand stroked her hair, sliding over the edge of her brow, over and over again. Charlotte leaned deeper against the warm bulk of the man behind her and continued.

"Our parents left us enough money to live on, but because we were unmarried, we were not allowed to live alone. A cousin moved into the house. Cousin Gareth. He wanted to marry me but I loathed him. One day he got drunk. He cornered me into a room and forced himself on me."

A gruff sound came behind her, a low rumble that held a mix of anger and sympathy. "I'm sorry," Thomas said. "No woman should have to endure that." The soothing hand kept up its gentle motion. "Does he know about the baby?"

"No," Charlotte replied. "I prepared for my journey in secret. My sisters know. I promised to write and let them know as soon as I had arrived safely."

"You can do that tomorrow. I'll ride to Gold Crossing and post the letter. The town has a post office. It operates at the back of the mercantile. Or, if you want to, we can send a telegram."

"A letter will suffice."

For a moment, they lay in silence. Then Thomas spoke quietly, his deep voice quivering with emotion. "When the child comes, it will be my child, and yours. It will have nothing to do with that man. I will love it as my own. I don't want anyone to know the child isn't mine."

The stroking hand had stilled its motion while he spoke, and now his fingers swept down to curl over her shoulder, pressing lightly, demanding a response. "Do you agree?" he said. "My child. My name. Everything else forgotten, as if it never happened."

Charlotte nodded. Without thinking, she eased her grip on the edge of the covers and reached up to her shoulder, to place her hand on top of Thomas's. He had a large hand, knotted with knuckles. She let her fingers slide over his but didn't speak. There were no words that would make justice to his kindness, no words that wouldn't add to the burden of her guilt.

"I think I'm getting sleepy now," she said and withdrew her hand.

"Sleep." His fingers briefly squeezed her shoulder, then lifted away. The mattress dipped as he shifted his hips. The thick forearm settled across her waist once more. The muscled body curled around hers, cocooning her.

Warm. Safe. Content.

Charlotte closed her eyes and let slumber steal over her.

Thomas woke to the first glimmer of dawn. Another sunny day. The thought registered before others rushed in. Charlotte lay in his arms, slender and warm. All night, she had snuggled up against him. He had intended to stay awake, but as the night hours wore on, fatigue had taken its toll and he had drifted off to sleep.

Reluctant to leave her, Thomas eased up on one elbow and leaned over his wife. He breathed in her scent and studied her sleep-soft features. His heart beat strong and steady. He'd known contentment before, but this was more. This was happiness. His whole body thrummed with it.

Never in his life had he looked forward to a new day as much as he was looking forward to today.

Not just to today.

To all his tomorrows.

With his wife by his side, and soon a child to call his own.

Charlotte stirred on the feather mattress. Her lashes lifted. Instead of fuzzy and unfocused, her eyes were bright and alert at once. Not hazel now, in the morning light, but green with a touch of brown in it. The color of a moonglow pear before it ripened.

She saw him leaning over her and smiled up at him. "You're sniffing at me like a hunting dog." She spoke softly, her voice husky and muffled with sleep, but he could hear the laughter in it.

"What do I smell of?" she asked.

"I don't know," Thomas replied. "I've been trying to figure it out all night." He took another deep breath, filling his lungs with her scent. "I smelled it in the water you left in the bowl by the stove after your wash. I used the water after you." He looked down at her, a smile tugging at his mouth as he marveled at her beauty. "Can you do that every night? Leave the water in the bowl so I can use it after you and enjoy the smell."

"It's lavender soap. I brought a cake with me."

"Lavender." Thomas nodded, settled on an instant plan. "I'll buy some seeds and sow them by the edge of the wheat field. We'll learn to make that soap. Much better than carbolic, or bear grease."

"Learn to make lavender soap." She burst into laughter. "Give me a chance. First I'll have to learn to make coffee." She peered up at him, mischief lurking in those eyes. "And cook breakfast. And do laundry. And use a scrubbing brush. I don't think making lavender soap comes very high on the list."

Thomas dipped his head and brushed a kiss on her forehead. She didn't flinch away. For a second, he let temptation flood over him. His gaze fastened on her mouth. Small and plump, vivid red against the pale skin. He eased closer, inch by inch.

No, he warned himself, and wrenched away.

It was more for his sanity than her protection.

A wise man did not build up an appetite, only to suffer from starvation.

"Time to get up, Mrs. Greenwood." He rolled away from her, flung his legs over the edge of the bed and got to his feet.

The bedding rustled as Charlotte wriggled around to look at him. He could feel her gaze on him. It skimmed him from head to toe, paused at the erection that strained inside the pajama bottoms and then moved up to linger on his shoulders and the expanse of his naked chest.

Thomas stood still. Let her look, get used to him. Bit by bit. A touch of color flared up to his cheeks as Charlotte kept up her inspection. He was not a vain man, had no idea if he was handsome or not.

He had thick yellow hair and even white teeth. His skin was smooth and his jaw square and his nose straight. His body was that of a healthy, hardworking male. But there might be too much of him. That might be a problem, and he could do nothing about it.

A portly man could try to slim down, but a man who was big and muscular could only hope that the woman he married liked his powerful frame. And from the rapt expression on Charlotte's face Thomas decided that she did.

With that thought, he grinned and stopped parading half naked in front of his wife. He snagged his clothes from the chair, hurried into the parlor and closed the door behind him, leaving Charlotte to get up in the privacy of the bedroom.

She heard the front door open and close. Charlotte darted out of bed and rushed to the window to peek out. Thomas was striding down the path toward the big barn she could see through the cottonwood trees. Of course. A farmer needed to tend to his animals. At Merlin's Leap, grooms had looked after the horses.

She hurried into the parlor in her nightgown. Water was heating on the stove. She dipped her finger inside. Warm enough. She scooped some into a bowl, rinsed her face and teeth. No soap in the morning. Her lips tugged into a smile as she recalled how her lavender soap had enchanted Thomas. She'd send him a box of the stuff as soon as she was back at Merlin's Leap.

Her smile faded.

Perhaps by then he might prefer not to be reminded of her.

But right now, she had to concentrate on earning her keep.

She dressed in the bedroom and hurried back into the kitchen to work on her relationship with Vertie, the green enamel cookstove. She opened the hatch with the iron poker. Added another piece of firewood. Took the coffee grinder down from the shelf. One handful of beans from the small jute sack. Round and round with the handle. The beans rattled, the grinder crunched. The heavenly aroma of freshly ground beans spread around the parlor.

Last night, while she'd been busy clearing the sticky mess from the floor, Thomas had made coffee from the last grains in the tin, explaining every step as he went along. Charlotte repeated the instructions in her mind and measured three spoonfuls of coffee into the pot. One per person and one extra for the pot. She added two cupfuls of water, then slid the copper coffeepot into the middle of the iron ring and said a quick prayer it would turn out all right.

Next step was breakfast. She'd make porridge. That must be easier than bacon or biscuits or whatever farming folk ate for their morning meal in the Arizona Territory. She found a tin of grain on the shelf. Was it wheat? Or oats? Could you make porridge with either?

Lips pursed, Charlotte measured three cups of grain into an iron pot, added two cups of water and set the pot to boil on another ring on the stovetop. Satisfied with her efforts, she started searching for a stirring spoon.

Breakfast was on the way.

Thomas would be proud of her.

Chapter Six

Thomas strode into the parlor. He could smell coffee and something burning. The table was set. Coffee simmered on the stove. Beside the coffeepot, a big cast iron pot made loud bubbling noises, like frogs plopping up and down in a muddy pond.

Charlotte spun around to face him. "I made you breakfast."

Thomas smiled at the pride in her tone. What more could a man ask for? A pretty wife and a meal on the table. He nodded and sat down, too overcome to speak. Charlotte flitted about in a flurry of green skirts and a white blouse. Her hair was coiled up on her head. Thomas hoped the curls would soon unravel to tumble down her back.

He watched, ready to interfere if she risked burning herself, or created some other calamity. She remembered to use a cloth to protect her hands as she poured out the coffee. Thomas peered at the black trickle that flowed into his cup. It had the consistency of tar. Perhaps he could eat it with a spoon.

"It might be a bit strong." The pride in her voice had faded.

"I like it strong." Bravely, Thomas took a sip. And managed not to grimace. He ran his tongue over his teeth to stop them from sticking together with the glue-like substance.

"Perhaps a bit too strong," he said and pushed the cup toward her across the table. "You might add a drop of water into it."

"Yes. Of course."

Charlotte plunged the steel dipper into the pail and poured some water into his cup. Thomas didn't have the heart to tell her that he'd meant hot water, not cold. He stirred the mixture. Lumps of coffee floated around the cup. He ate them with the spoon, trying to get the balance between coffee and water about right.

"What's for breakfast?" he asked.

"Porridge."

"Porridge?" he said, puzzled. "Not many people make it from wheat. Let me know if you prefer oats, and I'll get you some. I grow it for the horses."

"This is…wheat porridge." She waved airily toward the pot that had stopped rumbling like a volcano and was now making a sizzling sound. The burning smell had intensified. Whirling to the stove, Charlotte wrapped a cloth around her hands and prepared to lift the pot to the table.

Thomas jumped to his feet. "Let me do that."

"No. I'm doing this. Sit down."

Startled, he sank back into his seat. She might be small, she might appear fragile, but his wife could muster up an air of command if she wanted to.

He watched, muscles tense, ready to leap to her aid if she faltered. She managed to transport the heavy pot without mishap. All Thomas had to do was to reach across the table and shove a slate holder beneath the iron pot to stop the heat from scorching the tabletop.

Charlotte lifted the lid. A notch appeared between her brows as she peered into the pot. Holding the lid in one hand, she dipped a wooden spoon into the porridge. A stunned expression spread across her face. She put down the lid and gripped the wooden spoon with both hands. With a grunt and a heave, she levered a huge lump of something solid out of the pot.

Thomas positioned his plate beneath the object. It fell on the china plate with a splat. He poked at the thing with his fork. It had the consistency of rubber. "Is this how they make porridge in New York?"

"Err…it's not really porridge. It's called a… porridge dumpling." Charlotte passed him a knife. "You cut it into slices."

"I see." Thomas felt laughter tickle in his throat. He didn't want to hurt her feelings. He stole a glance at her from the corner of his eye. She was biting her lip. Her shoulders were shaking. He lost the fight and burst into laughter.

Charlotte swatted at him with the cloth she'd used to protect her hands. "It's a *porridge dumpling*," she managed between bursts of mirth. "Eat it."

"I'll eat a slice if you eat a slice."

Quick as a flash, she sat opposite him. "Challenge accepted."

She pushed her plate next to his, picked up a knife and reached over to cut a wedge and slipped it onto her plate. After pulling her plate back in front of her, she stared down at the wedge. Her features puckered in determination, and then she picked up the congealed lump of wheat and crammed a huge bite into her mouth.

Her eyes bugged. Her cheeks ballooned. She chewed. And chewed. And chewed. And finally she swallowed, with a shiver that rippled all the way down her delicate frame. Thomas rocked in his seat, laughter rumbling in his chest, his eyes streaming with helpless tears.

A dainty forefinger jabbed into the air. "Your turn."

Thomas dropped his gaze to the big dumpling on his plate. He cut a wedge and shoved it into his mouth. The stuff had the flavor of sawdust and the consistency of boot leather.

"You forgot salt," he said after he'd finished chewing and swallowing.

His wife lifted a single eyebrow. "I'll remember it next time."

Thomas burst into another gust of laughter. Charlotte joined him. Between them, they ate every morsel of the porridge dumpling.

Ten minutes earlier, Thomas had looked at his pretty wife and the table set for breakfast and thought, *What more could a man ask for?* If pushed for a reply, he might have said, *Tasty food to fill his plate*. Now he knew it didn't matter. His happiness was complete, even if he had to survive on porridge dumplings for the rest of his days.

Charlotte washed the breakfast dishes and Thomas dried them. She had never thought there would be such sweet symmetry in housework. Her mother had tried to explain the thrill of sailing on a boat with her husband, just the two of them, united against the elements. Charlotte had never understood, until now. A wave of nostalgia washed over her. She lifted a hand to dash a tear from the corner of her eye.

"It's all right," Thomas said softly. "It was a good effort."

"I'm not downhearted about the cooking. I was just thinking of my parents...of how it was for them, working side by side...the way we are doing now."

"Were they happy together?"

"Blissfully. We were all happy. A happy family. Our father was a sea captain, but he gave up the long voyages after we were born. He loved sailing, and so did my mother. I didn't, and neither did my sisters. Father often joked we must be changelings because we all got seasick on the boat." She glanced up at him. "You said you have five brothers. Were you a happy family?"

Thomas turned away to stack a plate in the cupboard. He knocked over the sugar bowl. "Darn it," he said, and seemed to forget her question as he focused on scooping up the sugar before it got ruined.

By the time they had finished tidying up after breakfast, sweat beaded on Charlotte's brow and trickled down between her breasts beneath her blouse. She peeked out through the window. Bright sunshine played on the leaves of the cottonwood trees.

"It's going to be another hot day," she commented.

"The summer will be here soon," Thomas replied.

She hesitated. "Would you mind if I took off my wool skirt and just wore a petticoat? I'm already sweltering, and I'd like to save my skirt for trips into town. I have nothing else to wear, just the two petticoats and one skirt."

"Wait here." Thomas gestured for her to remain in the parlor while he strode into the bedroom. She heard the blanket box lid creak open and then slam shut.

He returned carrying a bundle of clothing. "Try these on."

She took the garments, turned them over in her hands. It was a pair of sturdy denim trousers and a faded cotton shirt. "Whose are these?"

"Doc Timmerman's grandson stayed with me a couple of weeks last summer. He left those behind. You can use them if they fit. He was a strapping boy of thirteen. If he comes back this summer, he'll have grown out of them."

She looked up from the worn garments. "I'm surprised there's a doctor in Gold Crossing. Why did he stay when the town closed down?"

"The doc's really retired. He's around seventy. His wife is the same age. They decided they were too old to leave. Art Langley stayed because he can't afford to leave." Thomas shook his head. "Poor Art. He keeps hoping."

"Hoping for what?"

"Hoping that the town will burst back into life. You've met Art. He owns the Imperial Hotel. And the saloon attached to it, the Drunken Mule. And the mercantile. And the row of empty buildings beyond. Even the schoolhouse."

Charlotte recalled the innkeeper's amusement at her wedding. "Is he the gaunt man who likes to play solitaire and laugh at other people's misfortunes?"

"Don't hold it against him if he tries to find something to laugh about. Art Langley discovered the seam of gold and started the mine. He invested everything into the railroad spur. When the mine played out, he was left with barely enough to buy the buildings as people moved away. He spends his time trying to keep everything in good repair. He believes that one day someone else will find gold and then the music will play again and the whiskey will flow and the dancing girls will dance and the mine owners will pay him to use his railroad to haul out the ore."

Curious, Charlotte arched her brows. "Could someone find gold?"

Thomas shifted one shoulder in an indifferent gesture. "I guess it's possible. Art believes there's gold up there, and he knows a lot more about mining than I do. Dozens of prospectors roam around in the mountains. They are what keeps the saloon and the hotel and the mercantile going, and generate enough business for the doc to see out his days in Gold Crossing."

"It's sad," Charlotte said wistfully. "A whole town just…vanishing."

"Don't shed too many tears. If the mine hadn't played out, I couldn't have bought the farm. Land values plummeted. My operation is small. I trade with Art for things I can't grow or make myself. In the fall, I make a couple of trips to Jerome and Flagstaff to sell the wheat and the corn." His voice fell to a rough murmur. "I hope you understood you were not signing on for a life of luxury."

Charlotte heard the strain in his words. She flashed him a bright smile. "Let me go and try these clothes on. If they fit, I can dress like a proper farmer's wife."

Thomas waited, standing on the porch, leaning against the railing, taking deep breaths of the fragrant spring air. Sundown was his favorite part of the day, but sunup was not far behind, and he liked middle of the morning too, like this moment. The cow had been milked, the horses moved to pasture. The chickens were clucking contentedly around the barn.

"What do you think?"

He heard the voice before he heard the clatter of feminine footsteps across the porch. He turned around. The sensation that slammed into his chest was becoming all too familiar. Maybe he was developing a heart condition.

Poised on her toes, Charlotte pivoted a full circle and repeated her question. "What do you think?"

Thomas let his gaze drift over her. The denim trousers hugged the curve of her buttocks. The shirt swamped her. He could see at least three inches of pale skin above the loose collar. His gut told him that if he stood right beside her and looked down when she bent forward, he might get a peek inside the neckline.

"What do you think?" she asked for the third time.

Thomas allowed himself one final second of perusal. Best of all, her upsweep had failed to stand up to the swift change of clothing. Curls were unraveling to spill down past her shoulders. Delicate wisps framed her face, dancing in the breeze.

"That's good," Thomas said. "Just like a farmer's wife should look."

She gave a peal of laughter and racketed down

the steps, bubbling with excitement. "Let's go. I want to see everything. A complete tour."

Thomas showed his wife the beaver dam. She laughed and pointed in delight when she saw a flash of brown fur in the water. He showed her the lake. She strolled along the bank, seeking the best spots for swimming. He showed her the pomegranate garden with its fading blooms. She ran around, chasing the fragrant petals that floated like snowflakes in the air.

By the time he'd showed her the fields of wheat and corn, he had become painfully aware that his wife knew nothing about agriculture. She seemed to think farmers frolicked in the sun and Mother Nature took care of the rest.

"You have to plant the corn every year?" she asked, brows furrowed, head cocked in surprise. "It doesn't grow back in the spring on its own?"

Thomas clamped down on the twinge of disappointment. It was clear that she was an intelligent woman. New York had an excellent public library. He'd hoped she might have taken an interest in his profession, had prepared for her new life by reading a book or two.

He shrugged his shoulders and let his eyes dwell on her slender frame and tumbling curls. A man couldn't ask for everything.

"No," he said. "Corn doesn't grow on its own. You plant in May. Then you water. A couple of times a week should be enough unless it gets very hot. You harvest the crop in August."

Her face brightened. "Irrigation. That means watering, doesn't it? I promised to help. Show me how to do it."

"Later." He pointed at her feet. "You'd ruin your leather boots. It gets muddy by the pump. Travis Timmerman left behind a pair of old rubber boots. They'll be too big for you but you can pad them out with old newspapers."

He continued the tour by taking her into the barn. The big timber building was divided into two in the middle, with an entrance at both ends. The wood store and chicken coop occupied one end, the milk cow and the pair of horses the other.

The chickens, all white leghorns, were scratching about in the dirt, clucking and squabbling. Thomas shooed them out of the way and led her into the shadowed interior of the barn. Stacks of firewood stood on the right, and straw-padded perches lined the wall on the left.

He heard a frightened cry behind him and spun around, poised for a quick rescue, looking for whatever trouble his wife might have landed herself in this time. Charlotte was squatting on her heels on the earth floor, sucking at her forefinger. Next to her a hen danced in fury, flapping its wings and screeching.

"It bit me," she mumbled around the finger, scowling at the furious hen.

Thomas crouched beside her. "Show me."

She pulled her finger from her mouth and held it out to him. A dot of blood gathered at the tip. Slowly, Thomas lifted her hand to his mouth and kissed away the droplet at the fingertip. His eyes held hers. He could see a blush rise to her cheeks. Her hand was tiny in his, her skin soft. He could smell the faint scent of lavender.

What did it matter if she wasn't the helpmate he'd hoped for?

What did it matter that she'd more likely add to his workload than ease it?

He was no longer alone. That was all that mattered.

"Don't try to pet the chickens," he told her quietly. "They are like cantankerous old women. That one—" he paused to nod at the aggressor "—is getting on in years. She is no longer a good layer and she likes to hide her eggs."

"What's she called?"

Thomas smiled. *A chicken pecks her and she wants to know its name.* "Harrison." He pointed at the birds rootling and pecking on the ground in turn. "That's Tyler. Polk. Zachary. Fillmore. Pierce." Each bird wore a metal band on one leg, trimmed with a scrap of cotton in a different color, so he could easily identify them.

Her merry laughter tingled down his spine. "The presidents! You named your chickens after the presidents."

Thomas nodded. "I started from Washington but a few have died. Tyler and Taylor sounded too similar, so when it came Taylor's turn I used his first name, Zachary." He pushed up to his feet and pulled her up with him. "Your job will be to collect the eggs every morning."

"The eggs! Where can I find them?" She spun around to face the wall with the straw-lined perches.

"Sometimes they sit in plain sight on top of the straw," Thomas explained. "Sometimes you need to search around. Sometimes it could be anywhere. Harrison likes to hide hers between the stacks of firewood."

In a comical stalking motion, feet rising high, fingers curled like claws in front of her, Charlotte marched up to the wall and searched the nearest perch. "I've got one." She hurried back to him, as excited as a child on Christmas morning. A single white egg sat cradled in her cupped palm.

Her whole face lit up in a smile—eyes shining, cheeks dimpling, lips parting to reveal a row of pearly teeth. To Thomas, that smile delivered more warmth than the sun in the sky.

He took the egg from her, moved aside to prop it on the stack of logs.

Charlotte darted to the next perch and looked back at him over her shoulder while she searched about with her hand. "I'll get a little wicker basket to collect them in," she told him, full of enthusiasm. "Is that the right way to do it? Or do I need to collect them in an apron?" She lifted a single eyebrow, the way he'd seen her do before. "How does a proper farm wife do it?"

As she rummaged about without taking proper care, the egg rolled over the edge of the straw perch and crashed down to the dirt floor. Charlotte jumped back. She stared at the mess of broken shell and spreading white and yolk and uttered an unladylike word.

Thomas tried not to laugh as he observed her fraught expression. Something moved inside him, an odd sense of tenderness, like a warm flicker in his chest. With a rueful smile, he said, "A proper farm wife does it without breaking the eggs."

Four eggs! She had found four eggs, including the one she'd smashed. Now she knew what farming folk ate for breakfast. Thomas had told her that the hens laid an egg most days, except for the elderly Harrison. He'd warned her not to become attached, because if they wanted a proper Thanksgiving dinner, Harrison would end up in the pot.

When he mentioned Thanksgiving, she fell into silence.

Don't spoil today by worrying about the future, she told herself.

They took the eggs into the cabin. Thomas showed her one more time how to make coffee. Three spoonfuls. That was right. But the small spoons. Not the big. And level spoonfuls, not heaped. She was learning from her mistakes.

The porridge dumpling sat heavy in their bellies and they only had coffee and dried biscuits for lunch. Then Thomas took her to meet the milk cow. Charlotte followed him into the shadowed barn. The smell was different on this side of the building. The chickens had an acrid odor, but the stable had a more fertile smell.

"Muuu," the animal greeted them.

It was huge. An enormous lump of brown matted fur on four legs—legs that seemed far too spindly to bear its hulking weight.

"Milking her will be your job," Thomas said.

Charlotte slid her terrified gaze from the cow to him and back again.

"She's called Rosamund." Thomas walked up to the fur-coated brown monster and patted its flank.

"Muuu," went Rosamund.

Charlotte eased closer, hiding behind Thomas. She peeked past him at the animal, which was straining its head toward them. "Does it bite, like horses?"

"She won't bite. You can pet her nose. Like this."

Following his example, Charlotte held a flattened hand in front of the huge pink nostrils. Cool, damp breath brushed against her skin. A wet, slippery nose nuzzled her palm. Startled by the touch, Charlotte pulled her hand away.

"I guess you can't just press a button and the milk will come out," she said, eyeing the cow with a speculative look.

"I'll show you," Thomas promised.

She scooted backward, keeping safely behind Thomas as he moved away. He lifted a small wooden stool from a hook on the wall and set it down next to Rosamund. Then he turned toward her and pointed at the stool.

He wanted her to sit there.

Right under Rosamund's huge belly.

Charlotte inched forward. *Don't be a coward.* She slipped onto the stool. The wide flank of brown fur filled her sights. Surely, the animal would crush her, if it decided it was tired and wanted to lie down.

Thomas crouched behind her. His arms circling her, he reached for the pink udders that dangled from Rosamund's belly. His hands curled around two of the teats.

"You tighten your fingers one by one, starting from the top, and at the same time you pull your hand downward. Like this." His hand moved. A thin stream of milk spurted into the straw.

"You try," he said.

Charlotte leaned deeper beneath Rosamund's sagging belly and fisted her hands around the udders. She tightened her fingers and pulled. Nothing happened. No stream of milk. She tried again. Rosamund made an angry noise and shifted her enormous hooves. Charlotte shrieked and toppled back on the stool. She would have fallen over, but strong arms closed around her, steadying her.

She was lifted in the air. Thomas perched to sit on the milking stool and settled her between his muscled thighs. His arms on either side of her, he guided her hands back to Rosamund's udders and laid his hands on top of hers. His body surrounded hers, even more completely than it had at night when they slept.

Every trace of fear vanished. Rosamund was getting restless, grunting and stomping, but Charlotte could feel Thomas all around her—his chest against her back, his legs outside hers, his arms circling her. He was a barrier to keep away any threat of danger. As long as she sat snug in his lap, nothing could hurt her.

His fists closed over hers. Fingers squeezed.

One hand slid down. Milk rained into the straw. Thomas lifted his hands away from hers and she tried alone. Nothing. Rosamund protested, an unhappy bellow and the angry clomping of hooves.

"That's enough for today," Thomas said. He eased back, his arm firm across her waist, and rose to his feet, lifting her with him. He held on to her for a moment longer, while she found her footing, and then he released her and stepped away.

She turned toward him. "I can learn how to do it. I *will* learn."

He reached one hand to touch the curls by her face. "It's not important."

The gentleness of the gesture, the soft acceptance in his voice flowed like a magic spell over Charlotte. The restless noises of the cow, the smells of the stable, everything seemed to fade away. She was only conscious of Thomas. His eyes held hers, and again she could see a sharp, almost painful longing in them, like she'd seen when he'd brought her home in the wagon across the desert.

Something stirred within Charlotte. Something other than guilt. Respect. Admiration. Perhaps even envy. Thomas wanted so little in life. Just to grow enough food to survive on, and to live peacefully in his valley, with a wife by his side.

For a moment, she almost hoped that she could

be that wife. A temptation seized her, to lean into his touch, to rise up on her toes and move into him, to have his arms close around her in an embrace. To give something to him, instead of just taking from him—food, protection, guidance and affection.

Rosamund let out another angry bellow. Thomas flinched, as if he too had drifted into some inner world, detached from reality. He made a small, fraught sound low in his throat and turned away to soothe the restless animal.

Charlotte could feel her body trembling. What would have happened if the moment had not been broken? What was happening between them? Was it simply the idyll of two people isolated from others, like Adam and Eve, or was it more?

She did not dare to think about it. She must keep her distance. Anything else would only cause more problems, bring deeper hurt when she returned home to Merlin's Leap. And she *would* have to return, there was no question about it. Her duty was to her sisters, her responsibility as the firstborn something she must never forget.

As they left the barn and crossed the sunlit yard to the paddock where two horses grazed, Thomas's words played on Charlotte's mind. *It's not important,* he'd said when she promised she would learn how to milk Rosamund.

It's not important. As if he was resigned to her being incompetent, unable to deal with the farm chores. She would learn. Otherwise she would be nothing but a burden to him.

Chapter Seven

Charlotte sat at the long table in the parlor and composed a letter to her sisters. It had to say everything without revealing anything. Thomas had gone out to work on the vegetable patch after showing her the horses—the chestnut cart horse called Trooper and a blue roan quarter horse called Shadow.

The sun was low in the sky by the time Charlotte was happy with her efforts. She hurried to read the letter once more time before sealing it in the envelope. It was addressed to her—Charlotte Fairfax.

Dear Charlotte,
I hope this letter finds you in good health, and that you remember me, Miss Emily Bickerstaff, from those few weeks you spent at the Boston Academy for Young Ladies,

before you returned home to be educated by a governess.

I am writing on behalf of another student, Maude Jackson, whom you never met as she joined the Academy a year later. Her name is Maude Greenwood now. Her husband is a pioneer in the frontier region of our country. They live in Gold Crossing, Arizona Territory, and their hometown is the reason why I am writing to you now.

Teachers are very difficult to recruit out in the West. Mrs. Greenwood has contacted me to see if I might be interested in a position, but unfortunately I need to care for my elderly mother. However, it occurred to me that you might be interested in an adventure out in the territories.

If you are not in need of a position, perhaps your younger sister might be. I believe you mentioned she is only two years younger and has benefited from the same education. I am afraid I don't recall her name. However, if she were interested in traveling out West, Mrs. Greenwood would be extremely grateful to hear from her, as would everyone in the town of Gold Crossing.

Yours truly,

Miss Emily Bickerstaff

Charlotte let her mind stray back to the few miserable weeks she'd spent at the Boston Academy for Young Ladies. The formal, rule-driven world of the school had felt stifling, full of petty jealousies. The secluded valley that now surrounded her reminded her of the happy home Merlin's Leap had once been.

She cast aside her memories and raked one final glance over the letter. That would have to do. She daren't give any more details. Annabel would figure it out, and her sisters would write to her, addressing the letter to Maude Greenwood, care of the Post Office, Gold Crossing, Arizona Territory.

She had considered making the sender Maude Jackson, with just a mention of Emily Bickerstaff as a mutual friend, but that might arouse suspicion in Cousin Gareth, for young ladies of quality did not write to each other without getting an introduction first.

The biggest problems with the letter were the lack of sender's address and the prospect the post office might put marks on the envelope, revealing it had come all the way from the West. She hoped those would escape Cousin Gareth's notice, and that he would be too lazy to seek out Emily Bickerstaff to verify the facts.

Charlotte folded the sheet, slipped it into the

envelope and sealed the flap, just in time, for heavy footsteps echoed across the porch. The instant the door flung open, she bounced up to her feet and waved the letter in the air.

"I've written to my sisters. When can you go and post it?"

Thomas strode over to the kitchen counter and used the dipper to drink from the pail. Charlotte could see hurt and disappointment in the way he averted his face. Of course, he would have liked to have seen what she'd written, to be included in the family connection. However, it was just as important that he remained ignorant of the contents of the message.

She had hesitated before addressing the letter to herself. Thomas might study the envelope, see the name Charlotte and be puzzled by it. It couldn't be helped. It was more important to throw Gareth off her track. His suspicions were more likely to arise if a letter came for Miranda, who had never been away from home and was unlikely to have friends Gareth didn't know about.

For Cousin Gareth *would* intercept the letter. Charlotte had no doubt of it. However, in his efforts to discover her whereabouts, he was bound to share the contents with Annabel and Miranda, hoping to get some clues from their reaction. It was something Charlotte could not predict for certain, but it was a gamble she had to take.

Thomas wiped his mouth with the back of his hand. "Is the letter important?"

"Not really," Charlotte told him. "But I'd like my sisters to know that I've arrived safely and that the wedding has taken place."

"I'll ride into town tomorrow."

"There's no need to make a special trip."

"We need a few things from the mercantile anyway, and it's only an hour's fast riding. It takes longer in the cart." Thomas held out his hand. "I'll leave at first light tomorrow. If you give me the letter now, I'll get my saddlebags ready."

Charlotte felt her heartbeat quicken. She couldn't meet Thomas's eyes as she handed him the letter. He took it, studied the envelope. When he lifted his gaze back to her, a troubled furrow lined his brow, but he did not ask why her sister was called Charlotte Fairfax.

Charlotte prayed in her mind for him to remain silent. If he asked, she could tell him her middle name was Charlotte and she used it because she disliked Maude, and her sister was also called Charlotte and she was married to a man named Fairfax, but the thought of adding to her lies filled her with shame.

The silence in the cabin went on and on until it grew oppressive. Like so many times during the day, Charlotte could feel Thomas's assessing gaze lingering on her slim waist. The denim trousers made the flatness of her belly even more obvious.

He suspects. The thought flashed through her mind.

With a bright smile that hid her ill conscience, Charlotte hurried up to the kitchen cupboards. Chattering like a demented magpie, she banged doors and shuffled cardboard boxes and glass jars and small burlap sacks.

"I see that you mostly have dry goods," she said. "Do you know, they are preserving things in metal cans now? Meat and fruit and even fish. Not in glass jars, like people do at home, but in metal cans."

"I read the newspapers," Thomas said. "When I can afford one."

Charlotte fell silent. She'd already seen the small pile of carefully preserved back issues of the *Arizona Citizen* and the *San Francisco Call*. There had even been a copy of the *Matrimonial News*, with some advertisements circled in pencil.

"I know." She spoke into the depths of the cupboard. "I wasn't implying that you're a country yokel. I simply assumed that such things may not have arrived here, because of the cost of transport."

Thomas didn't reply. Charlotte stole a glance

at him over her shoulder. He was rubbing a hand over his eyes.

"Are you tired?" she asked.

He nodded.

"I'll cook for you."

"I'll cook. I'm more hungry than I'm tired."

There it was again. The dismissal that suggested she might be a pretty face but useless otherwise. Didn't he realize how much she wanted to be of help to him? Didn't he see how hard she was trying?

Charlotte shook off the surge of frustration. It was too nice an evening to brood, with a chorus of birdsong coming in through the open front door and the last rays of the sun gilding the grass and the trees. "Fine," she said, her spirits rallying. "But tomorrow, after you are back from town, you must show me how to irrigate the fields, and then I can help you with the task."

Thomas stopped fighting the doubts as he rode home from Gold Crossing where he'd gone to post Charlotte's letter. The envelope—the contents of which his wife had taken care to conceal from him—had been addressed to Charlotte Fairfax, Merlin's Leap, Boston, Massachusetts.

He'd married Maude Jackson from New York City.

And yet his wife had asked him to call her

Charlotte, and now it appeared that her sister was also called Charlotte, but with a different last name, Fairfax. Perhaps the sister was married, or they were half sisters, with a different father.

But there was more to it. Several times, he'd caught his wife talking about Boston when she referred to her home in the East. When she noticed the slip, she'd made some flimsy explanation about having moved from one city to another.

Who was she?

Was she Maude Jackson? If so, why did she answer to Charlotte?

Was she Charlotte Fairfax? If so, why write a letter to herself?

And the pregnancy? However hard he looked, he could see no sign that she was with child. Weren't women supposed to have funny cravings for food? And morning sickness?

But each time Thomas pondered the matter, he came to the same conclusion: being in the family way outside marriage brought such shame, no woman would tell such a lie. Lies went the other way round, denying a pregnancy.

The photograph of Maude Jackson burned like a silent protest in his pocket, adding to his turbulent thoughts. More and more he felt unable to reconcile the plain features and pinched expression in the picture with the beauty he'd married.

Thomas could only come to one conclusion.

For some reason, his wife was deceiving him.

The old pain flared up inside him. The pain of being excluded, of not being worthy, of being rejected. He'd grown up wanting to belong, wanting to be loved, and now a fear surged inside him, a premonition that nothing had changed for him.

He was being used, and he didn't know why, or even exactly how. Perhaps his wife had contracted to the marriage as a temporary solution, to conceal her pregnancy from family and friends, and she planned to leave him as soon as the baby was born.

As the thought formed in his mind, an idea struck him.

If she planned to leave, might she let him keep the child?

Resolve hardened within Thomas. Even if he failed to hold on to his wife, he'd fight to be a father to the child. That might help him heal—saving another human being from the burden of growing up unwanted and unloved.

Thomas found Charlotte waiting for him on the porch steps, dressed in her boy's clothing, a pair of big rubber boots weighing down her movements, like anchors on her feet.

"Did you post the letter?" she called out as

she clomped down the front steps, hurrying to Shadow's side before he had even dismounted.

He let his gaze drift over her upturned, expectant features. Already, the first stabs of disappointment and loss sliced through him. "Yes," he replied. "I posted it." *The letter to Charlotte Fairfax in Boston.*

"Good." Her smile appeared forced, lacking its usual sparkle. "I'm ready to go and see the irrigation pump." She stepped back and stomped her booted feet against the earth, as if to demonstrate her eagerness.

Thomas swung down from the saddle. "I'll take care of Shadow first. And I'd like a cup of coffee. I had lunch in town. Art Langley sends his regards. I bought more sugar and a bar of soap. The mercantile didn't have lavender. I got vanilla."

He dug in the satchel tied to his saddle and handed her the parcel. The soap had been much too expensive, but he wanted her to wash with it every day, so he could breathe in her scent while they slept.

Fool, he told himself. *The more you let yourself get used to her, the more it will hurt if she abandons you.*

"Thank you." Charlotte unwrapped the small cake of soap and held it up to her nose. Eyes closed, she inhaled a deep breath. "It's lovely. Just as nice as the lavender."

A sudden sense of desperation flooded over Thomas. He could not bear to watch. Every second, her beauty and her good humor and her childish enthusiasm about small things cut a bit deeper into his lonely heart.

"I'll see to the horse." He took Shadow by the bit and led the blue roan down the path to the barn.

By the time he came back into the cabin and sat down for a coffee, Thomas had his emotions under a semblance of control. Gruff and morose, he avoided looking at Charlotte as he gave brief replies to her questions about the folk in town, Art Langley and the doc and his wife and the few others who remained.

When his cup was empty, he rose to his feet. "Let's go."

Thomas strode along the path to the lake, too fast for Charlotte to keep up, and gained a moment of solitude to calm down while she scampered along after him in her big boots that looked like clumps of dried mud on her feet.

His valley. His home. He glanced up into the sky that spread blue overhead, watched the tiny butterflies dancing over the yellow flowers in the row of bushes that bordered the lake. He might end up alone again, but he belonged to a place, his own land. Like so many other times during the past six years, Thomas immersed himself in the task at hand. A man who kept busy had no time to brood.

"Careful." He reached out a hand to steady Charlotte as she jumped onto the small wooden jetty he'd built at the shore of the lake.

She craned forward to inspect the iron handle on the metal pipe that rose from the water. "It's like the well pump," she commented.

"It's exactly the same." He opened the timber storage box, took out the long hose he used for irrigation and gestured for her to step back. "Watch out."

She scooted back and craned her neck to watch as he joined one end of the long gutta-percha hose into the pump and clipped the metal sprinkler to the opposite end of the hose.

He pointed at the various parts of his irrigation system as he spoke. "When I crank the pump, water goes into the hose. Once the hose is full, the pressure from the pump forces the water out at the other end. The metal piece is a sprinkler, with holes to distribute the water over a larger area. I have two different sprinklers. For the vegetable patch, a curved one with holes at the top, so the water comes out like rain. For the corn, a flat one with holes at the side. Corn should be watered at the base."

Thomas looped the coil of the hose over one arm, stepped from the jetty onto the muddy bank and held out his other hand to help Charlotte down. Her slender fingers clung to his callused ones. He maintained the contact for a moment longer, even after she was safely on firm ground.

Then he strode up the bank, at the same time unraveling the coiled hose to stretch it out like a long snake along the ground. "The tricky part of the job is moving the hose," he explained. "Corn does not like to get waterlogged. You need to reposition the sprinklers every few minutes."

"Can I help?"

She was standing still, looking at him with the eagerness of an army recruit on the first day of parade. It stirred something inside Thomas, her keen desire to help him. That much of her at least was sincere.

"Your help might make a big difference," he told her. "I need to stop pumping when I move the sprinkler around, and the pressure goes out of the hose. If you do the moving, I can keep pumping all the time. Mind you," he added, "you can't just drag the hose over the rows of produce. You'd crush the plants. You'll have to lift it over the plants, or drag the hose back to the edge of the field and drag it out again."

"Show me." Her hands flittered in front of her

face with an impatient, utterly feminine gesture. "I want to try."

"All right."

Together, they rolled out the hose. Charlotte was darting and leaping around him, clumsy in her big boots, hindering as much as helping. Little by little, Thomas conquered the tension her hidden secrets had stirred up in him.

There was no point in spoiling the present by worrying about the future. If he allowed bitterness to make him surly, he'd ruin whatever time he had left with her. He wanted to build up memories, something he could look back on during the lonely nights after she was gone.

"I'll go and pump," he told her. "You keep an eye on the sprinkler."

He'd chosen the rows of cabbages and beets on purpose, because the upright sprinkler created a mist of rain. Anticipating the next few moments, Thomas hurried back to the jetty and put all his energies into cranking the handle of the pump.

Water gurgled in the pipe that came up from the lake. The hose filled out, like a snake that had been feeding. The kinks in it straightened. The hose grew taut with the pressure and the sprinkler at the other end burst into life. Just as Thomas had guessed, in her impatience Charlotte had been crouching over the metal piece, staring at the tiny perforations, waiting for something to happen.

A feminine shriek, as much of delight as of outrage, rippled around the sunlit fields as she bounced backward and toppled over on her behind. Even from the distance, Thomas could see the rivulets of water dripping down her face.

"You rotten egg," she yelled. "You knew that would happen, didn't you?"

Thomas pumped harder. A fine mist of rain rose over the field, sparkling in the sunshine. Charlotte remained sitting on the ground, her legs flung out, her hands braced against the dirt as she leaned backward, her face tipped up toward the rain. Her merry laughter rang in the air, mixing with the rainbow that formed over her.

Oh, the glorious sight of seeing his wife happy, of hearing her laugh. The pleasure of it quivered like an arrow through every part of Thomas. He didn't even mind the few heads of cabbage she had flattened beneath her rump.

For the rest of the afternoon, Thomas watched Charlotte frolicking in the spray as she moved the sprinklers around. The muscles in his arms and shoulders protested with the strain of pumping, but even then he didn't cease. He didn't give up until he knew that if he saturated the soil with any more water, he would risk rotting his crops.

* * *

That evening unfolded in easy companionship, adding to the happiness that held Thomas in its thrall. Under his supervision, Charlotte managed to cook an edible beef stew. She sang while she stirred the pot, her hair pulled into ringlets from the humidity of the sprinklers, her face flushed from the afternoon out in the sun and from the heat of the stove.

"What's the song?" he asked.

"It's a sea shanty." She resumed her singing. "Oh, have you heard the news, me Thomas?" Dropping her voice to a low rumble, she went on, "One more day." Then, back in her feminine voice, "We're homeward bound tomorrow."

She jerked her chin toward him. "Go on. Join in." She dropped her voice again. "One more day."

Hesitantly, he joined in. She sang verse after verse about a sailor longing to reach the home port, each verse followed with the refrain of "One more day."

When they came to the end, she gave him a wistful smile over her shoulder. "I told you, Papa was a sea captain. Sea shanties accompany sailors in their work. A leader sings the full verse, and then the sailors sing the refrain as they pull the ropes or deal with some other physical task. That's why the refrain has a punchy rhythm to it.

One. More. Day. Each word represents a heave on the rope."

Thomas asked the question that had niggled inside him while he listened to her singing. "Is the sailor in the song called Thomas?"

"No. He is called John." Another wistful smile. "But I was singing for you."

One more day. Thomas swallowed. Was she trying to tell him something? Was it a hidden message, a warning that his time with her was coming to an end? He brushed aside the thought. It was a song. Just a song about a sailor called John. Not about a lonely farmer called Thomas and his wife, whatever her real name might be.

After they had eaten, he went outside to take the horses into the barn and give the cow her evening milking. He returned inside to find Charlotte in bed, curled on her side beneath the covers. A lamp burned with a low flame on the nightstand.

Thomas undressed quickly, almost fearful that she might vanish in a puff of smoke if he took too long. Honoring his promise, he had slotted in the bundle board. Only six inches high, it separated them, but as they continued to share the patchwork quilt over it, he could feel the presence of his wife beside him. He blew out the lamp and breathed in the scent of vanilla from the soap she had used for her evening wash.

Outside, an owl hooted. The moon had risen high. Silvery light fell across the floorboards. He'd have to ask Charlotte if she wanted him to make shutters for the windows. He'd never bothered. He liked the moonlight at night, and the secluded valley rarely suffered from heavy storms.

As Thomas lay still, the doubts he had brushed aside while they irrigated the fields and worked at the kitchen chores swamped him anew. Each minute that went by, his feelings for Charlotte grew. Not just the sudden thunderbolt of her beauty, but she was spinning a web around him with her presence, with the joy she brought to the simple tasks, with the pride that she stirred in him over his role as a protector, his masculine strength acting as a rock against which her delicate femininity could be shielded.

Had he made a mistake agreeing to wait six months?

What would happen if he went back on his word?

What would happen if he lifted himself over the bundle board and took her here and now? Would it mean she'd have to stay? Surely, if he consummated the marriage, that would give him more rights, would tie them together more firmly as man and wife.

His mind flashed back to his childhood. *Don't,*

his instincts screamed. *Don't do it*. It might be possible to tempt Charlotte into giving her body willingly, but she would end up resenting him for being forced to stay if she had planned to leave. He had spent his childhood with a mother and father who didn't want him. He shied away from repeating the experience with a wife who'd been saddled with him against her wishes.

Charlotte stirred beneath the bedding, as if reading his thoughts.

"How long do you think it will take my letter to get there?" she asked.

He shrugged, sending the mattress into a gentle sway. "I don't know."

"How long does it take for your letters to reach your family in Michigan, or their letters to get to you? It might be more or less the same duration."

What could he say? *I haven't spared a thought to them since the day I walked out of the house for the final time?* No, that was wrong. He'd thought of them aplenty. But he didn't write. Why bother? They didn't want to know about him, and they certainly wouldn't write back, unless it was to tell him to stay away.

"How long?" Charlotte pressed.

He made a gruff sound. "Go to sleep."

Either his wife was tired or she got the message that the topic was out of bounds, for she fell silent. She huddled deeper beneath the quilt, and little by little the moon crept across the sky as Thomas lay awake, wondering how many more times he'd get to have *one more day*.

Chapter Eight

Charlotte scattered a handful of flour on the baking board and kneaded the lump of dough with the heels of her palms. A pot of rabbit stew simmered on the stove. Thomas had caught the creature in a snare and had gutted and skinned it, but she had done the rest.

She'd been married for almost two weeks now. Every morning she fed the chickens and collected fresh eggs from the barn. She knew how to boil laundry in the big iron cauldron and how to darn a pair of socks. She made excellent coffee. Some of the meals she cooked still turned out like the porridge dumpling, but not all of them.

Milking the cow had defeated her. Thomas had decided her hands were too small for the task. He had ordered her to stop annoying poor Rosamund. She was helping, though. Contributing to the running of the farm. She scrubbed and cleaned and mended and polished. In the afternoons, as the sun started to cool, she helped Thomas to irrigate the fields.

Every night she slept beside him.

Sometimes, Thomas reached over the bundle board in his sleep, his fingers tangling in her hair, as if to make sure she was still there. Once, she had woken up in the night to find herself half draped across the wooden barrier. Her head had been pillowed on his shoulder, her leg thrown across his, her palm resting on his bare chest. Gingerly, she'd eased back on her side, her heart thrumming, her nerves rioting, but Thomas had remained sound asleep.

It had been all too easy to get used to him. To his warmth, to his strength, to his kindness and patience. To his handsome features. To his powerful frame. To the slow smile that revealed an even row of white teeth and lit up his entire face. To the sparkle of humor that sometimes twinkled in his solemn gray eyes.

What if…?

What if…?

So far, Charlotte hadn't quite dared to let the thought form in her mind, but now it broke through, like excess water spilled from the reservoir over the top of the beaver dam.

What if she confessed to her lies and offered to make the marriage real? Would Thomas forgive her? Would he accept her as his wife despite the deceit?

She knew he'd suffered in the past. It was something to do with his family, the reason he'd left his home in Michigan, but she had no inkling of the details. He never spoke of his parents or his brothers, avoiding even the most casual of questions.

No, Charlotte decided.

He wouldn't forgive her.

He was scrupulous in his honesty, and he expected the same from others. Already, she felt he didn't fully trust her. He had guessed she was guarding secrets. Ever since she'd written home to Merlin's Leap without sharing the contents of the letter with him, she had felt a barrier of suspicion between them, as solid as the bundle board that separated them at night.

Charlotte sighed and kneaded the lump of dough against the baking board. What was the point of dreaming about a future with Thomas anyway? Her life was in the East, her duty with her sisters, and worry about them was spoiling the peace she had found in the small secluded valley.

Ten days had passed since Thomas went to post the letter to Merlin's Leap. She had no idea how long it would take for a letter to reach Boston…or if Cousin Gareth might confiscate the missive…or if Miranda might be unable to mail a reply.

Charlotte recalled her conversation with her sisters on the day she escaped. Miranda and Annabel had insisted Cousin Gareth would not take out his revenge on them but put his energies into finding her. Even if that were true, he might have been heavy-handed with them, believing they knew her whereabouts and attempting to force them into revealing what they knew.

She was desperate for news.

Desperate to know her sisters were safe.

Outside the cabin, Charlotte could hear the thudding of hooves and the jangle of a bridle and the creaking of leather as Thomas returned. She didn't like it when he rode into town and left her alone, but they only had the one saddle horse, the blue roan Shadow, and it would have taken too long to harness Trooper and go in the wagon.

Five minutes later, Thomas strode in and hung his hat on the peg by the door. The summer sun had bleached his hair golden and tanned his skin to the color of nutmeg. With the blue shirt he wore, his eyes looked more blue than gray.

"Everything all right?" he asked, glancing at her waist.

Charlotte nodded. More and more, he was eyeing her flat stomach with suspicion. She had considered padding out her midriff with a folded towel, but she had resisted the thought. It would be taking the deceit one step too far. She'd told a lie. She would not compound her dishonesty with acts designed to mislead.

Thomas tossed a newspaper on the table. "Brought you the *Citizen*."

Charlotte dusted the flour from her hands. "Can we afford it?"

"It's an old copy Doc Timmerman had lying around."

She hesitated before asking, "No mail?"

His brows furrowed. "You know it's too soon." He dipped his hand into his pocket, as if to count the coins he had left. "If you are worried, we could send a telegram."

She shook her head. "I'll wait."

He peeked into the pot bubbling on the stove. "Smells good."

While he unpacked his meager purchases, Charlotte fashioned a loaf from the dough and pressed it into the bread tin, which she slid into Vertie's oven compartment. As they sat down to dinner, they talked, the way they did every night at suppertime.

"Art Langley is up to something," Thomas said. "He is as secretive as a squirrel burying nuts in the ground. I wonder if he's taken up prospecting for gold again."

"He doesn't have time for prospecting," Charlotte pointed out.

From their evening talks, she knew every one of the eight permanent residents of Gold Crossing. There was Doc Timmerman and his wife, Dottie, and Reverend Eldridge, the ancient preacher who had married them, and Art Langley, who owned everything. He employed Manuel Chavez, the one-eyed card sharp who ran the saloon, and Gus Osborn, a widower in his forties who ran the mercantile.

Gus Osborn had a fourteen-year-old son, Gus Junior, who rode messages to the farms and ranches and the prospectors in the surrounding hills. Gus Junior was a bigger gossip than any nosy matron had ever been.

Last, but definitely not least, there was Miss Gladys Hayes, a spinster in her fifties who according to Thomas had stayed in Gold Crossing out of sheer stubbornness, refusing to leave the place where her brother lay in his grave.

The rest of the men who had crowded on the porch of the Imperial Hotel on her wedding day were ranchers and farmers and prospectors from the surrounding hills. The train came into Gold Crossing once a week, on Thursdays, and people chose that day to come into town, to pick up mail and get provisions, and to see who was arriving and leaving on the train.

Thomas scooped up the last spoonful of his rabbit stew. He pushed his plate aside and leaned back on the kitchen bench. "That was good," he said, rubbing one hand over his stomach. Then he returned to the earlier topic. "Art sure is up to something. Next time I go into town I'll have to look up Gus Junior and see if he knows anything about it."

Charlotte tried to ignore the small niggle of worry his words caused. She'd come to enjoy the peaceful existence in their valley. Anything outside seemed like a threat, like an intrusion. If only she could have her sisters with her. Then she'd be happy to forget about the outside world and never leave again.

Thomas wiped the china plate and reached to stack it in the cupboard. Doing the dishes, standing side by side, was a new addition to his growing list of favorite times of the day.

Charlotte was singing one of her sea shanties, and Thomas listened to the words. "Oh, my old mother, she wrote to me, my darling son, come home from the sea…"

The plate nearly slipped from his fingers. Had she chosen the song on purpose? He didn't want to hear any more verses, didn't want to listen to a song about a mother yearning for her missing son to return home. He cast around in his mind for something to say that would make her stop.

"I've been reading in the newspaper about a thing called electricity."

Charlotte ceased her singing and glanced up at him, her hands immersed in the dish bowl.

"Ever come across it?" Thomas asked. "I hear they use it in big cities to power the street lamps."

"I heard people talk about it in Bos— In the East. But I don't claim to understand what it means."

"It's something you can use for power. Edison Machine Works is advertising these little machines they call dynamos, or generators. When the generator goes round and round, it makes electricity. You can use the electricity to power a motor. I thought one of those generators could operate the motor for the pump. I could irrigate the fields on my own."

Thomas saw the stricken expression on Charlotte's face and cursed himself for being so thoughtless. Couldn't he have chosen a better example about the benefits of a generator? For the example he had chosen said: *I can manage without your help. I can replace you with a machine.*

He tried to smooth over the awkward moment by prattling on. "For the rest of the time, you could use the generator to power lamps. They have something called electric lightbulbs. I don't think they cost a lot."

Her voice was subdued. "What is this…electricity? Does it come in a bottle?"

"I don't think so. It's not like the steam they use for the trains, either, or the gas Art Langley uses for the lamps in his hotel. I'm not quite sure what it is. But I'd like to find out."

She spoke tartly. "What's the point, if you need to make it go round and round? You'll just end up cranking the generator instead of cranking the pump."

"It doesn't work like that. The generator makes the electricity slowly and stores it. You don't have to crank it by hand. The current in the creek would be enough to make the generator go round and round."

Charlotte shrugged. "I don't care much for the sound of it. I don't think it will ever catch on." She handed him the last of the cutlery and shook her hands with an angry flick of her wrists, hard enough to splash droplets up to his face.

"Anyway," she added in the sharp, determined tone that sometimes emerged behind her softly spoken ways. "I enjoy watering the fields. Why would I want to spend money on a machine that does something I like doing myself?"

She spun on her kid slippers and marched off

with a mutinous clatter of footsteps. Halfway across the room, she paused and tossed him a frowning glance over her shoulder. "I'm going to bed. Try not to stomp the house down when you come in."

Thomas lay in bed, stretched out on his back, arms crossed beneath his head. Somehow, a tension had crept between them, ruining his *one more days*.

It wasn't just him and his suspicions about her secrets. There'd been something wrong with Charlotte in the last couple of days. She was increasingly wrought. Tonight, she'd been snappy, edgy with nerves. And after he came to bed, she continued to toss and turn, emitting small huffs of frustration as she struggled to get comfortable beneath the quilt.

Thomas tried to get to sleep. But rest didn't come. He sighed, his breath rustling in the moonlit night. For the first time in six years, he had someone to help him on the farm, but because she kept him awake at night, he was suffering from fatigue now more than ever.

Hours passed. He lay in the darkness, chasing the elusive slumber. Just as the first rays of dawn lit up the sky outside, the bedclothes stirred. Thomas held his breath. Would it happen again? Twice before, Charlotte had become restless in the night, and had climbed across the bundle board to snuggle up against him.

He kept still while Charlotte wriggled over the small barrier between them. Her hair tickled his jaw as she tucked her head in the crook of his neck. Her hand slid onto his chest and halted there, the imprint of her palm burning on his bare skin. Her leg, bent at the knee, flung carelessly over his and hooked firmly across his thighs. The scent of vanilla filled every intake of his breath. The warm gust of her contented sigh brushed against his neck.

For what seemed like forever, Thomas lay motionless, apart from his heart that beat with such ferocity it surprised him the sound didn't awaken her. Slowly, he lifted his hand, let it settle over her hair, his fingers tangling in the ebony curls. Charlotte mumbled something in her sleep and eased her body half on top of him, one slim leg sliding between his, the edge of her hip butting against his arousal.

Thomas froze. When the first shock to his overloaded senses faded, he felt something sticky and wet against his thigh. With infinite care, he disentangled his limbs from hers, slipped away from her and lowered his feet to the ground. Standing up, he bent to her and lifted the edge of the patchwork quilt. In the faint light of dawn, he could see the dark stains on her nightgown and on the bedsheet.

Blood. *Dear God.* Terror clenched in his gut. He'd known all along there must be something wrong with the baby. It hadn't been growing, not the way it should have been. A woman approaching six months should have a rounded belly.

He shook her shoulder. "Charlotte. Wake up."

"Mmm…" She came awake slowly, resisting his efforts.

"Wake up," he said. "I think you're losing the baby."

"What?" She raised her head. Her hair was mussed, her body still languid, her eyes squinting with sleep. "The baby?" she muttered.

"You're bleeding. That's a sign of miscarriage."

She snapped wide-awake. Leaning up on the bed, she surveyed the dark smears that were spreading on the sheet and on her nightgown. "No." Her whole face crunched up as she shut her eyes tight, as if to block out the sight.

"I'll ride out and get the doc," Thomas said.

"No." Her eyes flew open again. She stared at him, panic flickering across her pale face. "No, Thomas—"

"I won't be long. I'll be back in an hour. Look…" He pointed toward the first dawn rays at the window, attempting to reassure her. "It's already daylight. The doc will be here in no time. It's going to be all right."

"Thomas—"

He leaned down, brushed a kiss on her brow, and then he pressed his palm to where his lips had touched. Her skin seemed neither feverish nor clammy. She'd be all right. She had to be all right, Thomas promised himself as he turned away from the bed to snatch up his clothing from the chair.

"Thomas, please, don't go…" Her voice was fraught.

Too focused on fetching help, Thomas did not listen. He had his trousers and shirt on in seconds. His gaze drifted over Charlotte as he fastened the buttons and pulled on his boots. Should he ride bareback to save one precious minute by not saddling Shadow? No, he'd ride faster in the saddle.

"It's going to all right," he said as he bent down for another quick kiss, this time on her lips. "You'll be fine, and there'll be other babies."

"Thomas, no!" She clung to his arm. "We need to talk!"

There was a shrill edge of desperation to her words. He wanted to haul her into his arms, talk to her, listen to her, sing one of those sea shanties with her, apologize for talking about electricity as if a machine could replace her, but now wasn't the time. His first priority was to get Doc Timmerman.

"You'll be fine. I promise," he called back from the door.

His footsteps clattered across the porch and down the path as he raced to the barn. "Sorry, boy," he said to Shadow as he flung the saddle on the horse. There was water in the bucket in the corner of the stall, and hay on the floor. At least he wasn't going to make a thirsty horse canter across the desert. As Thomas swung into the saddle and hurtled up the path, doubts bombarded his mind.

Had he done the right thing leaving her alone?

Should he have attempted to stem the bleeding first?

Made her coffee? Cold water?

Hot compress? Cool-compress?

He shook his head, frustrated at his ignorance of female ailments.

The right thing to do was to go and get the doc.

Charlotte buried her head in the pillow. This was terrible. Terrible. Her monthly flow was late. She'd assumed the stress of her situation was to blame and she'd been waiting, counting days, hesitating between confessing to Thomas and finding a way to wash the rags and keep them hidden from him.

And now this! Never before had her menses started with such a flood. No wonder her lower back had ached last night, and her mood had been so foul. How could Thomas not have guessed the truth?

With a strangled groan, Charlotte fisted her hands over the patchwork quilt. Growing up, she had resented how young women, at least those of her social class, were kept in ignorance of anything pertaining to the male body.

But could it be the same for men? Could it be that Thomas, who had grown up without sisters, had little understanding of the cycle of female bodies?

And now he'd find out the hard way.

A whimper of distress rose in her throat.

When the doctor hurried out to her and discovered the truth, she could just imagine his pitying glance at Thomas. There was no way to keep such a juicy scandal secret in a place like Gold Crossing. And when Gus Junior got hold of the story, he'd spread it around, until the hillsides rang with laughter at the naive and gullible Thomas Greenwood.

She could not let that happen to him.

She could not let him become an object of ridicule.

She had to make her escape, right now.

Something twisted in Charlotte's chest at the thought of leaving.

She would never dart through the mist of the irrigation spray in the fields again, would never feel the roughness of straw grazing against her fingers as she hunted for eggs in the barn, would never see another sunrise over the hills, would never spend another twilit evening listening to the rustling of nature's rush hour, would never get another chance to learn to milk Rosamund.

And Thomas! Charlotte burst into weeping now, harsh sobs racking her on the feather mattress. How Thomas would be hurt! Hurt and puzzled, but even in the throes of his grief he would worry about her, search for her, putting her safety before his own pain.

But what could be gained by staying? One day she would have to leave anyway, and the longer she stayed, the stronger the bond between them would grow, and the hurt would be even deeper when she finally left.

It was best to leave now. That way she could spare Thomas the public humiliation, and herself the shame and anguish of confessing to the deceit. Let him think she had married him because of the baby, and now that she had lost the child, she saw no reason to stay with him.

For a few more minutes, Charlotte allowed herself the comfort of tears. *Thomas, Thomas,*

I'm so sorry, I'm so sorry. I never meant to hurt you, but of course all along I knew that in the end I would. Thomas, Thomas, I'm so sorry. Her mind sang the words over and over again, like the refrain from a sea shanty.

Conscious of the pressure of time, Charlotte stifled her sobs and got out of bed. An odd lassitude had seized her, a sense of disorientation, as if she had been suffering from a bout of fever, and she had to force herself to hurry.

After doing her best to tidy up her disheveled appearance, she dressed in her pale gray blouse and petticoats and green wool skirt and matching jacket. The thick wool fabric was far too hot for the Arizona summer, but she could not leave her only respectable garments behind.

At the risk of wasting a few precious minutes, she made a pot of coffee and left it to brew while she rinsed the bloodstains out of her nightgown and packed the wet garment away, together with the rest of her possessions.

She carefully folded the shawl Thomas had given her and put it away in the blanket box in the bedroom. The only thing she took from him was the bar of vanilla soap, and she left her lavender one in its place.

While she drank a fortifying cup of the thick, creamy coffee, Charlotte calculated in her mind. The journey to the farm had taken about two hours in the cart, traveling at perhaps twice the walking speed. That meant four hours of steady walking. Six, or maybe even eight, if she faltered and had to pause frequently for rests.

However slowly she made her way, she ought to get to Gold Crossing in the afternoon. Tomorrow was Thursday. Until tomorrow afternoon, when she could take the train south to Phoenix Junction, she would need to find some safe place to keep out of sight—a feat that shouldn't be difficult in a town where more than half the buildings stood empty and boarded up.

"Goodbye, Thomas Greenwood," she whispered, and swept one final glance around the cabin. She left no letter. Nothing would be adequate to explain or excuse what she had done.

Outside, the sun had already leaped up on the horizon. Charlotte set off walking, the heavy leather bag bouncing against her hip. In the past two weeks, she'd explored the tiny valley, but she had never ventured out beyond the entrance road.

By the time she crested the hill and the dusty expanse of the desert landscape spread out in front of her, she was already sweltering inside her thick clothing. She looked ahead, searching between the stunted vegetation for the narrow ribbon of a trail toward Gold Crossing.

There was no trail.

She could see ruts from wagon wheels, lines

of hoof prints, even footprints. And all of them were overlapping, crisscrossing each other, and heading in different directions.

Refusing to be intimidated, Charlotte picked out the deepest set of wheel ruts. They were headed east. She recalled the drive out from Gold Crossing. The journey had been in one constant direction. She closed her eyes and tried to remember, tried to picture the day she arrived, tried to reach back in her mind for any recollections.

Perhaps the sun had been sinking on the horizon ahead?

Charlotte opened her eyes again and studied the landscape once more. If her memory served her right, they had been traveling west. Hence, the town must be to the east.

That would be easy. All she needed was to keep facing the sun that was rising on the eastern horizon. She was not a sea captain's daughter for nothing. She would not get lost.

She set off at a measured pace, to preserve her strength.

After less than half a mile, the tracks Charlotte had chosen to follow grew faint and then petered out altogether. She tried to keep her direction fixed but desert shrubs forced her to detour, her path weaving like that of a drunk. Rocks tripped her up. Cactus branches snagged the hems of her wide wool skirts.

An hour went by. The sun rose high overhead and she no longer had a firm idea which way was east. Doggedly she marched on. Her mouth became parched. She should have thought to take a canteen of water for the journey. It would not have been stealing, for she could have left the empty canteen with Art Langley at the Imperial Hotel before she boarded the train.

By now, there should have been some sign of Thomas and Dr. Timmerman riding in the opposite direction. But she'd seen nothing, had heard nothing, had felt no vibration in the earth beneath her feet. She'd been watching out, so she could drop down to the ground and hide out of sight as they thundered past.

Another hour went by. Perspiration beaded on her brow and trickled into her eyes, making her squint with the sting as she picked her way through the vegetation. Her lower back ached with every step. Her stomach cramped with her monthly cycle. She paused to take off her wool jacket, stuffed it in her bag and resumed walking.

When the sun reached the zenith in the sky, Charlotte knew she'd been walking at least four hours. Her tongue was thick in her mouth. Her eyes burned in their sockets. Her steps dragged. Sweat ran in rivulets down her back. Her pulse throbbed, a steady, painful thudding as her heart labored to pump blood to her tired muscles.

Something tripped her up. She toppled head-long to the ground. Her elbow smashed painfully against a rock. "Nothing broken, nothing broken." Charlotte muttered the words of reassurance to herself as she scrambled up, unsteady on her feet.

The sun was a ball of fire in the sky. The air shimmered in front of her eyes. She could feel her lips blistering, could taste the blood on them. Her legs gave and she fell to her knees. She struggled up, swayed on her feet, found her balance.

In her head, she sang, forcing her feet forward, one step at a time.

Oh, have you heard the news, me Thomas?
One more step.
We're homeward bound tomorrow.
One more step.

She fell. She got up. Time and again, she fell and got up.

And when she fell for the final time, when she no longer possessed the strength to get up and resume walking, she accepted the grim truth. She was a sea captain's daughter, and she knew how to keep on course. But she had made a mistake following those wheel ruts and assuming that Gold Crossing lay due east from the valley.

She closed her eyes, made another attempt to

let her memory drift back in time. She was sitting beside Thomas Greenwood on the hard bench of the cart. He was holding the lines, urging the chestnut gelding into a canter to make it up the slope ahead. Like a chill breaking through the desert heat, the memory flooded back to her.

Just before Thomas slapped the reins, he took a sharp turn to the left.

Instead of east, she should have been walking south.

Chapter Nine

Thomas leaped down from the lathered, panting Shadow and took the porch steps in two long leaps. The front door banged against the wall as he flung it open. He rushed across the floor to the bedroom   and froze at the doorway.

She was gone.

His feet became alive again. He strode to the bedside, boots thudding on the floorboards, and pulled aside the covers, as if not trusting what his eyes had already told him. The bloodstains on the sheets had dried to form stiff patches, but they were smaller than he'd feared.

"Charlotte," he bellowed, and hurried back to the parlor.

The coffeepot on the stove was still warm. A rinsed cup stood upside down on the counter. Surely a dying woman wouldn't pause to make coffee and rinse the cup? Surely if she was bleeding to death, there would be bloodstains on the floor?

Thomas went back to the bedroom, his gaze searching the plank floor. Nothing. No trail of dark drops. He took quick inventory of the contents of the room. Her clothes were gone, the ones she'd arrived in. Her leather bag was gone, too.

He hurried back outside. Shadow stood by the porch steps, waiting patiently. Thomas mounted, rode him to the creek. "Drink, boy," he said. Every second might count, but a dead horse would not take him far.

When Shadow stopped slurping and blowing and lifted his head, Thomas dug his heels into the horse's flanks and surged up the slope back toward the cabin. He jumped down one more time and went inside. He filled a canteen with water and bundled up a blanket and tied both to the saddle.

Then he was off on his way. As he crested the hill, he halted Shadow at the top of the ridge and scanned the barren landscape. Which way had she gone?

"Charlotte!"

"Charlotte!"

His frantic cries rippled across the desert. Only the wind replied.

Thomas marshaled his powers of reasoning. He had not seen any sign of Charlotte on his way back from Doc Timmerman's, and that must mean she had taken the wrong way. Or perhaps she was not aiming for Gold Crossing, but might be wandering through the desert without any aim.

Would her logic be impaired?

Did a woman lose her mind when she lost her baby?

Thomas didn't know. He didn't know anything about women, pregnant or otherwise, and now he cursed his lack of experience. For it might make a difference between finding his wife dead and finding her while she was still alive.

"Charlotte!"

"Charlotte!"

On the trail toward Flagstaff he spotted a row of dainty footprints in a soft patch of sand. When he went out that way, he brought back heavy wagonloads, such as the cookstove on his last trip, and the wheel ruts were deep. Perhaps she'd followed them.

Thomas urged Shadow into a canter and headed east, riding to and fro in ever-increasing semicircles, like ripples expanding on the surface of a pond.

"Charlotte!"

"Charlotte!"

His voice grew hoarse. The sun began to sink in the sky. Thomas ignored Shadow's tired grunts, merely pausing occasionally to rinse the horse's mouth with a drop of water from his cupped palm.

He ignored the painful rasp in his throat, the sting of grit in his eyes, the ache that throbbed through his muscles. But one thing he couldn't ignore was the fear that throbbed through him with every beat of his pulse.

"Charlotte." His croaky call no longer carried far.

He found his wife when the sloping rays of the sun cast long shadows across the desert and lit up the gravel with hues of red and gold. She lay beside a prickly pear covered in pink blooms. Crumpled on the ground, she was curled into a tight ball, the wide hems of her skirts fanned out about her. One of her arms was flung over her head, shielding her downturned face. The green bonnet hung askew on top of her unraveling upsweep.

Thomas slid down from the saddle, crouched beside her. "Charlotte."

She didn't move. Gently, he pulled her arm aside to reveal her face. Her skin was burned bright red. Her eyes were shut. Her lips were peeling and crusted with blood. He held the backs of his fingers to her mouth, felt the small puff of warm air.

She was breathing.

Thomas jumped up to his feet and hurried over to his horse. He untied the canteen from the saddle, went back to crouch beside Charlotte and unscrewed the cap. Slipping one arm behind Charlotte's neck, he cradled her head in the crook of his arm and pressed the spout of the canteen against her mouth. Her eyelids flickered but refused to lift.

"Charlotte. Look at me. Look at me. You need to drink."

He tipped the canteen to her lips but she was too weak to swallow and the water ran in rivulets down her chin. She tried to turn her head away. A faint moan rose in her throat.

Thomas lowered her back down, poured water into his cupped palm and trickled it over her lips with his fingertips. She made another moaning sound, stronger this time, and her lips parted. Thomas refilled his palm, managed to tip some water into her mouth. She shuddered, a tiny spasm racking her. At first, Thomas thought she was choking, that she would retch and spit out the water, but then her throat rippled in an awkward, labored swallow.

"That's it," he said. "A little more."

He kept trickling water into her mouth. After he had counted ten measures from his cupped palm, Thomas paused to let her rest. For a few moments, Charlotte lay absolutely still, her eyes closed. Then her tongue peeked out and slid over her lips, moistening the cracked skin. Thomas eased his arm around her shoulders and propped her up to a half sitting position, her back resting against the side of his thigh.

"Charlotte?" he said. "Can you hear me?"

"No doctor. No doctor." Her voice was a faint whisper. Her eyes remained shut. Thomas frowned. How did she know the doctor couldn't come?

"I'm sorry," he said. "The doc's up on Desperation Hill. A miner was trapped in a rock fall. He is too badly hurt to move, so someone rode into town to fetch the doc and he is still out there. Gus Junior has gone after him."

"No doctor. No doctor."

"Hush." Thomas stroked the loose curls that fluttered around her face. He adjusted her slipping bonnet to protect her skin from the last rays of the sun. "It's all right," he reassured her. "The doc's wife knows a lot about nursing. I'll take you into town when you feel up to getting on the horse. Drink a bit more first."

He held the canteen up to her mouth. She was able to drink properly now, swallowing in greedy gulps. He limited her to a few mouthfuls. She'd been without water for less than a day, so it was unlikely that she would retch, but the canteen was already half empty and he didn't want to risk a drop of it going to waste.

When he eased the canteen away, Charlotte reclined against his thigh and closed her eyes again. Thomas took the opportunity to survey her condition. One sleeve of her pale gray blouse was torn. The shadow from the green bonnet across her face gave her burned skin a purplish hue. Ignoring propriety, he lifted the hem of her skirts to peer underneath and saw streaks of blood on her petticoats.

Charlotte must have felt his bold inspection, for she emitted a distraught sound. One small hand came alive and flapped away his fumbling fingers with a surprising amount of strength.

Startled, Thomas swept his gaze back to her face. Her eyes were open. He'd never seen such anguish on a woman's face. Except perhaps once. On his mother's face, on the day he left his home in Michigan.

"I'm sorry," he said. "There'll be other babies."

"No." She exhaled a sigh that held as much frustration as grief. "No baby."

He uncapped the canteen and held it to her mouth. "Drink a little more."

Appearing to overcome her distress, Charlotte gripped the leather-covered canteen with both hands and clung tight when he tried to pull it away. He let her drink. She took deep swallows that rocked her body against the support of his thigh.

When she'd had enough, she slumped down, as if survival instinct had given her enough energy to consume the life-saving water but nothing beyond that. Thomas could see a dazed look enter into her eyes. Her eyelids fluttered down.

"I'll take you into town. Doc's wife will know what to do." He draped the canteen by its strap over his shoulder and eased onto his feet. Bending down to her, he gathered Charlotte in his arms and lifted her up.

He propped her across Shadow's back, and then he swung up behind her and settled her in his lap and set off toward Gold Crossing. He kept the pace to an easy lope. Speed was less important than not jolting her. She sat sideways in his lap, huddled against his chest. One small fist clung to the front of his shirt.

"Thomas... Thomas," she muttered.

"I'm here. You're safe." He wanted to ask why she had left the cabin, but it could wait. Perhaps the anguish of losing an unborn child muddled a woman's mind. Pity welled up inside him. Later, he would do his best to console her.

Her eyes flared open. Fever burned in them. Maybe sunstroke.

"There is no baby...never was any baby... This is just the normal flux a woman has every month... No baby...no miscarriage... Don't let people think..."

Startled, he stared down at her sunburned face. Her eyes closed again. The parched lips moved.

"No baby…no miscarriage… Don't let people think… They'll laugh at you…for believing… For not being able to tell… Flat stomach…no baby…"

Thomas stiffened in the saddle. He knew little of the world, and even less about women, but it was still insulting to hear it spelled out.

"I'm not…your wife…not Maude Jackson… She died…on the train… I took her ticket…your letter… Ran away… Hide…away from Merlin's Leap…"

"Who are you?" Thomas asked bluntly.

He knew the answer even before she spoke.

Charlotte Fairfax, Merlin's Leap, Boston, Massachusetts.

"Charlotte… Fairfax… Don't tell anyone… Ran away…away from Cousin Gareth…"

So, a small part of her story had to be true. How small a part, he'd have to wait and see. Thomas cradled his wife—not his wife, a stranger called Charlotte Fairfax—in his arms as he made his way to Gold Crossing. By the time they reached the doc's house, Charlotte was sound asleep. Thomas came up with a story of his own and told his lies to Dottie Timmerman.

Then he went out and slept in the yard of doc's small frame house.

He wanted to stay with Charlotte, but he knew that he had no right to.

No right to watch her sleep. No right to touch her. No right to kiss her.

For she was not his wife.

He *had* no wife.

He was alone again.

Charlotte came awake slowly. She was in a small room, with tiny pink roses on the wallpaper. The acrid scent of carbolic floated in the air. She lay between pristine linen sheets in a narrow bed. She wore a thick cotton nightgown, and she could feel a rag secured in place to trap her monthly flow.

She tried to move. A moan burst from her lips. Every muscle in her body ached. Her legs felt as if they might never support her weight again and the skin on her face felt as if someone had rubbed a sanding block over it.

"Good morning, dear." It was a female voice, pitched low. Accented, with a sharp, rolling *r*. Good *morrrning*.

Charlotte craned to look toward the doorway. A small woman, seventy if she was a day, bustled in, carrying a tray loaded with a teapot and milk jug and sugar bowl, and a pair of china teacups that matched the wallpaper. She wore a frilly pink dress. Her hair, soft and pure white, was arranged in a style that might have been fashionable thirty years ago, with ringlets dangling like icicles by her temples.

"It's good to see you awake, dear." She set the tray down on the bedside table, went to the window and pulled the lace curtains open. Bright sunshine streamed into the room.

Charlotte shut her eyes tight, then blinked them open and squinted against the light. It seemed around midday. She must have slept all the way through from last night, when Thomas found her. She counted in her mind. Eighteen hours.

The woman dragged a padded chair over to the bedside and flopped to sit on it. "I thought you might like a drop of tea and a wee chat." She picked up the teapot and poured. "I hope you don't mind that I took the liberty of giving you a wee tidy-up. A woman likes to be clean at her time of the month." She gave a forceful nod, as if agreeing with herself, then peered across at Charlotte. "Plump up your pillows, dear, so you can drink your tea. Or would you like me to re-arrange them for you?"

"No. I can do it." Charlotte adjusted the pillows and sat up against them.

"That's it, dear." The woman added milk, offered sugar and passed Charlotte the cup on a saucer. "You'll be right as rain," the woman went on. "I was worried earlier, when your husband rode in looking for the doctor. I thought he said you were having a miscarriage. Then he brought you in on that blue roan horse of his and put me to rights. He'd said *misadventure*. Silly me." The woman chuckled. "People say I talk too much and don't listen, and I guess they're right."

The innocent blue eyes widened. "I didn't introduce myself, did I? I'm Dorothy Timmerman. Dottie. The doctor's wife." Her head cocked to a mischievous tilt. "I'm fifty percent of the female population of Gold Crossing. That's counting by numbers. If you count by weight I'm only one-third, for Miss Gladys Hayes is twice the size of me."

Her lips pursed into a circle of disapproval that left no doubt about how one half of the female population of Gold Crossing felt about the other half. Then a look of eager curiosity chased away the frown and the softly rolling voice resumed its prattle, like a stream that couldn't stop its flow. "Your husband said you were bitten by some poisonous critter."

Dottie paused to take a sip of her tea, and Charlotte did the same, hiding her surprise and relief in the china cup. So, her incoherent ramblings had made some sense and Thomas had understood the situation. She was grateful for his quick thinking that had saved them both from embarrassment.

Dottie went on. "He feared it might have been a snake, so he made you lie still. With snakebite it's best to restrict movement. Then, when he got back home from trying to fetch the doctor, you were incoherent and thrashing about, so he brought you in. We decided it might have been a spider. Whatever it was, you appear to have shaken it off."

The woman gestured with her cup. "Thomas is sorry he tore your blouse. Your arm was stiff, and he wanted to take a look at the elbow where the critter bit you. The skin is too badly scraped to see any sting marks."

"I… I think I fell…"

"Doesn't matter, dear." A soft hand reached out to pat her arm. "You'll be right as rain in no time." Dottie picked up a spoon and stirred, looking a bit awkward. "I must say I was confused when I thought Thomas had said miscarriage…seeing as you've only been married such a short while."

"Two weeks." Charlotte felt a blush heat her cheeks. Plain talk was needed if she wanted to lay the groundwork for resolving their situation without any dishonor falling upon Thomas. "Mr. Greenwood and I agreed to a trial period. Marriage in name only."

Dottie gave a huff of dismissal and flapped her hand in the air. "I know all about that. Thomas told me." She lowered her voice and leaned closer. "He's sorry it didn't work out, but he knew from the moment he laid eyes on you that you weren't cut out for life on a farm. You're too delicate. I'm glad he sees it, too. It would be a tragedy if he kept you and then had to watch you wilt away from the hard work and childbirth."

"He…he told you it didn't…work out?"

Dottie nodded, white icicles quivering. "He said he'll put you up at the Imperial Hotel while he gets the money together for your passage home." The soft white hand reached out for yet another kindly pat. "It's for the best, dear. You'll learn to accept it and move on with your life."

Shaking her head in regret, Dottie heaved a sigh that sent the frills and bows on her pink dress fluttering. "Such a good man, he is, Thomas Greenwood. Since the two of you have agreed to annul the marriage, he didn't think it would be proper for him to sit by your beside. He's been waiting out in the yard, poor man. Didn't want to leave you alone until he knew you were going to be all right. He had to go home to milk the cow but he'll be back soon."

A knock sounded at the front door. Dottie bounced up. "That will be Gus Junior. He's come to let me know how soon the doctor expects to be back from Desperation Hill. You finish your tea, dear. I'll collect the tray later."

Dottie hurried out of the room. Charlotte heard the front door open. She heard a voice speaking in the awkward adolescent croak that marked the transition from a boy to a man, and then Dottie burst into another stream of talk.

Charlotte's fingers tightened around the china cup. *An annulment.* The marriage was probably not valid anyway, considering she had impersonated someone else, but an annulment would avoid any legal problems. She should be relieved. She should be grateful to Thomas Greenwood for having tied up all the loose ends so neatly, but instead an odd sense of disappointment niggled in her belly.

Could she truly have been so wrong? She had thought Thomas would be heartbroken when she left, but it seemed he was completely happy to free her from her marriage vows. He had no intention of fighting to keep her.

Could it be that her lack of expertise with the household chores mattered more to him than the companionship she had felt growing between them? Maybe he wanted to end the marriage, so he could find a different kind of wife.

Someone more capable.

Someone who did not deceive him and tell lies.

With a sinking feeling, Charlotte accepted the facts.

It appeared her husband was eager to be rid of her.

* * *

A tumult of feelings fought within Thomas as he alighted outside the doc's house and tied Shadow to the hitching rail by the porch. Of all the confused emotions relief ruled the strongest. Charlotte would be all right. Right behind the relief, eagerness to see her burned like a flame through him, but the bitter sting of anger overshadowed his pleasure.

He tried to brush aside the resentment.

He had suspected all along that she might leave him. Even if she had been who she said she was—even if she had been the woman who signed a contract to be his wife—he had feared from the moment he first saw her that she would be too delicate for the life he could offer her.

But that had not stopped him from hoping. Hoping she would prove him wrong. Had not stopped him from wanting. Wanting the marriage to last and be complete. Now he rejected those hopes and wants as nothing but foolish dreams.

So, considering he had predicted Charlotte would abandon him before the month was out, what difference it did make that she had never intended to stay? Thomas probed around in his mind and decided it made a lot of difference.

He'd been deceived. Tricked. Taken advantage of. Made into a fool.

That's why he was so angry with her. A man

who had in good faith put his heart and guts into an attempt to make something work did not like finding out that the enterprise had been doomed from the start.

His boots beat a short cadence against the floor as he followed the doctor's wife into the small room where he had carried Charlotte last night. Roses on the wallpaper. Lace curtains in the window. He thought of the rough log walls and uncovered windows of his cabin.

It had not been enough.

He had not been enough.

Charlotte was sitting up in bed, propped against the pillows. She looked much better now. No longer exhausted or anguished. Her skin was still pink but it had not blistered, and her lips were on the mend, shiny with a protective layer of grease.

Dottie walked out with a quiet comment. "I'll leave you two to talk."

She did not close the door after her. Thomas shifted on his feet and spoke in a low voice, the first words that sprang into his turbulent mind. "I'm sorry I wasn't here when you woke up this morning. I had to go and milk the cow. It's painful for the animal if you let the milk build up in the udders for too long."

Charlotte twisted the edge of the blanket in her nervous fingers. "You don't need to apologize..."

She took a deep breath, her shoulders rising and falling. "Dottie said you told her we were getting an annulment."

Thomas clasped his hat in his hands. Why prolong the agony of loss? Why torture his battered heart with a futile hope? Why keep the dream alive, just to see it die again in the end? Charlotte had never been suited to be his wife. He'd known it from the moment he first met her at the Imperial Hotel, but he had closed his eyes to the truth.

"Seems the right thing to do," he said gruffly.

"You seem to be in a hurry to get it done."

He let his gaze slide over her features. Such delicate beauty. He should have accepted right from the start that she was out of his reach, as far as the distant surface of the moon. He should have put her back on the train instead of marrying her.

"Why postpone?" he said.

"You are angry at me…"

The accusation in her voice cracked his hardwon control. "Don't you think I have a right to be angry?" he said through gritted teeth. "You took everything. My money, my care, my affection. You used me. Nothing was safe from you. Not even my dignity."

"I didn't mean to hurt you…"

"You managed it well enough."

"Please," she said. "Let me explain." She gestured toward the padded chair by the window.

Thomas hesitated, turning his hat in his hands.

"Please," she said again.

He sighed, pulled up the chair and sat down on it. Despite everything, when he rode back home in the morning to milk the cow, he had taken the time to wash and shave, and to change into clean clothes. Even now, it mattered to him what she thought of him, and he could not deny her the opportunity to say what she wanted. And, if he was honest to himself, part of him was curious to hear her explanations.

"Close the door," Charlotte said, in that firm voice she sometimes used.

Thomas glanced back at the open doorway. It was not proper, but he was too wrought up to care. He got to his feet, shut the door quietly and sat down again. He let his gaze drift over her once more. The thought that had been stewing at the back of his mind burst into the forefront of his consciousness.

Night after night, he'd slept beside her. What if he had claimed his husbandly rights? What if he had bedded her? Where would they stand now? Would she be forced to stay with him? Or would she leave anyway? Would he feel less empty inside if he had taken something from her, the way she had taken something from him?

"I'm listening," he said.

"I told you, my parents died four years ago. They drowned when their boat capsized in a storm. They'd only gone out for the day, but the weather changed suddenly."

"I'm sorry," Thomas muttered.

But at least your parents loved you while they lived.

"I already explained that my sisters and I were not allowed to live alone. A cousin came to live with us. He is a greedy, selfish man, and he has been trying to force me into marriage. He attacked me, and I knew he'd repeat his unwanted advances until he succeeded in ruining me. That's why I had to flee. To be safe from him."

Thomas nodded. He could see how Charlotte had tied snippets of truth into her lies, blending her own situation with that of Miss Jackson.

A pleading look entered her eyes. "I found Miss Jackson dead on the train…she had… I'm sorry, Thomas… She had taken her own life with an overdose of laudanum… I don't know why she did it. I took your letter and the railroad ticket and pretended to be her. It didn't feel so very wrong at the time. It seemed as if she was reaching out to me, helping me to find a place of safety. I didn't know she was a mail-order bride until you came to collect me. I had assumed she had entered into a contract for a teaching position."

Thomas shook his head. Was there no end to his misfortunes? The woman he'd contracted to marry, the plain woman he had chosen to be his wife because he wanted to save her and the child from ending up destitute, had taken her own life and the life of her unborn child rather than letting him take care of them.

He needed to be alone. He stood, hat in hand, and spoke harshly as his anger and hurt poured into words. "Why didn't you tell me right at the start? When I first came to collect you, and you discovered you were meant to be my bride, why did you keep pretending? Why didn't you tell me the truth and ask for my help?"

A guilty expression flickered across her sunburned features. "I wanted to. But you seemed so angry when I suggested breaking the contract. You told me that if I didn't marry you I had to pay back the cost of my journey. I didn't have any money, and I was confused and afraid. So I just went along with it. You must believe me. I never meant to hurt you. I thought I'd be able help to you on the farm, during the time I was there."

"Did you ever consider telling me?"

"Many times…but I…" She looked up, her eyes bright with unshed tears. "I was happy there, in your secluded valley. And you had made it clear you'd be…a gentleman…allow me a waiting period before consummating the marriage.

I didn't want to tell you, because I knew you'd send me away if you discovered I wasn't your wife in the eyes of the law. You'd have been too honorable to let me stay with you if there was no real marriage."

"What about the baby? Surely you understood it would soon become clear there was no child. Would you have told me then? Or would you have pretended you'd lost the child?"

He made an angry gesture at her, taking in her slender shape. "If I had not decided to fetch the doctor, would we still be at home in the cabin, with me rocking you in my arms, pouring my affection out to you, trying to console you because you'd lost the baby you were expecting?"

"I... I don't know. I hadn't thought that far..."

"No," Thomas said. "You hadn't thought further than the end of your pretty little nose." He tapped his hat against his thigh, propped it on his head and prepared to leave.

"No. Please, Thomas, don't go. I... I have something to ask."

Charlotte must have seen the incredulous expression on his face, for she flinched and hunched deeper beneath the covers. Thomas halted, not looking at her but staring at the tiny roses on the wall, his body rigid with tension.

"What more can you ask?" he said gruffly. "What do I have left?"

"Don't tell anyone I'm not Miss Jackson. Surely it makes no difference now? You can get your annulment, and it will be easier for me to remain safe if I continue to use her name. Cousin Gareth will be looking for me."

Thomas glared down at her from his height. Then his rigid posture eased and he exhaled a resigned sigh. Was there no end to his willingness to be a fool? "I guess it make no difference now," he said with reluctance. "I'll have to find out about an annulment. Maybe Reverend Eldridge can be persuaded to forget he even married us in the first place."

With that, he walked out. How insignificant, how transient his marriage had been. Like dandelion fluff floating in the wind. They would tear up a piece of paper, ask the reverend to cross out an entry in the church register, and it would be as if the union between them had never been.

Chapter Ten

Feelings Thomas had thought buried years ago surged within him as he took care of the evening chores. Those feelings gathered force while he cooked scrambled eggs for his dinner and ate them with two slices of bread.

The unworthy, unloved and unlovable little Thomas Greenwood. Sturdy and blond, so different from his lithe, dark parents and his brothers. Always in the way. Ignored by his mother, kicked around by his father, tormented by his brothers. The kindest emotion he'd received from the people around him had been pity.

Why? Why? Whose sins had he paid for?

After he'd tidied up the kitchen, he sat down at the table with a pen and paper and wrote a letter. He wrote quickly, not pausing to select his words.

Dear Mother,
I have to know. You have always refused to

answer questions about my father but now
I need to know. Who was he? What did he
do? What about him was so terrible that it
made you hate me? Why did you not love
me? Why could you not love me?

I must know. If you don't answer this letter, I'll write every week until you do.

Your son,

Thomas

PS. I farm my own land now, I am not
married and I have no children. I am in good
health and hope that all of you are the same.
My address is Gold Crossing, Arizona Territory.

PPS. There is no gold here. The mine
played out six years ago.

He read the letter and frowned. It was clear
from the way he wrote that he was ill suited for a
woman like Charlotte Fairfax. She had disclosed
scant details about her background, but it sounded
as though she came from a good family and had
benefited from a formal education.

A grim smile tugged at Thomas's lips as he recalled his thoughts while he drove to Gold Crossing to collect his bride. *I don't want a beauty, for
a beautiful woman will put on airs and graces
and expect to be waited upon.*

However, that was exactly what he had ended

up with, a delicate beauty unable to even make a cup of coffee without creating havoc in his cabin. He hardened his heart against the memories and got up to fetch an envelope.

Tomorrow, he'd ride into town and post the letter. He'd take the opportunity to look in on Charlotte at the same time. Even though they were getting an annulment, he still felt responsible for her. Thomas refused to acknowledge the longing that flooded over him at the thought of seeing her again.

Spinsters could be very vexing, Charlotte decided. Miss Gladys Hayes had appeared at the doorstep of the doctor's house before they'd even finished breakfast. After hearing about the plans to annul her marriage to Thomas, Miss Hayes had decided that any further encounter between the pair of them needed to take place under the supervision of a chaperone—a role for which she felt amply qualified.

So, instead of allowing Thomas into the house when he rode up on Shadow, Charlotte had been required to greet him on the canopied porch of the Timmerman residence, where they were now seated on a hard bench, squinting into the sun, dust clogging their nostrils.

"I'm glad to see you are up and about," Thomas said.

"Let's take a walk." Charlotte stood, wincing at the stiffness in her legs.

Every step might be an effort, but Dottie and the other fifty percent of the female population of Gold Crossing were sitting in the parlor with the window open, listening to every word of her conversation with Thomas.

It seemed to Charlotte that Gladys Hayes and Dottie Timmerman had little in common and certainly shared no mutual admiration. However, due to the lack of other female residents in Gold Crossing, they had little choice but to tolerate each other.

Charlotte took Thomas's arm. She'd missed him. It had felt strange to sleep alone at night. She'd been cold. Cold and anxious and a little lonely.

"How many eggs did you find this morning?" she asked.

"I didn't look."

She halted. "But you must look! Polk likes to watch while you search her perch. She is very proud of her eggs. And Zachary occasionally lays two. And Harrison is getting very clever about hiding hers…"

A wave of homesickness washed over her. But not homesickness for Merlin's Leap. For the tiny secluded valley, a world of its own. Charlotte rushed into a breathless stream of words. It seemed very important to make Thomas understand everything she had forgotten to tell him yesterday.

"I know I have caused you a lot of pain and inconvenience. I am truly sorry for having deceived you. I genuinely assumed that having a wife for a few months would be better than not having a wife at all. I hoped that I could add to your life, create some homely comforts. I thought I was helping with the chores."

"You were helping. Trying to, anyway." His tone was grudging.

Just the words she wanted to hear. It might have been like pulling teeth, but he had admitted that she had made a contribution. That she had been an asset. Charlotte launched into putting her plan into words.

"Even though I need to live in town, now that you are getting our marriage annulled, I've decided that I might come out every afternoon and help you irrigate. I will borrow a horse from Dottie and ride over."

"It rains more often in July and August. I can manage."

"And…" She took a deep breath. "I will help you acquire another mail-order bride. You might like to put an advertisement in the *Matrimonial News*. I can help you choose."

Even as Charlotte spoke the words, an odd

resentment twisted in her belly. The thought of Thomas marrying another mail-order bride didn't sit right at all.

She sneaked a glance at him from the corner of her eye. He was such a handsome man, so steady and big and powerful. She imagined the delight of some unknown bride when he appeared to fetch her from the Imperial Hotel.

The happy moments they had spent together flickered through Charlotte's mind. The fun and laughter. The quiet times in the evenings. Everything Thomas had taught her about farming. All the care and concern he had shown for her.

Would some other woman fit so well in his rustic cabin? Would some other woman try as hard as she had? Would he…? That nasty feeling in her belly flexed its claws. Would Thomas like some other woman better than he had liked her?

It would be ill advised for Thomas to rush ahead and marry some other mail-order bride without her help, Charlotte decided. It was nothing personal. It was simply that he deserved better than a woman chosen at random from a catalog.

A wonderful idea struck her. "I know, Thomas. Why get a bride in a bag, so to speak, when you can have the benefit of a wider selection? When it's safe for me to return home, you must come to Boston with me. We'll put an advertisement in the newspaper and interview the applicants in person."

There. That sounded much better now. She could veto any bride until she had made sure they had found a suitable one. And the prospect of returning home to Merlin's Leap seemed far more tempting if she pictured Thomas by her side.

Thomas's arm went rigid beneath her fingers that rested in the crook of his elbow. "I think I'll do better selecting a wife without your help." He glanced down at her from his towering height. "The kind of wife I need. A farmer's wife. A strong, capable woman. Someone who knows how to cook and clean and doesn't tell lies to her husband or run away and get lost in the desert."

The Timmerman residence was the last house in the row that made up the town. They'd been walking away, toward the desert. Now Charlotte came to an abrupt halt, as if her feet had been nailed to the rough gravel ground.

So, he truly did think she'd been useless as a wife.

She'd helped with the irrigation. She had tamed the chickens so that they let her pet them, at least Polk and Tyler did, but Thomas didn't give her any credit for it. All he would remember after she was gone was the porridge dumpling.

"I think we've walked far enough," she told

him curtly. "My legs are still sore from when I got lost in the desert." She tried to turn back, tugging at his arm, but Thomas stood on the spot, rooted as firmly as one of those giant redwood trees they had in California.

"Wait." He dipped a hand in his coat pocket. "A letter came for you."

He held out a small white envelope. Charlotte took it from him, saw it had been opened. She studied the writing. It was addressed to Maude Greenwood. She looked up at him, accusation in her eyes. "You've…you've opened it."

He nodded, a quick, angry dip of his chin. "I didn't know if it was for you or for the woman who died on the train. I opened it, in case it was meant for her."

"Yes…yes, of course." Charlotte peeked inside the envelope and pulled out the single sheet. It was in Miranda's handwriting.

Dear Mrs. Greenwood,
I hope you don't mind that I take the liberty to reply to your letter addressed to my sister Charlotte. I am very sorry to inform you that Charlotte has passed away. She was traveling to meet relatives when she suffered some kind of food poisoning on the train. She is buried in the small cemetery here at Merlin's Leap.

A teaching post in the territories sounds like a wonderful adventure, however, as I am now the oldest, I have inherited Charlotte's responsibilities. As much as I might enjoy seeing more of this fine continent of America I am not free to travel out to the West.

I believe that the best way for you to secure a competent teacher is to send funds for someone to cover the cost of their trip.

Best of luck in your search for a suitable teacher.

Yours truly,

Miranda Fairfax

"They think I'm dead." Charlotte lowered the letter and spoke in a stunned whisper. "Not Miranda and Annabel. They know I'm really Miss Jackson, but somehow Miss Jackson has been mistaken for me. Officially, I'm dead."

The enormity of the news rendered her mind numb, and then thoughts broke through, filling her with horror. Could it be…could it be that for a while, until they saw her Emily Bickerstaff letter, even her sisters might have believed she was dead?

Charlotte imagined their anguish at such news. In her mind she could hear their wails of grief, could see them slumped in mourning. How must they have felt, not knowing for certain, wondering how she might have met her end?

And Cousin Gareth…? Her brows drew into a frown. Did Gareth know the truth? Had it been a genuine mistake, or had he somehow contrived to have her declared dead? And if it was part of his intrigue, why might he have done it?

Charlotte's fingers fisted around the letter as the full horror of the situation became clear to her. Despite the hot sun overhead, a chill ran through her. "I'm safe now." She spoke in a low voice, her throat tight with fear. "But Cousin Gareth might go after Miranda. He might do to her what he was trying to do to me."

Lifting the letter, Charlotte reread the last sentence.

I believe that the best way for you to secure a competent teacher is to send funds for someone to cover the cost of their trip.

Of course. The message was clear. Miranda was asking for funds. Charlotte took a deep breath and released it on a shaky sigh. "If only I had some money to send to her, it might help her escape."

Beside her, Thomas said something, but Charlotte was too distraught to pay attention to his words. Guilt racked her, guilt and remorse. "It's

my fault. All my fault. I was wrong to imperson-
ate Miss Jackson. Terribly wrong. I hurt you, and
now Miranda is in danger. The only good thing
that came out of it is that poor Miss Jackson is
buried at Merlin's Leap where my sisters will
mourn for her and her unborn child."

Charlotte raised her gaze to Thomas, tears
brimming in her eyes. Why didn't he bundle her
into his arms? That had been the safest place
she'd ever known, being warm and snug in his
embrace. Now she longed to lean against his
strength. But he just stood there, staring past her,
a strained expression on his face.

Behind Charlotte came the crunch of approaching footsteps. Thomas nodded and touched
the brim of his hat. Charlotte spun around. The
two halves of the female population of Gold
Crossing were marching toward them, parasols
raised, determination stamped on their features
as they embraced their chaperone duty.

"Go away. *Shoo*," Charlotte muttered under
her breath.

But of course, they didn't. The pair of them
took up positions a few yards behind her and
Thomas, making it impossible for her to discuss
the situation with him. And, even more annoy-
ingly, the presence of the chaperones prevented
any possibility that she might seek comfort in
his arms.

To his credit, Thomas tried to keep up the small talk as they strolled along. He mentioned the weather, how hot it was. He said he had irrigated the crops last night, and told her how long it had taken him on his own. Then he slid his fingers beneath his collar, tugged at it and said how hot it was. He snatched down his hat, beat it against his thigh and said July and August were always the hottest months of the year.

Then he said his goodbyes and made his escape.

Charlotte watched him go and scowled at the chaperones.

There was such a thing as taking one's duty too far.

Thomas drove the wagon back from Flagstaff. The trip had taken two days. Gus Osborn in Gold Crossing operated savings accounts where you could deposit and withdraw cash or gold, and you could buy and send money orders, but you couldn't apply for a loan. To borrow money, Thomas had needed to go to the bank in Flagstaff.

When he arrived home in the early evening, he took care of Trooper and unloaded his purchases from the wagon. He milked Rosamund, fed the chickens, collected the eggs and took a walk around his fields.

Once the chores were done, loneliness closed

in around him. He'd gotten used to Charlotte's laughter rippling through the cottonwood trees. He'd gotten used to her chasing the chickens around the yard and prattling to them. He'd gotten used to her merrily leaping over the rows of cabbages and beets. He'd gotten used to those sea shanties she sang as they worked together, irrigating the fields.

She is gone, Thomas told himself. Charlotte had never truly been his, would never be his. He didn't have a wife. Perhaps he never would. So, why had he toured the stores in Flagstaff and wasted money on lace curtains and china teacups with a rose pattern on them?

In the cabin, the silence sounded too loud in his ears.

He went out, saddled Shadow and headed into town.

He'd call on Charlotte. He could tell her how Polk had followed him around as he searched for the eggs, and how he'd found Harrison hiding one in an old boot in the corner of the barn. He'd tell her how much longer it took him to irrigate the crops without her help.

But first, he stopped by the mercantile.

Gus Osborn was a short, stocky man in his forties. He had thick dark hair, as untamed as a wire brush, and a face that no woman would ever call handsome. He tried to cover up his bulbous nose and his thick lips with a bushy beard.

"What can I do for you?" Gus said. He put down the book he'd been reading and rose from the stool he'd been perched upon. Despite his rough features, Gus Osborn seemed an educated man, polite and well mannered.

"I'd like to send a money order," Thomas replied.

Gus Junior drifted out from between the shelves of merchandise, munching on an apple. At fourteen, the boy was on the cusp of turning into a man. He resembled his father, but on him the shine of youth softened the features that looked too harsh on his father.

Gus Osborn took the slip of paper Thomas handed out to him.

"Sorry to hear your mail-order bride didn't work out, Mr. Greenwood," Gus Junior said. His voice broke on a funny croak. His face flushed scarlet. An angry rash covered the skin on his jaw. Thomas assumed it was evidence of his first attempt at shaving.

"That's two hundred and twenty dollars," Gus Osborn said.

Thomas counted out the money. The eleven double eagles clinked on the counter, each sound twisting in his gut. He'd borrowed too much money from the bank. He was risking losing his farm, something he'd sworn never to do.

Gus Junior edged closer. "Sending for another bride, Mr. Greenwood?"

Thomas gritted his teeth. It was none of their business. He glanced at the boy and said, "You think a man should give up trying if he fails the first time?"

Gus Osborn frowned at his son. "Of course not. I'll send this at once."

"You do that." Thomas spun around and strode off.

"Mr. Greenwood!" Gus Junior called after him.

Thomas whirled back. What was it now? The boy was a pest. The only reason Gus Junior got away with his gossiping was that his father had instilled in him such polite manners that people were mollified by them. And of course there was the fact there was no one else in Gold Crossing to ride out with messages.

"If you are looking for Mrs. Greenwood … *err*… Miss Jackson—I don't rightly know what she's called now—she is no longer at the doc's house. The doc came back from Desperation Hill yesterday. He declared she's all fine and dandy. She is at the Imperial Hotel now. Mr. Langley expects you to pay her bill."

Thomas nodded, grunted something in response. He hurried out to the Imperial Hotel, his footsteps thudding on the boardwalk as he jumped from porch to porch in his haste to see Charlotte. He pulled the double doors open and stormed through, as impatient as on that first day, when he'd come to collect his bride.

Two heads bent together at one of the oak tables in the lounge. An elegant, jet-black upsweep, huddled next to a masculine cut in dishwater brown. In front of Thomas's stunned eyes, Art Langley appeared to be drooling over Charlotte Fairfax, and Charlotte was swooning beside the richest man in Gold Crossing, as if she were already a free woman.

A new sensation, an altogether unpleasant one, surged within Thomas. He'd felt faint stirrings of something similar as a boy, when he'd watched his parents dote on his brothers the way they never doted on him, but those were pale imitations compared to the claws of jealousy that now sank into his gut.

Thomas strode up to the pair. Where were the chaperones when you needed them? He'd been looking forward to telling Charlotte that he'd sent for her sister, but now the information remained locked up inside him. If people in town thought he'd ordered himself another bride, it might help salvage a shred of his pride.

Charlotte jumped up. Her eyes were sparkling and her cheeks dimpling. Excitement shone in every inch of her lovely features.

"Thomas," she cried out. "Where have you been?"

"Went to Flagstaff."

"Please, sit down." She gestured at the chair opposite her, where Art Langley was already rising, his lanky frame unfolding like a puppet on a string. "Art was just about to get back to work," she added.

Thomas took the seat. He bounced his hat against his thigh. Art Langley winked—*yes, winked*—at Charlotte before returning to stand behind the counter. He picked up a deck of cards, shuffled them, spread a selection over the counter. Thomas gave an indignant huff. *Art was just about to get back to work,* Charlotte had said. Was playing solitaire now called work?

"Tell me about your trip," Charlotte prompted him.

Thomas stopped scowling at Art Langley and groped in his mind for something to tell her about Flagstaff. He mentioned the patches of snow that glittered at the top of the mountain. He told her it was one of the biggest towns on the railroad west. Of course, the Gold Crossing spur came on a different line, from the south, out of Phoenix Junction.

Then he ran out of things to say.

They couldn't have been talking more than five minutes when Miss Gladys Hayes appeared. She lowered her ample frame into a chair at the next table. Once she had settled there, she pulled out a half-finished sweater from her small carpet bag and soon had the knitting needles clicking. Every few seconds, she cast a beady eye at them, all fired up to do her chaperone duty.

Thomas let his gaze shuttle to Art Langley, who was flipping over his cards, and then he slid it back again to Miss Hayes. He was about to ask the grouchy spinster why she'd failed to interfere when Art had been as good as devouring Charlotte in public, but then the woman piped up, as if she could read his mind. Thomas shuddered at the thought.

"Mr. Langley works here. He has a reason to be here. A reason other than romantic aspirations."

Romantic aspirations?

The words made Thomas feel as uncomfortable as a worm on a hook. He supposed it was true. Somewhere in the hidden corners of his mind he still held on to his dreams of a wife and children of his own.

It occurred to him that this public scrutiny was what a man had to put up with when courting a woman. Only, most men who suffered through this torture of supervised small talk could expect to gain a wife at the end of it. He was losing one.

Chapter Eleven

It had been a joy to see Thomas again. Charlotte could tell his anger at her was fading. She would have liked to enjoy a longer visit with him, but Miss Gladys Hayes was a more effective deterrent against impropriety than any enraged papa with a fully loaded shotgun might have been.

When the sound of Thomas's departing footsteps had died away, Art Langley rejoined her and continued his amazing revelation.

His big secret, the one Thomas said he'd been guarding like a squirrel hoarding nuts, was a plan to revive Gold Crossing. Art had entered into a contract with a Widows and Orphans Association in San Francisco, to bring out sickly children who would benefit from a spell in the dry desert climate.

He would convert the Imperial Hotel into an orphanage, and he was offering her an opportunity to run a school—not part of his original plan, but now that a qualified teacher had become stranded in Gold Crossing, it might be an added benefit to encourage the association to send out more children.

According to Art's thinking, widows would accompany the orphans. Prospectors starved of female company would marry the widows and, as if by miracle, Gold Crossing would have an influx of new families. That would mean increased business for the mercantile, and the growth would snowball from there.

Having seen some of the prospectors, Charlotte had her doubts the widows would want to marry them, but one never knew. The important thing was that Art's proposal offered her a place to stay until May the following year, when it would be safe for her to return home to Merlin's Leap.

She launched herself into a business negotiation. "Ten dollars a week."

"Five," Art countered.

"Ten. Where else can you get a competent teacher?"

"Seven. No school on Saturdays."

Charlotte pursed her lips. No school on Saturdays. That meant she could visit Thomas on his farm. On Sundays, her position would require her to attend a church service, assuming that from now on there would be one held each week.

She was just about to nod her agreement when Art spoke again.

"All right. Ten dollars a week. If you sleep in the schoolhouse."

"But it's only one room." She'd seen the tiny cabin, situated just past the church, a short distance apart from the row of buildings that formed the single thoroughfare of the town.

"There's space for a cot behind the teacher's desk. The potbellied stove has a flat top you can cook on. I'll give you an extra blanket that you can hang up from the ceiling to separate the cot from the schoolroom."

"Done," Charlotte said.

They shook hands on the deal, and she hurried out to the schoolhouse to begin her preparations. She wouldn't be forced to set out into the world after all, seeking a new safe harbor to hide in. She could remain right here in Gold Crossing. Close to Thomas. That last thought rippled through her mind, bright and sparkling. Everything suddenly seemed better. Even the ramshackle buildings along the street seemed to stand straighter.

Charlotte craned up on tiptoe on a rickety desk, holding a blanket to the schoolhouse ceiling. The first lot of children would arrive on the

Thursday train, which meant she only had two days to prepare her accommodation. Ten feet away from her, across the small cabin, Gus Junior was holding up the other end of the blanket and banging nails into the rafters.

He pulled another nail from his mouth and spoke around the ones that remained clamped between his teeth. "It's a good thing you got this job, Miss Jackson, now that Mr. Greenwood has sent for another mail-order bride. He would not want to keep paying your bills at the Imperial Hotel."

The world around her went gray. Thick, suffocating gray, as the blanket slipped from her fingers and fell on top of her head.

"Miss Jackson, are you all right?" She heard the anxious question and the sound of scrambling feet. An instant later, the blanket lifted and Gus Junior's homely face stared at her.

Charlotte sneezed. A shudder rippled down her body. The desk rocked beneath her feet. She climbed down to the safety of the solid timber floor.

"What did you say?" she muttered.

"I said, it's a good thing—"

"Never mind." She silenced him with a flap of her hand. She didn't want to hear those words repeated. But she couldn't stop them from buzzing in her ears.

Sent for another mail-order bride.

What had she thought? That Thomas would court her in her true identity as Miss Charlotte Fairfax from Boston, not Miss Maude Jackson from New York City. That, instead of taking a bride in a bag, he would *see* her. *Choose* her.

Of course he wouldn't want her. She was incompetent. Too fragile. Everyone said so. She didn't even come with the free extra of a baby on the way. She was not a practical farm wife. She made friends with chickens and danced over the rows of cabbages and beets, singing sea shanties. She would never have agreed to put Harrison in the pot for Thanksgiving dinner, and Thomas knew it.

He'd already sent for another bride.

The thought drenched over her like a winter downpour, icy and unwelcome. Charlotte straightened her spine in the haughty way her governesses had taught her to do. She would show him. She would show them all. Fragile, hah! Hamish Fairfax's daughter was made of sterner stuff than that. She would stun them all with her success as a schoolteacher. She would show Thomas what he'd let slip through his fingers. When his new bride arrived, he'd realize he'd traded down, not traded up.

"Are you all right, Miss Jackson?"

"Huh?" Charlotte blinked, the wild thoughts scattering.

"You were staring at the wall and muttering. Your fists were clenched. I thought you were going to sock me one. It's not my fault you dropped the blanket. I wasn't pulling on it. It was just too heavy for you to hold up."

Charlotte silenced Gus Junior with a sharp look and climbed back up on the desk. "It's not too heavy. I'm not fragile. Let's get on with it."

Her first night in her new home. Charlotte moved the little jar with wildflowers from one desk to another and surveyed her domain. Home, workplace and sanctuary, all in one. A fire glowed in the potbellied stove. The blanket hung from the ceiling. Coffee brewed on the stove in a pot she'd borrowed from Miss Hayes, who might not be such a dragon after all.

It was a sweet little cabin.

There was only one thing wrong with it.

She was lonely. *It's just homesickness,* Charlotte told herself.

She closed her eyes and tried to imagine the crash of the ocean against the rocks at Merlin's Leap and the steady blinking of the lighthouse on Merlin's Point. But instead, her imagination came up with the clucking of chickens and the clunking of the irrigation pump.

It hit her then. She didn't miss Merlin's Leap. She didn't miss the ocean. Not one bit. She didn't care if she never saw either again. The ocean had stopped being a friend after it had taken her parents. Merlin's Leap had stopped being a home after Cousin Gareth had turned it into a prison.

All she missed was her sisters.

And Thomas.

Oh, how she missed him.

What was that? A sound outside. The tinkle of metal. A pebble rolling on gravel. Charlotte snuffed out the lamp on the teacher's desk and crept to the window. The night was overcast, with no moonlight. A shadow passed mere yards behind the building. Then it vanished. Gravel rolled again. Something big and heavy was moving in the night.

She was not fragile. Not afraid.

Her mouth dry, her heart hammering, Charlotte eased the door open and slipped out through the gap. Keeping her footsteps light, she felt her way round the corner of building in the darkness. Lamplight spilled out through the windows of the Imperial Hotel and the saloon, but it was too far to reach out to the schoolhouse.

"Ouch!" She tripped over something big that lay on the ground, and toppled over it in a flurry of petticoats and flailing arms and legs. Strong hands closed around her waist and broke her fall.

"Easy now."

Thomas.

She tried to fling her arms around his neck in the darkness but missed and ended up bashing him in the face with her elbow. She could hear his grunt of pain.

"It's me, Thomas," he whispered. "Don't hit."

He thought she was fighting him.

Charlotte stilled her motion and whispered back, "What are you doing here?" Her eyes were adjusting to the lack of light. She could see the pale circle of his face. The big looming shape she'd seen was Shadow, standing a few yards away.

"I'm doing chaperone duty," Thomas replied.

"You're...what?"

Thomas plunked her down on her rear end beside him. He scooted up to a sitting position, his bulk looming beside her in the darkness. She heard the rasp of a match, saw the flare of light. There was a clink of glass against metal. Then a steady flame burned inside the storm lantern he was holding up.

"Have you seen this?" he asked, and passed her a handbill.

The single page resembled a wanted poster. It said *Gold Crossing Informer* in big letters on the top. The headline beneath read: *The Female Population of Gold Crossing Skyrockets*.

In the light of the storm lantern, Charlotte read the article that followed. It mentioned the new schoolteacher, Miss Maude Jackson, and referred to an unspecified number of unattached females arriving on the Thursday train.

She looked up at Thomas. "Who did this?"

"Gus Junior. It seems he wants to make a career out of spreading gossip. He wrote out twenty of these by hand and has been riding around selling them for two bits each. Every prospector in the hills is heading into town. Some have come down a day early and are drinking and gambling. There's a carnival atmosphere in the saloon."

Warmth flooded through her.

Thomas had come out to safeguard her.

To protect her from the invasion of woman-hungry males.

"Oh, Thomas." She sighed, her dreamy smile hidden by the night.

"That's right," he told her. "It's there, black and white in the newspaper, that our marriage has been annulled. We'd better make it right. I've spoken to Reverend Eldridge. He'll see us first thing tomorrow morning."

Charlotte opened her mouth in protest, then closed it again without a sound. He'd not come to protect her. He'd come to absolve himself from responsibility over her.

"Go back inside," Thomas said. "I'll sleep out

here. I'll see you in the morning." Sitting like a big rock on the ground, he curled one hand over her elbow to help her up and used his other hand to hold the lantern high, illuminating her path back to the schoolhouse.

Charlotte lay awake all night, trying to understand the melancholy that had taken hold of her. She knew her marriage must be annulled. It was not legal. She had been impersonating someone else. Thomas was doing her a favor by not hauling her in front of a judge and jury to stand trial for fraud.

An annulment was the perfect solution.

So why did she feel such a sense of loss?

In the morning she was ready and waiting when Thomas came banging on the schoolhouse door. Daylight had barely dawned. Despite sleeping the night on the ground, he didn't look rumpled. That…steadiness…was part of his appeal, it occurred to Charlotte. Instead of letting the storms of life buffet him about, he stood firm and forced the storm waves to crash about him.

He had offered her his strength, but from today she would have to stand on her own.

During the walk to the tiny white church neither of them spoke. Thomas was taking long strides and Charlotte had to break into a run to keep up with him. He seemed in a great hurry to complete the business of annulling their union.

They found Reverend Eldridge sweeping the floor, reaching between the pews. He straightened and peered at them through the thick lenses of his spectacles.

Thomas held out a folded piece of paper. "We've come about the annulment."

Charlotte craned her neck to inspect what he was offering to the reverend. Of course. The certificate of their marriage. How careless of her to let him keep it. She should at least have insisted on a copy for herself.

The preacher scratched his ear. "Did I marry you?"

"Four weeks ago tomorrow," Thomas confirmed.

"Let me see." Reverend Eldridge shuffled to the small altar. He pulled out a ledger from beneath the embroidered altar cloth and studied the pages. With a population of eight in town, and the residents of the surrounding farms and ranches and mining camps mostly bachelors, Charlotte didn't expect there would be many records of marriage or baptism, only the occasional funeral.

The reverend looked at them with a frown lining his forehead. "I don't have any entries here in the last three months."

Thomas scowled at him. "I paid you two dollars and you did marry us."

"Here, in my church?"

"No," Charlotte cut in. "On the porch of the Imperial Hotel."

One age-mottled hand rose and scratched the sparse white hair by his temple. "I must have forgotten to write it up in the register. Let me see your document." The preacher held out his hand. Thomas passed the marriage certificate to him.

The reverend glanced at it and nodded. "My signature." He peered up at them again. "Must have clean slipped my mind by the time I got back to the church." He tore the piece of paper in two and handed out a half to each of them. "Here. It's done." He gave a chuckle. "If you change your mind, you can stick the marriage certificate back together and I'll record it in the ledger."

Charlotte studied her half. It said: "...ude Jackson."

She looked up at the preacher. "Just like that?"

He smiled, a vague, absent smile. "What?"

"The annulment. Just like that?"

He sent her a puzzled frown. "What annulment?"

Thomas gripped her arm, said thank you to the reverend and hauled her out of the church. When they got to the schoolhouse, he came in-

side after her, without waiting for an invitation,
or even asking for permission.

She'd never seen him like that. His powerful
body was rigid, his face as hard as granite. He
looked just like she imagined a soldier might look
when charging into a battle where he expected
to meet his death.

He bent down to the potbellied stove, opened
the hatch and used the poker to stir the ashes,
his half of their marriage certificate crumpled
in his fingers. Then he put down the poker, uncurled his fist and tossed the piece of paper into
the belly of the stove.

Charlotte watched the marriage certificate
catch flame and curl up and vanish. Without
a word, Thomas held out his hand. Sometime
ago she had speculated that the will of Thomas
Greenwood might be more potent than hers, and
she'd been right.

As if against her will, her arm moved. Her
fingers released their grip on the piece of paper
she was holding. She blinked back a tear when
Thomas threw her half of the marriage certificate into the flames, and she witnessed the formal proof of their union dissolve away.

Thomas still hadn't spoken.

He stared at the cooling ashes for a long moment, until the last of the orange glimmer had
died. Then he whirled on one boot heel and

strode out without sparing her even the briefest of glances. *Just like that?* She'd asked the preacher about ending their marriage. Thomas, with his abrupt parting, had given her the answer.

Just…like…that.

It was done. Finished. Over with. Thomas pointed Shadow down the desert trail, planning to use the hard riding to heal his broken heart.

It's better this way, he told himself. If he felt such terrible emptiness after less than a month of marriage, how awful might he have felt if their union had gone on for longer before it came to an end?

His thoughts leaped ahead to the evening. The orphans and widows would arrive on the afternoon train. The town was in an uproar. He'd have to take care of the animals on the farm and come back for the night, to make sure Charlotte was safe, all alone in the schoolhouse.

He was just about to kick Shadow into a canter when he heard the thunder of hooves from the direction of the town. Thomas brought Shadow to a halt and craned around in the saddle. He adjusted his hat brim and squinted at the cloud of dust that billowed between him and the buildings in the distance.

A rider hunched low in the saddle was catching up. Thomas recognized Gus Junior. The boy had the best horse in town, a black mustang he used in his business of delivering messages to the surrounding ranches and mining camps.

Gus Junior reined in alongside Thomas. The boy was panting for breath. His homely features crumpled with worry and his sallow skin seemed unusually pale.

"Mr. Greenwood, Sam Renner is coming into town."

Thomas snapped to attention. "How do you know?"

"I rode out to Desperation Hill yesterday." Gus Junior's voice cracked, and it was more than the usual adolescent croak. The boy was close to tears.

"It's my fault," Gus Junior went on. He reached into his shirt pocket and pulled out a folded piece of paper. "I've been selling these."

Thomas took the sheet, unfolded it. It was a copy of the one-page newspaper he'd already seen. *Gold Crossing Informer.*

"Sam Renner got hold of a copy and read it." Gus Junior's voice cracked again. "He knows there's women coming into town. He's already set off down the hill." His eyes pleaded at Thomas. "It's my fault. If I hadn't started the newspaper…" He gave a forlorn shake of his shaggy head. "It's my fault."

"It's all right, Gus," Thomas said gently, and

handed back the copy of the *Informer*. "You did nothing wrong."

"I wrote the newspaper…"

"Sam would have heard about the women anyway. Now we can figure out when to expect him, and we can be prepared."

Gus reined in to control a nervous sidestep by his mustang. "Your wife… I mean Miss Jackson… she is small and dark, with curly hair, just like that Frenchwoman who took Sam Renner's gold…"

Thomas spoke calmly. "It will take Sam about a week to walk into town. I'll be there. I'll see that Char— Miss Jackson is safe."

Gus Junior's expression brightened. "I'll help you protect her."

Thomas racked his brain to find a way to keep the boy out of harm's way without insulting his masculinity. "No," he said. "I need you to stand aside for now. That way, if something happens to me, you can step in and protect her."

"Right." Gus nodded. "If Sam Renner kills you, I'll step in."

Thomas said nothing. What a world they lived in, if a boy of fourteen talked so casually about death. No wonder Charlotte didn't want to stay around any longer than she had to.

Gus Junior cleared his throat, then spoke awkwardly. "Mr. Greenwood, do you think I should stop publishing the newspaper? I mean, am I stirring up trouble?"

Stirring up trouble? Thomas suppressed a groan. More like whipping it up with the force of a hurricane. However, it was clear the boy needed something to occupy him. The newspaper was ideal, for it provided an outlet for Gus Junior's curious mind and allowed him to reach out to other people. The citizens of Gold Crossing would just have to learn to cope with his meddling.

"No, Gus," Thomas replied with a mixture of encouragement and resignation. "You go on and keep right at it. This town needs a newspaper, and you are just the man to provide it."

They said their goodbyes. Gus Junior wheeled his mustang around and headed back into town. Thomas set off down the trail at an easy lope, no longer needing the challenge of breakneck speed to distract his mind.

Sam Renner was coming into town.

Seven years ago, at the height of the boom in Gold Crossing. Sam Renner had owned a struggling mine. One day, while working down in the mine shaft in the flickering light of a storm lantern, he hit his pickaxe into a solid rock of gold.

According to Sam, it would have been one of the biggest nuggets ever found in the history of mining, around eight pounds, the weight of a newborn baby, but the blow from his pickaxe had shattered it into fragments.

Sam collected the fragments into a jute sack and rode into town. Art Langley urged him to deposit his fortune in the hotel safe, but Sam clung to it, showing off his treasure and paying for his purchases in gold.

He took up with one of the saloon girls, a small Frenchwoman from New Orleans, paying for her to be his exclusive consort. When they went to live at the mine, the Frenchwoman saw there was no cabin, no well, no stove, no bed, nothing.

On their first night under the stars, she waited until Sam had fallen asleep by the campfire, and then she took out the pearl-handled revolver she had insisted he buy her for protection and put a bullet in his back.

Three days later, another miner found Sam, unconscious but still clinging to life. The gold and the woman were gone. Sam survived, but the bullet had lodged in his spine. The doctor refused to operate. It was too dangerous.

Sam was not able to ride, for the jolts on horseback might kill him. He roamed around the hills, walking in a crablike limp, dragging one foot. He scraped a living by trapping and hunting, surviving on what he could kill and eat.

In six years, Sam Renner had turned into a ghost

with long straggly hair, dirt caked on his clothing and the burning look of insanity in his eyes.

From mining camp to mining camp he limped, looking for the woman who had betrayed him—a small woman with dark, curly hair. He carried a big skinning knife he sharpened every night by the campfire. And he told everyone that when he found the woman he was looking for, he'd gut her like a fish.

Chapter Twelve

Thomas shouldered his way through the throng of men on the station platform in Gold Crossing, looking for Charlotte. A head taller than most, he got a good view over the forest of hats—bowlers, Stetsons, slouch hats, even a top hat. There had to be almost thirty men waiting for the train.

At the far end of the platform, Dottie Timmerman and Gladys Hayes sat on wooden chairs, bedecked in gowns with ribbons and frills, parasols twirling overhead. Manuel Chavez, the one-eyed card dealer from the Drunken Mule, stood beside them, holding a gleaming trumpet in his hands.

The whistle of the train blew in the distance. A plume of steam rose like a white ribbon against the blue sky. The iron rails began to vibrate. The men cheered and surged toward the edge of the platform, fighting for the best position.

Thomas cast one final glance around, satisfied that Charlotte had remained away. *Not out of good sense,* he thought ruefully. She must be busy putting the finishing touches on the schoolhouse.

The train rolled in, screeched to a stop. Manuel Chavez lifted the trumpet to his lips and blew out a fanfare. Gus Osborn and Gus Junior held up a banner that said *Welcome to Gold Crossing.* Art Langley, looking officious in a frock coat and with a mayor's sash across his chest—he was the one wearing the top hat—stepped forward to make an official welcome speech.

The train door opened. A small, dapper man carrying a fancy leather suitcase in one hand stepped down and glanced around him. "Blimey," he said with a delighted grin. "Didn't think you was so happy to see me."

"Where's the women?" shouted a man in a long duster.

"And the orphans!" yelled Gladys Hayes from the end of the platform.

"There's no one but me." The small man lifted his case higher. "Ed Newland at your service. I drum business for Newland Distillers. No more rotgut but fine bottled whiskey with assured quality." He shook his head in wonder. "Best welcome I've ever had. I guess you folks care about your whiskey."

"There's no women?" Art Langley asked.

Newland shook his head. "Not as much as a petticoat."

A man in a black suit rushed toward the train. "I don't believe you," he shouted. "I'll see for myself."

The crowd of men roared in agreement. Thomas watched as they surged forward, fighting each other to climb into the single car behind the steam engine. He could see them through the train windows, hurrying up and down the corridor, peering beneath the seats, as if the widows and orphans were playing hide-and-seek with them.

Only a minute later, the men emerged one by one through the door.

"There's no women."

"Langley, you bastard. You fooled us."

"You just wanted to fill the saloon and sell your liquor."

"I want my money back," shouted the man in a black suit.

"I want my money back, too!"

"And me. Four dollars I spent on a bed and dinner!"

The chorus of men cried out how much Art Langley had fleeced them with his false promises about women arriving. The crowd surged into motion, heading toward the Imperial Hotel. One of the men picked up a rock and hurled it through a small side window. The tinkle of shattering glass mixed with the yells of angry males.

"Gentlemen. Gentlemen." Art Langley rushed ahead and stood on the steps, arms raised, like a politician on the campaign trail. "I assure you, the women will arrive. I have a signed contract from the Widows and Orphans Association in San Francisco. There must have been some delay."

"We'll burn down your saloon."

Thomas saw a flash of alarm in Art Langley's eyes, but the lanky businessman showed no other sign of panic as he addressed the furious crowd.

"Gentlemen, I assure you—"

Another rock hurled through the air. It hit Art Langley in the shoulder. Thomas pushed forward. Enough was enough. He climbed up the steps to stand beside the beleaguered mayor of Gold Crossing.

"Enough of that!" Thomas roared. "Are you men, or a bunch of stray dogs on the scent of a bitch? You should be ashamed of yourself. If there had been any women on that train, they would have locked the doors and gone straight back to San Francisco, without ever setting foot in this town."

The crowd stilled but he could hear their angry murmurs.

Thomas went on. "If Mr. Langley says there's widows and orphans coming, then there's widows and orphans coming. And I'm sure there's something he can do to compensate you for the inconvenience of a wasted trip."

Art Langley flashed a strained smile. "Free drinks! Free drinks for everyone at the Drunken Mule." He pulled out a pocket watch on a chain from his waistcoat and flipped the lid to check the time. "It's three o'clock now. Drinks will be free for the next hour, until four o'clock."

Like an advancing army, the men surged up the steps and into the hotel. Thomas stood aside. Free drinks didn't sound like such a good idea to him, but at least he had prevented a riot before the men switched their attention to Gus Junior and blamed the boy for spreading false rumors in his *Informer*.

Thomas sat alone by the window at the Drunken Mule, leaning back in the chair and lazily sipping from a glass of whiskey. Around him, the crowd was thinning. The miners were hardworking men, not inclined to waste daylight hours in a saloon, and only a few of them had benefited from the free drinks to excess.

"Listen to this, fellers!"

Thomas peered into a shadowed corner where three miners sat together. Two were dressed in worn jackets and canvas trousers and bowler hats they kept on even indoors. The third looked like a gentleman, with a gray broadcloth suit and neatly clipped dark hair.

One of the bowler hats was talking. He was studying something on the table before him. Thomas pushed up to his feet and craned for a look. It was a copy of the *Informer.* He settled back down in his seat and listened as the man read out loud.

"'It is with regret that we announce the marriage between Mr. Thomas Greenwood, of Gold Crossing, and Miss Maude Jackson, from New York City, is to be annulled. Miss Jackson has taken employment as a schoolteacher until she can make arrangements to return to her home in the East.'"

Thomas felt his ears burn. It sounded so trivial, the way it read in the paper. His shattered dreams had been reduced to a single paragraph under the heading *Matrimonial and Family News.*

"It's that sodbuster's mail-order bride," the well-dressed miner said. "The one who came in on the train a month ago."

"I saw it." It was the taller bowler hat, the one who had been doing the reading. "They were married right there." He jerked his chin in the direction of the porch outside.

The smaller bowler hat spoke with a thick German accent. "I hear the sodbuster turned down a thousand dollars for her."

"She was a beauty," the well-dressed miner said. "Worth a million."

The tall bowler hat pushed to his feet. "Well, if she is no longer married to that sodbuster, what are we waiting for? There's a woman, right here. Let's go and call on her. The schoolhouse is a little way back from the church."

Thomas stiffened. But it was resentment, not fear. They seemed good men, decent men. If they wanted to call on an unattached female, he had no right to stop them. No right at all. He waited for the three miners to troop out of the saloon. Then he got up, tossed back the rest of his drink and followed them.

Charlotte heard the banging on the school-house door. She'd been drawing a map of the United States on the chalkboard, copying it from a book. She'd got the southern border right, and the West Coast didn't look too bad, but the Eastern Seaboard was going all crooked, and drawing Florida made her blush.

"Come in," she called out and put away the piece of chalk.

Gus Junior had already been to tell her that the widows and orphans had not arrived. She vacillated between relief and terror—relief because her competence as an educator would not be tested just yet, terror because if the orphans did not come, she'd be out of a job.

The door flung open and three men crowded into the tiny room. Two wore bowler hats and the rough work clothing of miners, the third a neat gray suit. All three wore tall boots that clattered against the floor.

"Gentlemen." Charlotte inclined her head. "How can I help you?"

It never crossed her mind to be afraid. Papa had often brought his ships' crews home to Merlin's Leap. She'd known dozens of disreputable-looking sailors, and had discovered that most of them possessed hearts of gold, or at least of silver.

The taller man in a bowler hat puffed out his chest. "We've come a-callin'." He had pock-marked skin and hollow cheeks, as if he'd been starving. He could be no more than twenty. A boy, really. An eager, overexcited boy.

Charlotte smiled. "You are most welcome. Perhaps you'd like coffee."

"Coffee would be very nice," said the man in a gray suit. "I'm Stuart. Jenkins. These fellers are Mortenson and Rathke."

"Nice to meet you," Charlotte replied. "I'm Miss Jackson."

"Howdy, Miss Jackson."

"I'll put the coffee on." Eyes sparkling with mischief, she clapped her hand to her mouth.

"Whoops. I only have one cup. And there is no-where to sit. The desks are too small. You'll get stuck if you cram into them."

"'Ve fetch table and chairs from the hotel." The shorter man in a bowler hat, Rathke, spoke in a clipped accent.

"Oh! *Sind Sie Deutscher?*"

"Osterreicher."

"Splendid." Charlotte flashed her visitors an-other bright smile. "I'll put the coffee on. You can fetch a table and chairs. Put them outside, and we'll have a garden party. Don't forget to bring three more cups."

She watched them clatter away on their booted feet and set to work. As she was measuring coffee into a pot, the hair at the back of her neck prick-led. She spun around and saw Thomas leaning against the door frame, arms crossed over his chest. He was wearing his Sunday suit and a flat-crowned black hat that looked new. So, he had been to meet the train, too. Her back stiffened. Wasn't two brides enough for him?

"What do you want?" she said.

She hadn't quite forgiven him for burning their marriage certificate, or—if what Gus Junior had said was true—for sending for a second mail-order bride even before she had returned home to Merlin's Leap.

"Just came by to see everything is fine," Thomas replied.

"I see." Charlotte gave a brief nod, ashamed of her sharp tone. Thomas had plenty of reason to be angry with her. She needed to be understanding. She was at fault in their situation, not him. "I'm about to have a garden party," she informed him. "Would you like to join in?"

Thomas did not move from the doorjamb. "Did you buy that tin of coffee?"

"No," she told him. "Miss Hayes gave me a bit, to get me started."

Thomas made a noncommittal sound. Charlotte frowned. She suspected coffee would be terribly expensive to buy. Everything seemed to be.

Art Langley had paid her for the first month in advance. She had spent four dollars on a plain green cotton dress, the one she wore now, and two dollars on a straw bonnet. That only left four dollars for supplies until she got paid again.

Outside, she could hear banging and curses and friendly squabbling.

The Austrian miner appeared in the doorway. "Table is ready."

"Fine," she said. "I'll join you in a minute."

The coffee boiled in no time. She carried the pot outside, taking a small slate writing tablet with her to use as a pot holder.

The men were lounging in wooden chairs at

one of the square gambling tables from the hotel. Five chairs. Four men. Three cups. Charlotte poured and passed out the cups, leaving Thomas till last.

"Whoops," she said with an artificially sweet smile. "We seem to have run out of cups."

Thomas dipped one big hand into the pocket of his unbuttoned suit jacket, pulled out another cup and set it on the table. There was a hard edge to his smile.

Charlotte poured for him and resisted the temptation to create a spill. She put the pot down, dashed back inside to fetch her own cup and filled it with the last dregs from the pot—she had only allowed for three guests—and sat down in the vacant seat.

"Well, gentlemen," she said brightly. "This is nice."

She took a sip from her coffee. It was nothing but grounds. The sun burned down on her head. Flies buzzed around her. The tension in the air was thick enough to slice with a knife.

"What are you doing still hanging around her, Greenwood?" the hollow-cheeked boy said under his breath. "You had your chance and you couldn't hold on to her. Now clear off and let us have our turn."

"I'm seeing that Miss Jackson gets to return safely to the East where she belongs," Thomas replied. "It's clear she isn't cut out for the life here. I'm sending her back because I don't want to see her worn to death from farm chores and childbirth."

Charlotte nearly choked on the coffee grounds.

The hollow-cheeked boy, Mortenson, made an expansive gesture with his coffee cup. "When I strike it rich, I can buy her silk and lace and diamonds and furs. She'll have a houseful of servants and she'll never need to set foot in the kitchen."

Thomas lifted his eyebrows. "And until then? Until you strike it rich?"

The young miner shifted awkwardly in his seat and said nothing.

Thomas took a sip and put his coffee down. "Until then you'll expect her to live in a tent, which is freezing at night and sweltering during the day. She'll spend her days doing laundry in a muddy stream and cooking on a campfire. Even I could offer her more than that."

The well-dressed miner, Jenkins, spoke. "Greenwood, I mean no criticism, but if the marriage has been annulled, perhaps you should stay away from Miss Jackson and give her the opportunity to meet another man who might suit her better."

"Gentlemen," Charlotte said. "Mr. Greenwood and I bear no ill will toward each other."

"Fine," Thomas said, narrowing his eyes at

Jenkins. "I paid two hundred dollars for her passage. You are welcome to court her, but first you must pay me back my two hundred dollars."

A dark flush rose on the other man's face. "You talk as if women could be bought and sold."

"Isn't that what's going on here?" Thomas took another sip from his coffee, his movements perfectly calm. "Mortenson here wants to buy her with gold he hasn't even found yet. You want to buy her with a fine education that has no value on the frontier."

"My educational credentials are worth more than a few acres of fields scratched out from the wilderness. I have a degree in Latin and Greek. I—"

Thomas cut him off. "Latin and Greek?" He tilted his head to one side, as if considering the matter. "I think there's a Greek cook in one of the mining camps. Yes, your education might be of some use, if you come across the Greek fellow."

Jenkins surged to his feet. "Now, look here…"

"I will find gold," Mortenson said.

"The heck you will," Thomas replied.

Mortenson lifted his half-empty coffee cup and tossed the contents in Thomas's face. Thomas didn't cry out, didn't swear, didn't say anything. He didn't even flinch. Slowly, he unfolded to his full height behind the table.

Charlotte held her breath. He seemed so formidable, the slow certainty of his motion more daunting than any threats. It occurred to her that she had always thought Thomas a peaceful, calm person, but maybe it was because he had always taken care to appear so in front of her.

Mortenson circled the table and charged with his fists raised. Thomas stepped aside. When the boy lurched past him, Thomas grabbed the collar of his jacket with one hand, the seat of his pants with the other and lifted him in the air. The boy kicked and thrashed. One of the blows connected with a thud against Thomas's cheek.

Charlotte jumped up and down. "There's no brawling here," she yelled. "You are my guests. I'm a lady. There's no brawling here."

No one listened to her.

Brawling was exactly what they wanted.

Thomas didn't like fighting. It didn't seem fair. His size, strength and reach gave him an advantage which tipped the balance in his favor. But sometimes pressure built up inside a man, like the steam builds up inside an engine, and then a man had no choice but to let it out before he did something worse.

The three miners ganged up against him. Thomas didn't mind. It evened the odds a bit. But not much.

Jenkins danced and dipped and darted about,

delivering quick jabs. The man had the benefit of some boxing training, Thomas could tell from his fancy footwork. The Austrian, Rathke, was the most tenacious. Mortenson fought dirty. The tooth marks on Thomas's arm were proof of that.

Rathke charged at him again, head dipped low. Thomas tensed his stomach muscles and took the impact. Behind him, Mortenson jumped onto his back. The man's arms came around Thomas's neck in a suffocating hold. In front of him, Jenkins danced and weaved. Thomas felt a blinding blow on the crest of his cheekbone.

Enough.

Time to end it.

He brought up his left knee and heard a crunch when it connected with Rathke's nose. The Austrian staggered back, blood pouring from his broken nose.

One down.

Next, Thomas curled his fingers around the arms that held his throat in a chokehold. He gripped tight and made a sudden twist, bending low at the waist. The force of the motion sent Mortenson spinning over his head. Thomas let go and Mortenson landed in a sprawl in the dust.

Two down.

In front of him, Jenkins bounced on the balls of his feet, delivering his little jabs. Lacking patience for such finesse, Thomas waited for his moment. When Jenkins lowered his left arm, creating an opening, Thomas waded in with his right, then followed with a left hook that lifted Jenkins into the air. Thomas pulled his right arm back for another blow but there was no need. Jenkins crumpled to the ground.

Three down.

"Go," Thomas said to Rathke, who was standing to one side, spitting blood.

"Ja, ja, ich gehe."

Thomas spoke no German, but the man's hasty retreat said enough. On the ground, Jenkins groaned. Thomas reached down to pull the man up to his feet. This one, he could respect.

Making a halfhearted attempt to beat the dust from the man's clothing, Thomas shoved him on his way. "Go," he said. "And don't come back."

He turned to Mortenson, who lay sprawled on the ground, a dazed look in his eyes. Thomas picked him up by his collar and the seat of his pants and threw him after the others. "Don't forget your friend."

His breathing was harsh. His pulse pounded in a frantic beat. Pain throbbed in his cheek and his cut lip and his grazed knuckles. His muscles were hurting from the blows and his left arm stung where the bastard Mortenson had bitten him hard enough to pierce his skin, even through the clothing.

Somewhere at the edge of his blurred vision Charlotte was hovering, clenching and unclenching her fists. She'd been yelling something about not fighting in front of a lady. Thomas felt a quick burst of shame. What would she think of him? He took pride in being a peace-loving man, and now she had seen him engage in a brawl.

"Thomas! Thomas!"

"Huh." He shook his head, like a bear coming out of hibernation. He heard the patter of small feet on the gravel. Cool hands closed around his face.

"Are you all right?" Charlotte asked.

He looked down at her. She was looking up at him. There was worry in her eyes, and something else that made them sparkle, bright and full of life.

"I'm fine," he said.

Charlotte let out an exasperated sound, something between a snort and a gust of laughter. "You're a mess. Your suit is torn, your lip is bleeding and I wager you'll have a black eye. Don't tell me you're all right."

Thomas felt himself being shoved backward. He didn't resist. After a few shuffling steps he bumped against a chair behind him, and sank into it.

"Stay there," Charlotte said. "I have hot water on the stove."

Exhaustion swept over Thomas. He tipped his head back. The sun was low in the sky. It was past six o'clock. He'd have to get going soon if he wanted to ride home before dark.

Charlotte returned outside, carrying a bowl of water. A small linen towel hung over her arm. She set the bowl on the table, dipped the cloth into it and bent over him.

"Close your eyes."

Thomas did as he was told. Gently, she bathed his face, her fingers searching out the cuts and grazes, the hot water easing the sting on his skin. Thomas lifted his lashes a fraction and watched her. She leaned closer, studying the bruise on his cheek.

He could slide his hand behind her head and pull her closer, and they would be kissing. He had only kissed her once, on their wedding day. He should have kissed her when he could. When he had the right. He should have bedded her, when he had the right. She couldn't have left him then. She would have been forced to stay with him.

And now, he could pull her down to him and kiss her, out in the open, for anyone to see, and the whole town would know it was not over between them. *She* would know it was not over between them.

The aggression of the fight still pumped through him, driving needs that had festered inside him ever since he first laid eyes on Charlotte. The force of the temptation frightened him. All he wanted right now was to tumble her into his lap and tear off her clothes. Thomas closed his eyes, clamping down on the temptation, clamping down on the need.

"I'm sorry," he said, to break the tension of the silence.

"What for?"

"For fighting in front of a lady."

"Your right hook is weak and your footwork could be quicker."

He opened his eyes. "What?"

Charlotte gave him a smug smile. "When we were children my sister Miranda took boxing lessons from an Irish stable lad. I couldn't. He said I was too small, with small hands." She flattened her palm against his chest and shoved. "Lean back. I'm not finished."

She went on applying the hot water to his battered cheek. "Aren't you going to apologize for trying to sell me for two hundred dollars?" she asked.

"No."

"Are you still angry with me?"

"Don't I have a right to be?"

Charlotte didn't reply, merely continued her

ministrations. A cool evening breeze had picked up. Golden orioles were darting about in the prickly pears behind the schoolhouse, chirping merrily. At the Imperial Hotel, Manuel Chavez was playing his trumpet.

Charlotte gave a forlorn sigh. "Oh, Thomas. I wish…"

Thomas reached up a hand and curled his fingers around her wrist. "I wish, too."

For a moment, it seemed to him they were communicating without words, her pulse beating frantically beneath his fingers. Should he fight for her? Should he ask her to stay? Should he forgive her lies and deceit, accept she had acted because she had no choice? Could he trust her with his life, his dignity, his heart?

Clouds had drifted in front of the setting sun and twilight was falling quickly. The mournful sound of the trumpet drifted on the breeze. Thomas recognized the song. It was a Mexican ballad about a lost child. His child, the child he had hoped for, had been lost before it was even born. A child that had been no more than a mirage. A marriage that had been no more than a lie.

He couldn't ask her to stay. It would take too great a toll on his pride. If she wanted to stay, she should ask him. It would cost her much less.

Thomas waited…waited…waited for her to

ask, her frantic pulse beating beneath his fingertips. Charlotte shook herself, as if awakening from a dream. She pulled her hand free, poked at his gaping sleeve and spoke in an artificial tone of brusque efficiency.

"Your coat is torn. It was your only good suit."

"Doesn't matter."

"When I get back home, I'll order a new suit for you from a Boston tailor and mail it over. I'll have to take your measurements before I go."

Thomas fell silent. It was no use thinking he could ask her to stay. It was no good wishing. Wishes were two a penny. He pushed up to his feet.

"I'd best get going. It will be dark soon." He adjusted the torn sleeve of his coat. "There is something I need to tell you. This is really important. There is a man, Sam Renner, up in the hills. Years ago, a small woman with curly dark hair stole his gold and shot him, leaving him for dead."

Thomas looked around for his hat, spotted it on the ground. As he bent to scoop it up, the pain in his sore muscles made him wince. He knocked the crown of the hat back into shape with his fist and propped the hat on his head.

"Sam Renner has lost his mind. He is searching for her, the woman who stole his gold, but any small woman with curly dark hair will do. He won't be able to tell the difference. If he gets you cornered, he'll kill you. He is infirm. He can't ride. He moves around on foot. He has a bad limp. He drags one foot and moves very slowly. Keep your eyes open. Keep your wits about you. If you see a limping man around fifty coming toward you, run away from him. Do you hear me? Run. He is slow, and he can't catch you up."

Charlotte stared at him with worry stamped on her face. "Does he have a gun?" she asked. "I can't run against a gun."

Thomas hesitated. He didn't want to frighten her but perhaps it was better that she was afraid. "Sam Renner has a gun but he won't use it to shoot you."

"Why not?"

"He wants to slice you open with a skinning knife and tear out your guts."

Chapter Thirteen

Thomas cranked the handle on the irrigation pump, ignoring the protests from his battered muscles. For several days now the sun had baked the land with a relentless heat. To save his crops, he had to irrigate every few hours.

He missed Charlotte terribly. He hadn't truly appreciated how much help she'd been. More than that, her cheerful presence had turned the chore into a joy.

Thomas straightened, massaged his aching back. Everything seemed to be going wrong at once. Rosamund had developed an infection in her udders. His cabbages were infested with some kind of pest he'd never seen before. It made him realize he still had a lot to learn about vegetable farming.

During the nights, restless dreams plagued him. Sometimes he was sitting in a chair outside the schoolhouse, and Charlotte lay languid in his lap. She was wearing the green cotton dress he'd seen her wear at the garden party, with a row of tiny buttons on the front.

One by one, he slipped the buttons free, and then he slid his hand inside the bodice to cup her breast. The shape of it fitted perfectly in his hand. He'd known all along it would. Even in a dream, the pleasure left him breathless.

At other times, he dreamed of Sam Renner waving his knife, and Charlotte standing like a pillar of salt, waiting for the blade to bite into her flesh. *I'll gut you like a fish,* Sam Renner was shouting. Just before the knife flashed, Thomas would jolt awake, his body shaking, his skin coated in a layer of icy sweat.

Every morning, every afternoon, he wanted to saddle Shadow and ride into town to see Charlotte, but he couldn't afford the time. Not if he wanted to keep his farm.

A rider thudded down the path toward the lake. Thomas jumped off the jetty and headed out to meet him. It was Gus Junior on his mustang. It was the second time the boy had ridden over, to bring news of how Sam Renner was progressing in his journey down from Desperation Hill.

Gus jumped down from the saddle. "Howdy, Mr. Greenwood."

"Howdy, Gus." Thomas stroked the shiny black flank of the horse.

"He's past Burnt Pine," Gus Junior said. "Half-way to Hansen's Creek. I seen him myself."

Thomas considered the landmarks on the trail he knew from his days of prospecting. "He is going slowly. I doubt he'll make the Thursday train."

Gus Junior frowned. "Mr. Greenwood…how does Sam Renner know your wife—I mean Miss Jackson—is small and dark with curly hair? I didn't put anything about it in the newspaper."

"He doesn't." Thomas unrolled the shirtsleeves he'd rolled up to crank the irrigation pump. "Do you want coffee, Gus?"

"I'd kill for a coffee." The boy looked flustered. "I didn't mean…"

"It's all right, Gus." Thomas gave the horse another pat and got a friendly whinny in return.

"Sam Renner isn't coming into town for Miss Jackson," Thomas explained. "He is coming to see the women arriving on the train. With any luck, none of them will resemble his French-woman, and he'll go off on his way again. Or he might remember what he read in the newspaper about a new schoolteacher, and decide to take a look at her, too. We don't know the way his mind works. With a madman one never does."

"I'll keep an eye on him for you, Mr. Green-wood. I'll ride up the trail every day, and when he is close to town, I'll come and let you know."

Thomas nodded, hiding his concern. There was no point in upsetting the boy.

"That's a good plan, Gus. I'm grateful for your help."

Sam Renner made his clumsy way down the trail, bedroll and rifle dangling over his shoulder. Every step, agony sliced through him. He studied the ground with care, looking out for roots and stones that might trip him up, for the jolt of a fall might kill him.

Finally, she was back.

Madeleine Jacquinot. He let her image form in his mind. Long black curls, laughing brown eyes. Dimples in her cheeks and the devil in her heart.

He had offered her everything. His money, his love and his trust. And she had paid him back by pitching him into hell.

By the side of the path, Hansen's Creek made a merry ripple. Tiny birds hopped on the rocks by the edge of the current. Once, Sam had taken delight in the wonders of nature. He'd even enjoyed the hard work of a miner, burrowing like a mole deep into the crust of the earth, coaxing Mother Nature to give up her treasures.

But now his days were filled with agony and hate.

There was gold in his mine, he was sure of it. But his crippled body did not allow him to dig for it. Others had tried but the gold was too well hidden in the folds of the mountainside for anyone to find.

At the crossing of Hansen's Creek Sam paused for a rest. Carefully, he lowered himself to a sitting position on the ground. A week ago, he'd walked into a mining camp, to beg for a bag of salt to go with the rabbits and wild turkeys he lived on. One of the miners had been reading a newspaper, and Sam had borrowed it.

It had been right there.

Madeleine Jacquinot was back. It had to be her. Madeleine had told him about her past. She'd gone to a convent school in New Orleans, had trained to be a teacher, but in her first position as a governess there had been an incident with the master of the house, and she'd been dismissed in disgrace. No one else had employed her, which had sent her down the path of a saloon whore.

Sam had saved her from that path.

And she had paid him back by betraying him.

Maude Jackson, she called herself now. People did that, when they changed their name. Picked the same initials. Some did it for sentimental reasons. Most did it because they might have scratched their initials on something and wanted the letters to match the new name.

When Sam got the revelation that his treacherous lover had returned, he asked someone what day of the week it was, and since then he had counted the days. Today it was Wednesday.

Sam's face puckered, like on a child about to burst into tears.

He'd be late. He wanted to get into town for Thursday. The commotion that accompanied the arrival of the train would give him an opportunity to sneak up on Madeleine without getting noticed.

From higher up along the path came the rattle of a wagon. Sam struggled to his feet and turned to watch the approaching vehicle. A farm cart, and on the bench sat a farm boy, no more than eighteen, clad in homespun.

The boy pulled on the lines. "Whoa."

The cart horse, a buckskin with a white diamond on its nose, whinnied and came to a restless halt, eyes flashing in fear. Sam's mouth twisted in dismay. Even animals shunned him now. They could smell the hate in him.

"You go to town, old-timer?" The farm boy spoke with an accent.

"Yes," Sam replied. "I have a woman to see."

The boy grinned. "I hope you been saving your money."

A surge of bitterness rolled through Sam at the veiled reference to his crippled body and grimy clothing and long straggly hair. The one dignity he had clung to was to remain clean shaven, but that was only because he wanted to test the sharpness of his blade.

"I already paid her," Sam replied. *She took all I had.*

The boy scooted along the bench to make room. "Hop on, mister."

Sam stared at the bench, frowning. The boy must be a newcomer who didn't know he couldn't take the jolting of a cart. But today was Wednesday. For six years, he'd lived with no other thought on his mind but revenge, and nothing must stand in his way.

Carefully, not twisting his spine, Sam crouched to pick up his bedroll and rifle and threw them over his shoulder. "You have to help me up to the bench. I'm not as agile as I used to be."

He slipped his hand inside his unbuttoned duster and curled his fingers around the hilt of his long skinning knife. A ride into town wouldn't be enough. He needed the cart to sneak up on Madeleine.

The farm boy tied the lines around the brake and hopped down. He came to stand beside Sam and wrapped one arm around him, to help him up. When their bodies pressed together, Sam pulled the knife out of his belt and slammed it into the belly of the farm boy.

The blade sank to the hilt. The boy emitted a strangled groan and sagged against him. The warm flow of blood spurted over Sam's fingers. The horse neighed, stomped its hooves, but remained on the spot, too well trained to bolt.

Sam jerked his knife free and thrust the lifeless body of the farm boy away from him. He wiped the blade clean against his shirt and slid the knife back in its sheath at his belt. Then he scrambled up to the wagon bench.

The jolting might kill him, but he didn't care. There was nothing for him to live for except his revenge. He'd drive into town, and if he survived the journey, he'd do what he had dreamed of doing for six long years. He'd kill the woman who had stolen his gold and pitched him into hell.

Charlotte was just about to blow out the small oil lamp on the teacher's desk when she heard a wagon draw up outside the schoolhouse. Her heart seemed to lurch in her chest.

Thomas! He'd come! He'd come to wish her good luck as she embraced her teaching career with the orphans arriving on the train tomorrow afternoon.

In truth, she'd been annoyed that he hadn't found the time to visit her. Particularly if there was a madman on the loose. Although by now she had come to understand from Gladys Hayes that Sam Renner was little more than a myth. He hadn't been seen in town for years.

However, she'd been scrupulously following Thomas's orders. During the day, she remained out in the open, where she could see anyone approaching. After dark, she stayed in the schoolhouse and kept her door locked and bolted.

From Gus Junior Charlotte had learned Rosamund was ailing and there were maggots in the cabbages and the lack of rain required constant irrigation. Knowing that Thomas had been tied up with pressing matters eased the sting of his neglect of her. She really should be out there, helping him, and she would tell him so.

But now Thomas had come to see her. Unlike their first meeting at the Imperial Hotel, Charlotte had the presence of mind to consider her state of undress before she opened the door. She pulled the blanket from the cot and wrapped it around her shoulders, covering up her flimsy nightgown.

Then she hurried over to slide the bolt and unlock the door.

Her fingers were still gripping the key when the door flung open, smashing into her. She staggered backward. A gust of chilled air blew into the room. From the darkness a hunched form lurched inside, a long duster flaring about his legs.

She could smell him. Even before her horrified eyes recorded the details—long, straggly hair streaked with gray, dirt caked on his clothing, boots so worn she could see toes poking through—she could smell him, the thick stench of a destitute man who had almost ceased to be a human being.

He stepped into the room, an awkward swaying step that had his shoulders rising and falling when he dragged one foot behind him. He reached out one arm and swung the door shut. His other arm rose, as if in a salute. And gripped in his fist Charlotte could see a long, lethal-looking knife.

"Madeleine," he said. "I've come to kill you."

Terror slammed into Charlotte. Her senses sharpened. Time stilled. She had never felt pure panic before, and it left no room for fear. Her mind seemed crystal clear, her thoughts rational, her body poised for action.

Sam Renner. He was not a myth after all.

But he was supposed to arrive on foot.

"Mr. Renner," she said softly. "I'm afraid you are mistaken. My name is…my name is…" The lie froze on her lips. "My name is Charlotte Fairfax. I'm not the one you are looking for."

"Beautiful Madeleine." He stepped closer to her. The sharp, acrid odor of his unwashed body filled her nostrils. "You betrayed me. You stole my gold and crippled my body and turned my life into a nightmare. I'll do the same to you."

Charlotte backed away and crashed into the desks that blocked her retreat. The blanket fell from her fingers as she fumbled blindly at the desks, weaving her way between them, not daring to take her eyes off the man advancing upon her.

Sam Renner came after her with his swaying gait, the knife poised to strike. Lamplight glittered on the blade. Twice they circled the tiny room, Charlotte fumbling her way backward, Sam Renner following, like some kind of a macabre dance.

Then she tripped over the blanket that lay in a heap on the floor. With a cry she stumbled. Sam Renner reached out and grabbed her by the arm and swung her around. Gripping her with one hand, brandishing the knife in the other, he ushered her toward the log wall of the cabin until her back slammed against it.

"Don't fight," he said. "Or I'll slice you open."

Grunting with effort, or perhaps with pain, he dug in his pocket and pulled out several coiled strips of rawhide string. One at a time, he raised her hands above her head and tied her wrists to the wooden pegs on the wall where the children would hang their coats. Then he squatted by her feet and tied her ankles together.

She could kick him. Topple him backward and escape.

But even as the thought rose in Charlotte's

mind, it was too late. Her feet were trapped. Sam Renner straightened and surveyed her. She stood in front of him, dressed in her flimsy nightgown, ankles bound, arms flung wide and tied to the hooks, as if crucified.

His gaze drifted down her body.

"Beautiful Madeleine. Always beautiful."

"I'm not your Madeleine. My name is Charlotte."

Cunning flashed in his eyes. "Charlotte, Madeleine. Frenchwoman's name." He took a step forward. "You won't fool me with your lies. Never again." He took a step back and lifted his knife. "I'm going to gut you like a fish."

"No. Please."

"Please?" He tipped his head back and laughed, a horrible, cruel laugh filled with bitterness. "You put a bullet in my back and left me for dead and stole my gold and now you say a pretty please and expect me to fall at your feet again."

"It was not me. It was someone else."

Ignoring her, Sam Renner leaned forward. His face loomed in front of hers. The smell of his stale breath surrounded her. In his eyes she could see the fire of insanity. Spittle formed on his lips as he spoke to her with a burst of passion.

"Since that day, my life has been hell. I live like an animal. I crawl like a crab, I eat like a scavenger. I'm in constant pain. I have no future. The only pleasure I have left is taking my revenge. I'm going to gut you like a fish."

He drew back a step and raised his arm. The blade glinted in the lamplight and began its descent toward her belly.

"Wait," Charlotte yelled. "The gold. Don't you want your gold back?"

The knife ceased its motion. "You have my gold?"

"Why did you think I came back?"

Confusion flickered across Sam's face. "Why *did* you come back?"

"I hid the gold before I left Gold Crossing. I had to come back for it." Quickly, desperation guiding her mind, Charlotte spun her tale. "I hid it in a hole in the ground under an apple tree. I came to get it, but the tree must have died. I can't find the right spot. That's why I took the job. I needed to stay around and search for the gold."

"You have my gold?"

"Yes. And if you kill me, you'll never find it."

She could see indecision hover on Sam's grimy features. And then something flashed in his eyes. Not hate. Not anguish. But hope. A faint glimmer of hope that there could be a measure of restitution. That life could be worth living again.

Charlotte snuffed out a spark of pity. She forced herself to look at the knife. She imagined the blade sinking into her gut, imagined the pain, and imagined the blood spurting from the wound. The fleeting sense of shame she had felt for tricking the poor demented man vanished in an instant.

Reaching up with both arms, Sam used the tip of his knife to cut the rawhide straps that bound Charlotte's wrists to the coat hooks. She held her breath, muscles tensed, waiting for him to crouch down and cut the tie around her ankles. When the straps fell away, she'd smash her knee into his face and make her escape.

Without turning her head, Charlotte stole a glance at the door. Sam had not locked or bolted the entrance. Her feet were bare, which might slow her flight on the rough gravel ground, but whatever her speed, it would be greater than his. She'd have no trouble making it to the safety of the Imperial Hotel, where a handful of men had already gathered to wait for tomorrow's train.

But Sam didn't crouch down. The knife poised in one hand, he fumbled inside his long duster and brought out a coil of braided rawhide rope. He shook the coil loose, and she could see a loop at one end of it.

Reaching up once more, Sam slipped the loop over her head and yanked the sliding knot to tighten the noose around her neck. Only when he had her safely caught with the rope did he squat before her and snap the cord that tied her ankles.

"Let's go," he said.

"My shoes. Let me put on my shoes. And my clothes."

Sam jerked the rawhide rope. The noose cut off her air.

"You go as you are," Sam said.

Taking wheezing breaths, Charlotte slid her fingers beneath the rope at her throat and managed to ease the pressure against her windpipe.

"All right," she rasped. "All right."

Sam jerked the rope once more but she was prepared, her fingers tugging back against the impact, protecting her throat from the bite of the noose.

Charlotte made her way to the entrance, took one hand away from her throat and pushed the door open. The night air was cool. Darkness covered the landscape. A few yards away, she could see the looming shadow of a horse and cart. In the sky, a million stars twinkled, cold and uncaring. Halfway down the street, she could see the steady burn of gas lights at the Imperial Hotel, and at the far end, the yellow square of the doctor's window shone like the beacon, promising safety.

She would lead the way toward the hotel. When they were close enough, she would yell and throw her weight against the rope and attempt to break free. Even if the noose cut off her air, someone would come. Someone would hear her. It took a few minutes for a person to choke to death. Someone would come.

Behind her, Charlotte heard the scrape of Sam's shuffling footsteps. An instant later, a circle of flickering light fell around her. He had picked up the small lamp in the cabin and was holding it high to illuminate their way into the darkness.

"Get going," he ordered.

Charlotte set into motion. The gravel bit into the soles of her bare feet, but she ignored the pain. A thorn made her cry out. The rope jerked around her neck.

"Be quiet," Sam hissed.

"Sorry," she said in a low voice. "I stepped on a thorn."

He made a grunted reply that might have contained a shred of sympathy. Encouraged by that small evidence of his humanity, Charlotte increased her speed. She had planned to walk in a semicircle, in an attempt to disguise her destination, but now she pointed her feet directly toward the lights of the Imperial Hotel.

The rope jerked, hard. She came to a halt.

"Not that way," Sam said. "The apple orchard was next to the church."

There had been an apple orchard! Despair washed over Charlotte as she thought of the layout of the town. The small white church was the one building in Gold Crossing that lay even farther away from the other buildings than the schoolhouse. Farther away from the lights. Farther away from safety.

"Keep going," Sam said.

He was forgetting to whisper now. She would argue back, keep him talking, in the hope that he might raise his voice enough for someone to hear. Even as the thought formed in her mind, a burst of music floated through the darkness from the Drunken Mule, making Charlotte understand how unlikely the prospect would be.

Hope ebbed inside her. Why prolong the agony? Why not end it here?

Her feet stopped moving. She uncurled her fingers from the rope around her neck, letting the pressure bite into her throat.

"Keep going," Sam said. The rope jerked, but only a little. And then she felt the prick of the knife at the small of her back. "If you don't find the gold, I'll gut you like a fish."

Terror gripped her once more, and with it came a renewed spark of survival instinct. Oblivious to the sting of gravel and thorns beneath the soles of her bare feet, Charlotte set into motion again. The circle of lamplight danced and flickered around her, creating a play of shadows on the ground.

Ahead, she could see the small white church looming like an oasis in the darkness. Behind her, she could hear the sounds of Sam's awkward progress—the drag and scrape of his infirm foot, the rustle of his long duster as he swung his body in each laborious step. Even in the midst of her terror, she couldn't totally shake off her compassion for the man.

"Here," Sam said, and jerked her to a halt.

Charlotte stilled, tried to draw calming breaths. She raked a glance around her. They were beside the church, on the opposite side from the small graveyard. The ground was covered in coarse tufts of grass. When Sam moved the lamp in a wide arc, she could see a few stumps and gnarled roots on the ground, evidence that there might once have been an orchard.

"Dig," Sam said.

"Dig?" Charlotte straightened her spine. "What with?" She put out her hand, trying to keep it from shaking. "I need your knife. The ground's too hard to dig with my bare hands."

For a fraction of a second, she thought she'd get away with it. Then Sam laughed that horrible, bitter laugh of his. "You don't get away with your wiles no more, Madeleine."

Not taking his eyes off her, he bent to prop the lamp on the ground. Then he reached into a pocket on his duster and brought out a metal eating utensil, a spoon with a serrated tip that also allowed it to be used like a fork. *Spork*, Charlotte had heard someone call them.

"Dig." Sam pointed at the ground. "Here."

Charlotte took the spork he held out for her. Sam moved closer, letting the rope go slack.

"Dig," he said. "Find my gold."

Charlotte sank to her knees and struck the spork into the ground. The earth was softer here, evidence of past cultivation, and she managed to scoop out a spoonful of dirt.

Again and again, her arm swung, spooning out the dirt, creating a hole in the ground. Despite the effort the night chill made her shiver. When she twisted to toss aside the loose earth, her flimsy nightgown tore where her knees trapped it against the ground. Mud covered her hands and forearms. When she struck hard with the spoon, grit flew up into her face. She could feel it grinding in her teeth, caking inside her nostrils, stinging in her eyes.

When the hole was big enough to bury a small treasure chest, Sam jerked on the rope.

"Stop."

Kneeling on all fours, Charlotte ceased her digging. Too exhausted to scramble up to her feet, she folded one knee beneath her and slumped to sit on the ground.

Sam picked up the lamp and lifted it high. Charlotte watched, all thoughts of escape forgotten. Her lungs were heaving, her muscles throbbing, her hands shaking. Sam took a step to the left, to the right, illuminating the tufts of coarse grass beneath his feet.

"Here," he said, and set the lamp on the ground again.

The rope jerked. Charlotte scrambled back to her hands and knees. Her fingers tightened around the handle of the spork. Her arm began to rise and fall, scooping out the dirt. Digging, digging, digging, one spoonful at a time.

High up in the sky, the stars twinkled. Down the street, merriment went on in the saloon. Charlotte dug, her knuckles bleeding, the flimsy nightgown clinging to her body, mud coating her skin, tears of terror and despair streaming down her face.

Minutes turned to hours. *Thomas, Thomas,* she thought, *I'll never see you again. I'll never see my sisters again.* How long did she have? Until midnight? Until dawn? How long would it take before Sam understood they were digging for a treasure that did not exist?

Chapter Fourteen

Thomas rode down the trail in the darkness, letting Shadow pick the way. He'd planned to get into town in daylight. After all, tomorrow was Thursday, and although some of the miners had decided no women would arrive, others were still hoping and had come down the hill to meet the train. Thomas didn't want Charlotte alone in the schoolhouse with a bunch of woman-hungry males roaming around.

He ought to have set out earlier, but Rosamund's condition had taken a turn for the worse. For a few hours, Thomas had feared he would need to put the cow down, end her suffering. But then the fever had broken, and Rosamund had not protested when he had gently milked her, easing the pressure in her udders.

The light in the window of Doc Timmerman's house guided Thomas into town. The doc and his wife turned in early, but every night the doc filled a lamp and left it burning by the window, to help people find him in case of an emergency.

Past the boarded-up homes, past the mercantile, past the noisy saloon Thomas rode, eager to reach the schoolhouse and sleeping Charlotte.

He dismounted twenty yards away, tied Shadow to a hitching rail outside an empty store, unsaddled the horse and took down his bedroll. He'd walk the rest of the way, so the clatter of Shadow's hooves would not wake her up.

By the schoolhouse something big loomed in the darkness. The soft neigh of a horse greeted Thomas. He took out a match, stuck it against the sole of his boot and held the flame high. A buckskin horse. And a farm cart. He recognized neither, but in the darkness one horse and farm cart looked very much like another.

Thomas shook out the match before it scorched his fingers. He felt his way through the darkness to the schoolhouse door and gave it a light tap. The door slid open. He struck another match and held it high.

Instead of neat rows, the dozen desks stood askew, as if there had been a brawl. Quickly, Thomas counted the days since his last trip into town, ticked them off in his mind. No mistake. Thursday was tomorrow. The children had not arrived yet, could not have wreaked havoc in the classroom.

Worry twisted in his gut. Who had come for Charlotte? It could not be Sam Renner, for he was still three days away, and whoever had caused the disarray in the schoolhouse had arrived by cart. It had to be that man from Boston who was after her... *Cousin Gareth,* Thomas recalled.

He lit another match, searched for a source of light in the cabin. There was no lamp on the table, but he spotted one on the wall, fastened to a bracket with a reflector behind it. Not bothering with the niceties of unscrewing the bracket, Thomas wrenched the lamp free, taking care not to break the glass or spill the oil.

He lit the flame and continued his inspection. On the floor near the entrance he found a few strips of rawhide that had first been tied together with knots and then cut open—evidence that someone had been held captive.

Fear surged in him now, sharp and cold, but Thomas pushed it aside. People saw him as a calm, placid person, but they failed to see the effort that went into it. Ranting and wailing did no good when disaster struck but a cool head might.

He eased the door open, stepped outside and held the lamp low, at knee height. On the ground he could see tracks—a scrape mark from a man who dragged his foot. Terror banded around

Thomas, squeezing his chest. He sank to his haunches, studied the ground, saw a small depression in the sand, the imprint of a bare foot.

Straightening, Thomas surveyed the darkness around him.

There had been no blood in the cabin. And there were footprints.

If Sam Renner had been desperate enough to steal a cart and risk death from the jolting of the ride, what would he do when he found the woman who had ruined his life? What would he do? What would Charlotte do?

She'd pity him. Try to plead with him. And when that didn't work, she'd come up with some ruse to stay alive for a few moments longer, gain time to escape.

Something caught Thomas's eye. A muted light, unmoving, down on the ground. As he strained his eyes, the small sphere of light rose in the air, swung left and right. Then it descended back to the ground and stayed there, unmoving, partly obscured by the clumps of vegetation.

The churchyard. A shudder ran through Thomas. Could it be that Sam Renner was out there in the darkness, digging a grave? Had he killed Charlotte and now had the decency to bury her remains?

Using the lamp to illuminate his path, Thomas strode toward the churchyard. He tried to keep his steps silent, but he knew the sound of pebbles rattling beneath his boots might alert whoever was digging in the night. Anyway, the lamp he carried would give him away, if someone happened to glance his way.

It took him a moment to figure out the faint circle of light did not come from the cemetery, but from the patch of ground where there had once been an apple orchard. The drought had killed the trees one summer when Reverend Eldridge forgot to water them.

When Thomas got closer, the sight that met him filled him with a mix of horror and relief. Charlotte was alive. She was alive. But she was on all fours, with a rope tied round her neck, like a dog on a leash. The only garment she wore, a flimsy nightgown, was torn and streaked with mud.

For a fraction of a second, Thomas took in her slender frame barely hidden by the clinging fabric. Pity and rage at her wretched state welled up in him. Ruthlessly, he clamped down on the emotions and focused on the man holding the rope, Sam Renner.

In his other hand Sam was holding the big skinning knife, and he was staring intently at something down at his feet. But it appeared to Thomas that Sam's rapt attention was not on the half-naked Charlotte, but on the hole she was digging in the ground.

Thomas cursed himself for not carrying a belt gun. No one in Gold Crossing did. It was the 1880s and civilization had arrived in the West. Most towns had an ordinance that prohibited the carry of firearms within town limits. Men carried rifles for hunting, but he had left his in the saddle boot, an oversight for which he now bitterly blamed himself.

But his saddle was only twenty yards away, and Art Langley kept a shotgun behind the bar. Thomas measured the distance to the Imperial Hotel. Then he caught a flash of movement from the corner of his eye and realized Sam Renner had noticed him.

Holding the lamp high, Thomas marched out of the darkness. "Don't know what you're digging for, stranger, but you'll never find it with a woman digging for you. Let me help."

He shone the light on Sam's face, but lowered the lamp when he heard Charlotte's cry of pain and understood Sam had jerked on the leash, tightening the noose around her neck. Thomas stepped back and fought to keep his tone friendly.

"Order your woman to move out of the way and I'll dig you a hole as deep and wide as you want."

"What will you use for digging?" Sam asked.

"What has she been using?" Thomas shone the light on Charlotte. She was cowering on the ground. She appeared to be close to breaking point, but she had enough control not to give him away. She held up a metal spoon.

"You'll need to give your woman a drop of water and a rest," Thomas said to Sam. "She looks just about done in to me."

"Go find a shovel," Sam said. "There's gotta be one for digging graves."

Thomas hesitated. He did not dare to leave Charlotte alone with Sam. Sam might decide that he no longer needed her, now that he had someone else to do the digging.

Thomas bent down. "What's the soil like? Is it firm or soft?" He scooped up a fistful of dirt from the small mound Charlotte had created with her digging. As he straightened, he tossed the dirt into Sam's eyes and then charged at the man.

The knife flashed, and Thomas felt it plunge into his side, glancing from his ribs. Behind him, he heard Charlotte cry out. Had Sam jerked on the rope? Was the noose tight around Charlotte's neck? Had her air been cut off? Fear knotted in his chest as he knew he had to fight, not only against Sam Renner, but also against time.

Thomas wrapped his arms around Sam, hauling the man high against his chest and shaking him, the way a hunting dog might shake a rat in its jaws. He felt another slash from the knife, this time a long gash at the top of his shoulder. Gathering all his strength, Thomas tightened his hold like a vise. He heard the sound of cracking ribs, and then Sam snapped taut and emitted an anguished roar. An instant later he went limp, sagging against Thomas, the heavy weight of a lifeless man.

Thomas dropped the body to the ground and grabbed a lamp. He held it high, saw Charlotte sitting on the ground. He sank to his knees beside her.

"Charlotte! Are you all right? Can you breathe?"

"Yes. Yes." She had already loosened the noose around her neck and was now lifting it over her head.

"Let me help." Thomas untangled the rope from her hair and tossed it aside.

"Is he dead?" Charlotte asked, peering at Sam's crumpled form.

"Yes." Thomas spoke quietly. In all his days he had never yet killed a man, and despite everything the tragic fate of Sam Renner troubled him. "He had a bullet in his spine. It could have killed him at any time. It must have become dislodged when we struggled."

"Oh, Thomas, it was so awful. He was crazy. He thought I was some woman called Madeleine, and, the one you mentioned that had stolen his gold. He said he'd gut me like a fish but I tricked him into thinking I had buried the gold and he made me dig and dig and dig and I prayed you would come..."

"I'm here now," Thomas said.

And then Charlotte was in his arms, sobbing against his chest. Thomas bundled her into his embrace and held her tight. She was safe. She was safe. With the night darkness cool and silent about them, Thomas cradled her to his chest and looked up into the sky and thanked the Lord, promising to forgive all the hardships of his life, all the broken dreams, because none of them mattered if Charlotte was safe.

"I want to see him," Charlotte said to Dottie Timmerman, who even at midnight looked immaculate with her old-fashioned icicle curls hanging by her temples.

Dottie clucked her tongue with disapproval. "You are filthy, dear. The doctor is sewing up Mr. Greenwood's cuts. In your current state you are unhygienic. He'll not allow you into the treatment room until you've had a bath."

Charlotte sighed. She was wrapped up in an old horse blanket and standing in an empty bathtub in the middle of the kitchen. In her unhygienic state she had not even been allowed into the bedroom with pink roses on the wallpaper.

"Is the water hot yet?" she asked for the tenth time.

Dottie dipped a finger into the big iron pot on the stove. "Lukewarm."

"That will do," Charlotte said.

"No it won't, dear. You are shivering. I didn't waste a glass of the doctor's expensive brandy just to let you catch your death from a cold bath." With that Dottie poured another slug of brandy into the pair of glasses lined up on the kitchen counter and handed one of them to Charlotte.

Charlotte drank, knocking back the measure in a single swallow, the way sailors did. Liquid fire down her throat. She opened her mouth and let out an unladylike fire dragon breath, and then she burst into a giggle.

"Getting tipsy, are we?" said Dottie. "That's not a bad idea, dear. You've had a wee bit of a shock. But it's all right now, dear. That farmer of yours came and rescued you just in the nick of time." Dottie adjusted her curls. "Just like a dime novel, it was, with a beast from the moors—or desert, of course, in this case, for there are no moors here, of course, not like *Jane Eyre*, or *Wuthering Heights*, and of course Mr. Greenwood is fair, unlike Heathcliff, or Mr. Rochester, but…"

Charlotte let the prattle roll over her. After Thomas killed that poor demented man, he'd picked her up in his arms and carried her to the doctor's house. In some odd way, she had almost wished the distance had been greater. He'd carried her so effortlessly, and she'd felt so safe in his arms, so safe after that man… Her eyes misted… That poor man. How terrible his life must have been…

"The water is ready," Dottie said. "I'll pour and leave you to your bath."

Dottie filled the bottom inches of the big enameled tub and retreated. Charlotte hurried through her bath. After Thomas carried her in, the doc had inspected her bruised neck and the scrapes on her knuckles and the pinprick cuts from the tip of the knife on her back, and then he had handed her into his wife's care and led Thomas away. She had not realized Thomas was hurt. She had to find him. *Sew up his cuts,* Dottie had said. Sam Renner must have cut him with his knife, and she hadn't even noticed.

Mud and dirt rinsed off, the stinging in her raw knuckles easing, Charlotte clambered to her feet and dried herself with a linen towel and dressed in the thick cotton nightgown Dottie Timmerman had put out for her. Then she set off to find Thomas in the treatment room.

Masculine voices came through the closed door. Charlotte flung it open without knocking. Thomas sat on the edge of the treatment table, stripped to the waist, only threadbare long johns hiding his lower half. When she burst in through the door, he snatched a towel from the table beside him and wrapped it around his torso, covering himself from armpit to waist.

"Thomas!" she shouted. "You are hurt." She halted her charge a step before she could hurl herself into his arms. An angry red line, already closed with a row of neat stitches, ran across the top of his shoulder.

"I haven't quite finished with him," Doc Timmerman said. Tall, with gray hair, he liked to wear a white coat that marked him as a medical man, something not many doctors in the West bothered with.

Thomas lifted his brows. "Could you give us a moment, Doc?"

Doc Timmerman balanced on the balls of his feet. "Five minutes," he said. "Then I'll come and finish. I don't want to stay awake all night patching you up." He walked out of the room, but he did not close the door.

"Oh, Thomas." Charlotte edged closer to where he sat on the edge of the treatment table, looking so big and strong and masculine, and, heavens, so...so...*naked*. She felt light-headed, from the events, from the liquid fire of the brandy that throbbed in her veins. "You are hurt."

"It's only a scratch."

"A scratch?"

She moved closer still. Her hand crept up and her fingertips traced the curve of his shoulder. Despite his size there was something sleek about him. His belly was flat and his waist trim, which was not obvious through the clothing he wore for the farm chores, and she hadn't really noticed it before, except maybe when she sometimes stole a peek when he undressed for the night, or got out of bed in the morning.

"You have lovely shoulders," she said. "Wide and strong. Like Samson."

"Samson came to a bad end, if I recall. And it was because of a woman." There was a rueful edge to his tone.

"Oh, Thomas, you are still angry with me." She peered up at him between her lashes and blushed. Heavens, she was standing so close to him, that broad, naked chest right in front of her face. "Of course, you have a right to be angry," she added. "I lied and cheated, and now you have been hurt rescuing me. I'll make it up to you, I promise."

"How will you make it up to me, Charlotte?"

Heavens, there was a new husky tone in his voice. She'd never heard it before, except perhaps on the day of their wedding, when he'd kissed her. Her lips puckered at the memory.

"A kiss?" Thomas said. "Is that what you are offering?"

She looked up at him. He was so close, she could feel the heat from his naked chest and smell the clean, antiseptic scent of whatever the doctor had used to clean the wound in his shoulder.

"Kissing is for engaged couples," she said primly. "We're not engaged."

"We used to be married."

His gaze held hers now and, good heavens, his hand came up and slid behind her neck, his fingers tangling in her curls, and then he eased her closer, closer, closer. Charlotte lowered her lashes, and then she felt the warm puff of his breath on her lips.

A fist rapped on the open door. A throat cleared. Charlotte jumped back so abruptly her nose bumped Thomas on the chin. She whirled about, the loose cotton nightdress flaring about her feet, embarrassment burning on her face.

"I need to finish with him," Dr. Timmerman said, fighting not to smile. "And then you must get some rest, Miss Jackson. You'll have a busy day tomorrow, with the orphans arriving on the train."

Thomas waited until Charlotte was out of the room and then he peeled away the towel he had used to hide the more serious wound in his side. The doctor poked and prodded, pulling the gaping sides of the cut together.

"You are a lucky man, Mr. Greenwood. Although it looks nasty, it is just a flesh wound. If the blade had glanced the other way from your ribs, it would have gone into your belly and might have pierced vital internal organs."

"I saw the blade strike," Thomas said. "I had time to shift aside."

The doc took out more string for sutures and held the tip of the needle over a flame for a few seconds to sterilize it.

"Looks like your marriage is far from over," the doc commented.

Thomas tensed himself against the pain as the needle punctured his skin.

"I understand you think Miss Jackson is too fragile for life out in the West," the doc went on. "That hard work and childbirth might send her to an early grave."

Thomas gave a grunt of pain as his only reply. It was the excuse he had given to Dottie Timmerman to salvage his pride, but somehow in the days that followed he had come to believe the explanation himself.

"That's what people said about my wife, when I first brought her here." The doc glanced up from his task with a smile. "And look at her now. She loves it here. I'd be happy to return to the East, where some of our children live, but she won't go." He cut the string to make another suture. "Small, fragile women sometimes turn out to be tough and brave. I think that bride of yours proved it tonight."

That bride of yours. Thomas mulled over the words while the doctor finished his ministrations and left him alone to sleep on the narrow cot in the treatment room. Maybe he should forgive Charlotte. Heck, maybe he already had. Maybe there was a chance for them, if she would be prepared to stay in the Arizona Territory instead of returning to the East.

But one thing Thomas knew for certain. If he ever married again—Charlotte or anyone else—there would be none of that *six months from now*. If he married, his marriage would be real and for keeps, with his wife in his bed, starting from the wedding night.

Chapter Fifteen

Charlotte tapped her finger on the map of Europe. "What country is this?" She tried her sweetest smile. "Come now, children. Next to France? Right above Italy?" She put a stern demand in her voice. "The little country with high mountains called the Alps? Where they make excellent watches and send soldiers to the Vatican to protect His Holiness the Pope?

Nothing. Eight blank faces stared at her. Charlotte exhaled a sigh. She'd planned to dazzle the population of Gold Crossing with her success as an educator, but it would never happen.

Perhaps the inattention of the children had something to do with the way she sometimes lapsed into silence when she remembered how Thomas had almost kissed her. Or when she recalled the sight of his naked chest right in front of her eyes.

Two weeks had passed since Thomas rescued her from Sam Renner. Up by Hansen's Creek, the body of a farm boy had been found. He'd been on his way into town in the cart Sam Renner had used to charge up to the schoolhouse. It pained Charlotte to know that although she'd escaped with only minor injuries, Sam Renner's lust for revenge had cost the life of an innocent young man.

Despite the grief Charlotte felt for the farm boy and his family, the memories of the horror had faded quickly. Somehow, the sense of safety from being carried in Thomas's arms had left a more lasting impression than the nightmare of a noose around her neck and a madman's knife flashing before her eyes.

The morning after the ordeal, Charlotte had slept until midday at Doc Timmerman's house, her exhausted body needing the rest after the shock and all that effort of digging holes with nothing but a spork.

When she finally woke up, Thomas was already gone. According to Dottie Timmerman, he'd fetched his horse and ridden out at the first glimmer of dawn. That afternoon the widows and orphans had arrived on the train, and since then Gold Crossing had been as if a hurricane was sweeping through the town.

Twice in the past fortnight—once on a Thursday

and once during the Fourth of July celebrations—
Charlotte had seen Thomas ride in on Shadow, but
both times she'd been surrounded by a crowd of
unruly children, unable to have a private conversation with him.

Why had he tried to kiss her? Had he forgiven
her? She longed to ask Gus Junior about the other
mail-order bride Thomas was supposed to have
sent for, but pride kept her silent.

"Miss Jackson, can we go now? It's Thursday."

It was little Jessica, one of her pupils, the one
who showed the most promise on the path of
learning. The other children had caught on to it
and always sent Jessica to ask for concessions,
such as ending the lessons early when the train
was due.

"Go," Charlotte said. "And it is Switzerland.
Remember that. Switzerland, to the east of France
and to the north of Italy."

She was talking to their backs. The little mon-
sters were already trooping out of the classroom.
Charlotte went after them to close the schoolhouse door and then she collapsed to sit on the
nearest desk.

She had eight children in her school, six boys
and two girls, aged from seven to twelve, and
none of them were the least bit interested in
learning, except perhaps little Jessica. Most of
them were out of the city for the first time in

their lives. They didn't want to be shut up in a classroom, at least not on sunny summer days.

Two widows had accompanied the orphans. Mrs. Duckworth, a rail-thin redhead in her fifties, was a stout defender of moral values. She had already made friends with Miss Gladys Hayes. It was clear that Mrs. Duckworth would make no contribution to Art Langley's revival plan for the town—that the miners would marry the widows and start families, which would add to the population.

The other widow, Mrs. Perkins, was a pretty, voluptuous blonde in her late twenties. Her son, Timothy, a half orphan, was one of the children she was teaching. Mrs. Perkins might prove that the revival plan was feasible after all. Two prospectors were already courting her. The mercantile had ordered chocolates and little trinkets that were suitable as sweetheart gifts.

Out in the distance, Charlotte could hear the shrill whistle of the arriving train, but instead of going to watch she got on with chores. She needed to mend the green wool skirt she had scorched against the potbellied stove. The schoolroom was so small she was always bumping into things. She had barely finished the task and pulled the skirt back on when someone came banging on the door.

"Miss Jackson! Miss Jackson."

Charlotte recognized the voice of Timothy Perkins, her most unruly pupil.

She went to the door, opened it. "What is it, Timothy?" The boy's mother insisted that he be called by his full name, not Tim or Timmy.

"There's a man who wants you at the Imperial Hotel." Timothy spun on a grimy bare heel and hurried off.

With the arrival of the children, Gus Junior's monopoly on messenger services had been broken. Gus Junior was now dedicating himself full-time to newspaper publishing. The *Informer* came out at random intervals, whenever Gus Junior came across some piece of news that he hoped people might be willing to pay for.

Puzzled, Charlotte made her way to the Imperial Hotel. The lobby was crowded. Mrs. Perkins was having afternoon tea with one of her suitors. Mrs. Duckworth and Miss Hayes were on chaperone duty. Art Langley was playing solitaire at the counter. Gus Junior was hawking the latest issue of the *Informer* at the little newsstand he'd set up in the corner.

There was one more occupant, a well-dressed stranger who sat alone at a table near the door. Small and slender, with a beaked nose and receding chin, he had a pair of nervous eyes that flitted about. He cast a quick glance in her direction.

Appearing to lose interest in her, he resumed drumming his fingertips against the tabletop.

Timothy ran to the man. The child stuck out his cupped hand in an unmistakable gesture of demand and pointed at Charlotte with his other hand.

The stranger's darting eyes snapped wide. Incredulity flickered across his features. He jumped to his feet, charged up to Charlotte, grabbed the bodice of her pale gray blouse with both hands and shook her hard enough to make her teeth rattle.

"What have you done with Maude?" Hysteria edged his voice. "Where is Maude?"

Dear God. For once in her life, Charlotte regretted that despite her frail appearance she possessed a sturdy constitution. She would have given anything to escape into a swoon.

Art Langley dropped his playing cards and hurried over. "Is there a problem?"

The stranger shoved Charlotte aside and turned to face the room. "Is there a problem? Is there *a problem*?" he yelled to everyone at large. "This woman is not Maude Jackson."

"Please." She touched the man's shoulder. "I can explain."

He ignored her calming gesture and drew a pistol from beneath his suit jacket. He didn't aim the barrel of the gun at her, or at anyone else in the room. He just flung his hands about, carelessly waving the weapon in the air.

"Where is Maude?" His eyes rolled in his head, the whites flashing, like on a horse about to bolt. "What have you done to her?"

Charlotte swept a frantic glance around the room. Art Langley had eased back to the reception counter, where he kept a short-barreled shotgun. The man sitting opposite Mrs. Perkins had pushed aside the lapel of his coat. His fingers fondled the handle of a revolver in a leather holster at his hip.

Since the Sam Renner incident, and since the arrival of the widows and orphans, the previously somnolent little town of Gold Crossing seemed to have plunged right back into the lawless frontier era of a decade ago. Even Gus Junior wanted to carry a gun, in defiance of his father's orders.

Footsteps. The creak of timbers on the porch. Charlotte turned around to look just as the doors swung open. A man appeared on the threshold, tall and broad, a hat in his hand. Golden hair glinted in the sun.

Thomas.

Of course. It was Thursday. He usually came into town on Thursdays. And now he stood there, silhouetted against the bright daylight, his broad chest filling the door frame, making him into a target even the most incompetent of shooters would find difficult to miss.

As far as Charlotte knew, Thomas didn't possess a sidearm, only a rifle for hunting, and he didn't carry it around town. He was unarmed, defenseless, and once again she had brought danger upon him.

"What have you done to Maude?" the stranger yelled, spinning back to face Charlotte. His eyes glittered with a crazed look. Even when he didn't speak, his mouth was working, as if he needed to chew up every breath he inhaled.

Scowling at Charlotte, the man waved the gun in his hand. When Charlotte didn't reply, he followed the direction of her anguished look, and understood she'd been staring at the newcomer who stood on the doorstep. Jumping to the wrong conclusions, the man aimed his cocked pistol at Thomas.

"Where is she?" he screamed. "Where is Maude?"

Charlotte could see Thomas tense his muscles, getting ready to tackle the deranged stranger. In her mind, she saw him leap forward, saw the bullet puncture his chest, saw a crimson stain spread on the front of his shirt. She had to speak up now. It was no use hoping for a more private moment.

"Dead," she said in a voice that rasped with terror. "Miss Jackson died from an overdose of laudanum on the train to Chicago. I stole her tickets. She is dead. Dead by her own hand because some man abandoned her, leaving her all alone with a baby growing in her belly."

As soon as she'd blurted out the words, Charlotte winced. She'd spoken without thought, out of turn. The secret of poor Miss Jackson had not been hers to reveal to the world. But she'd been angry on the woman's behalf, angry on behalf of every woman who had shared the same desperate fate.

The stranger collapsed to the floor. He huddled down on his knees, rocking back and forth. "I'm the one." His harsh, guttural sobs echoed around the room. "I am...the one...who abandoned her..."

The lobby hushed into silence, like a stage play interrupted. Only the stranger crumpled on the floor by Charlotte's feet kept talking. He rocked his body to and fro on the floor, his frantic gasps forming into words. "My father...didn't approve... She was only a maid...maid in my father's...house... Oh, Lord... I killed her... I killed her..."

Suddenly, his slumped form stirred into motion. His hand came up to his head. The barrel of the gun lined up against his temple. "I killed her...killed her."

From the corner of her eye, Charlotte caught a blur of motion as Thomas lurched forward and dived down toward the man. His right arm curled around the stranger's shoulders while his left arm flung upward and dislodged the gun from the man's clasp just as the weapon fired.

The shot reverberated around the lobby. The acrid smell of gunpowder exploded into the air. The gun clattered down and skidded along the floorboards.

Feminine screams. The scrape of chairs. Blood trickled from a jagged wound at the top of Thomas's arm. The man sitting opposite Mrs. Perkins leaped out of his seat and snatched up the fallen gun. The deranged stranger slumped against Thomas's chest. It seemed as if the two of them were embracing, the way they knelt facing each other on the floor, with Thomas's arms around the man to stop him from toppling over.

"Get the doctor," Charlotte shouted. She rushed up to Thomas, bent over him, pressed her hand to the bleeding wound at the top of his arm. Her head swiveled about, left and right, searching the crowd of stunned spectators for someone who could help.

She spotted Timothy Perkins. "Timmy, get the doctor."

The boy didn't move. He remained hovering between the tables, eyes gleaming with fascination. "Silver dollar, Timmy," Charlotte called out. "A whole silver dollar if you fetch Dr. Timmerman."

The boy glanced in her direction, came to life and edged toward the door, the power of commerce more potent than the lure of watching the unfolding spectacle.

Beneath her hands Charlotte felt Thomas move as he adjusted the weight of the man leaning against him. He tipped his head back to look up at Charlotte and sent her a shadow of a smile.

"I'm fit to walk," he told her. "And stop what you're doing, pressing down on my wound. It hurts." Rising to his feet, he slid the stranger's arm over his shoulders and draped the inert body against his side.

"Is he dead?" Timothy called from the door.

"Fainted," Thomas said. "Run along. Tell the doc we're on our way."

Charlotte watched Thomas haul the unconscious stranger toward the entrance. Her pulse was racing, her body trembling. Her breath came in rapid bursts. She tried to follow Thomas out into the street but someone grabbed hold of her and shoved her into a chair.

She didn't resist. The room dimmed around her, a swoon perilously close. But even then, she couldn't ignore the truth that had revealed itself while she saw the stranger's gun aimed at the big blond man standing in the doorway.

She'd never felt such fear, such agony of loss.

She was in love with Thomas Greenwood.

Perhaps she'd already known it when she sobbed against his chest after he rescued her from Sam Renner, or when he tried to kiss her in Doc Timmerman's treatment room. Or even earlier, when she walked out of his valley because she couldn't bear to bring ridicule upon him.

She loved him.

She had denied the knowledge because she had felt her duty was to her sisters, but what grown woman put her sisters before a husband, before a family of her own? Miranda was feisty and would forge her own path, and Annabel would grow up and mature to find her own way in the world.

She needed to leave her sisters to follow their own destinies. She needed to make Thomas understand. Understand and forgive her. And it would help their future if she could stop bringing deranged madmen to attack him.

For an instant, Charlotte believed she might truly have succumbed to a swoon. Around her, voices soared around the hotel lobby, but she could not make out a single word. She wanted to go to Thomas, but every time she tried to rise from the chair, someone pushed her back into it.

People came and went. Finally, when her head had cleared enough for her to flap aside the concerned hands of everyone and get up to her feet, Art Langley pulled her aside.

"I've got Mr. Wakefield upstairs."

"Mr. Wakefield?"

"The man who came looking for Miss Jackson. He had only lost consciousness. Doc Timmerman looked him over and let him go." When she tried to break away and head for the door, Art scowled at her. "Mr. Wakefield has questions for you."

Of course. Charlotte swallowed. More than anything, she wanted to go to Thomas. She wanted to wrap her arms around him and tell him that she wanted to live with him in his secluded valley, away from the rest of the world. She wanted to be a farm wife with chickens and a milk cow and a strong, steady husband who slept by her side every night.

It didn't matter if her name was Maude Jackson or Charlotte Fairfax.

She wanted to be Mrs. Thomas Greenwood.

Charlotte sighed and let her heavy mantle of duty settle on her shoulders. She might want to go and see Thomas, but she owed it to the stranger to tell him as much as she could. He deserved better apologies and explanations than the angry words she had flung at him in front of the curious crowd.

She clasped Art's arm. "Thomas. How is he?"

"It was just a flesh wound. The doc's patched him up. One more incident, the doc says, and he'll give Greenwood wholesale rates. Greenwood is resting in the doc's spare room. You can see him after you've spoken to Mr. Wakefield."

Art led her upstairs, where the stranger huddled in an overstuffed armchair. His eyes were red rimmed, his face ashen. Charlotte sat in another chair beside him, introduced herself by her real name and told him everything she could remember.

"It's my fault," Mr. Wakefield said, sobbing.

"Not yours alone," she consoled him. "Your father shares the blame, for rejecting her. And if Miss Jackson had waited for you, if she'd had more faith in you..." Charlotte groped in her mind for the right words of comfort. "I'm sure she knows now, in heaven, that you came after her. That in the end you stood by her and would have married her and taken care of her and the baby."

Mr. Wakefield's weeping showed no sign of ceasing. "At first... I thought she'd died on the train...like you said... A body of a pregnant woman was found... But then some other man came...identified the dead woman as his cousin... Some rich man...from a Boston seafaring family... The police sent for him because he had reported his cousin missing and they found a silver cross on the body with the missing woman's name and a birth date engraved on it…"

A shiver ran over Charlotte. Of course. Cousin Gareth. The silver cross she had hung around the neck of poor Miss Jackson, like a blessing, had led him to her trail. For on the back of the cross an engraving said *Charlotte, 4th May*.

Now she understood how it had come about that Cousin Gareth had been able to claim the body of Miss Jackson as hers, and why she was presumed dead, just as Miranda had indicated in her reply to the Emily Bickerstaff letter.

But Cousin Gareth must know she was alive. There was no possibility that Miss Jackson, who had straight, light brown hair, and who stood several inches taller and weighed at least thirty pounds more, could be mistaken for her.

Clearly the mistake had been deliberate. But why had Gareth done it? What was his plan? Did he continue to pin his intentions on her, or had he now revised his plan and set his sights on Miranda?

Charlotte's hands tightened in her lap. If only she knew more of what was going on at Merlin's Leap! She'd been wrong to think her escape did not put her sisters in danger, but it was too late to regret it now.

Miranda is strong, Charlotte consoled herself. *She'll manage Cousin Gareth better than I ever could.* She wished she could write or telegraph, asking for news, but it would only serve to raise suspicion. Her sisters knew her address and would write when they could. She would just have to wait to hear from them.

Brushing aside her own worries, Charlotte focused on the distraught young man sitting beside her. "Mr. Wakefield," she said. "There has been a mistake. It is my doing, but I hope something good has come from it. My cousin claimed the body of Miss Jackson, assuming it was me. The body is buried in the cemetery at Merlin's Leap, my home in Boston. Your fiancée is buried in consecrated ground, and my sisters mourn for her. They know it is not me in that grave. It is Miss Jackson they pray for, which means she is not alone in death."

"How could your cousin make such a mistake? Has he never met you?"

"He has, Mr. Wakefield. Indeed, he has. And I am sure he made no mistake. I believe he did it on purpose. I think it may be part of his intrigue about the family fortune—a fact that I implore you to keep a secret. People in Gold Crossing don't know I come from wealth. If they did, one of the miners might sell me out to the Pinkerton detectives I expect are following on my trail."

Mr. Wakefield's nervous eyes ceased their flickering. He swallowed, a quick ripple of his pointed throat. Then a faint smile. "So my family is not the only one to put money before happiness and the lives of others..."

"Certainly not." Charlotte drew a calming breath. "Mr. Wakefield, I expect you will wish to visit the grave of Miss Jackson, and I would be happy to give you directions to Merlin's Leap, but I beg you, until my birthday next year, until May fourth, could you pretend it is me you are visiting? I shall write to my sisters and let them know you might be coming. Then, once I have returned home, we can replace the headstone and have the name of Miss Jackson engraved on it."

"I think I'd prefer to wait for a bit. Perhaps I'll come and visit later, after you have returned home and put up the memorial for Maude."

"That would suit me very well," Charlotte said softly.

Mr. Wakefield fidgeted in his seat. "Miss Fairfax... I'm sorry about..." He pointed his finger like a gun and waved it about, imitating how he'd threatened her with the weapon. "I bear no ill will," he went on quietly. "If anything, you helped Maude...showed her kindness and respect in death."

Charlotte wiped away a tear. "I'm not blameless. Far from it. I caused you to travel all the way out here in false hope. And I blurted out her secret when I had no right to do so."

"Maybe the journey did me good. And secrets always come out anyway." He held out his hand. "I wish you well, Miss Fairfax."

"And I you, Mr. Wakefield."

Charlotte took his hand, felt the trembling of it, although the young man was succeeding in pulling himself together. Perhaps she should remain longer with him, Charlotte thought, but she was eager to see Thomas. She left Mr. Wakefield at the Imperial Hotel and hurried over to the doctor's house.

Thomas was outside by the hitching rail, mounting on Shadow. He held one arm stiff, and she could see the white of the bandage peeking through the tear in his shirt.

"Are you all right?" she asked.

"I'll live."

"Are you going?"

He didn't meet her eyes. "I have chores to get on with."

"Are you angry with me?"

He finished tying on whatever he'd purchased at the mercantile and turned to face her. He shot her a sharp glance from beneath the brim of his hat. "Do you think I enjoy being shot at and humiliated in public?"

"Humiliated… I…" She took a deep breath. "What have I done that is so very wrong…? I didn't kill poor Miss Jackson."

"No. But you lied and deceived, and now you've

spilled her secrets to the world." Thomas tugged at the stirrup strap, although it didn't need straightening. "It was one thing to have our marriage annulled because you didn't suit for the life out here. It's another thing for everyone to know that you fooled me from the start. And I never intended to announce it to the world that I had arranged to marry a woman who carried another man's child. I had my reasons for it, but they were my own."

"I…" Charlotte closed her eyes, then blinked them open again and saw the stark, angry expression on Thomas's face. Every word he said was true.

"Mr. Wakefield has forgiven me," she said quietly. "Can't you?"

"Mr. Wakefield will leave on the train next Thursday and can put today behind him. I live here. Today will be part of all my tomorrows."

Making no more comment, saying no more goodbye, Thomas mounted on Shadow, wheeled the horse around and rode away from her.

Chapter Sixteen

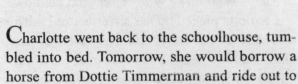

Charlotte went back to the schoolhouse, tumbled into bed. Tomorrow, she would borrow a horse from Dottie Timmerman and ride out to Thomas and make him listen. She'd tell the children there was no school and leave first thing after breakfast.

She'd find a way to earn his trust and forgiveness. Then she'd persuade him that she was the only suitable bride for him and they would figure out an honorable way to release him from any contract with a second bride. Next, she would convince him she was competent with farm chores. And finally, she would make him understand that she loved him.

Four steps. Difficult. But not impossible.

All night, Charlotte tossed and turned on the narrow cot behind the blanket curtain, trying to come up with a workable plan. In the morning, she woke up fuzzy headed, and had barely finished dressing when someone was banging at the door.

Oh, no. Not again. She hurried to the door, pulled it open. It was Timothy Perkins, clutching a breakfast biscuit in his hand. "They want you at the Imperial Hotel." He took a bite out of his biscuit, whirled on his feet and skipped away.

They? Who *they*? Who could want her now?

Charlotte picked up her silver-backed mirror and checked her reflection. Her face was pale. Dark shadows beneath her eyes gave her a wanton look. Flyaway curls framed her face, but she decided not to take the time to repair her upsweep.

Nerves shot through her belly as she left the schoolhouse and hurried along the dusty street to the Imperial Hotel. In the lobby, two square tables had been pushed together. Behind them, three people sat in a row.

Gus Osborn.

Gladys Hayes.

Art Langley.

"This is the meeting of the town council of Gold Crossing," Miss Hayes boomed. Dressed in a purple gown that strained at the seams, she was sitting in the middle. The short, squat Gus Osborn on one side and the tall, gaunt Art Langley on the other looked like a pair of unmatched bookends flanking her.

"Gold Crossing has no town council," Charlotte remarked.

"With the rapid expansion of the town, it was deemed appropriate to establish one," Miss Hayes informed her. And then she launched into a speech about moral values and how a schoolteacher formed the minds of the young generation and needed to be above reproach.

"Did you not live with Mr. Greenwood as man and wife under false pretenses?" she trumpeted, bosom heaving, layers of chins wobbling. "Did you not assume another woman's identity? Did you not lie and deceive?"

"I... I..." Charlotte faltered. What could she say? It was all true.

The knot in her stomach tightened as she listened to Miss Hayes pronounce her unworthy and terminate her employment as a schoolteacher. Gus Osborn and Art Langley looked sheepish but said nothing in her defense.

Charlotte fought back. "It will take months to find another teacher."

"The school will close for the summer vacation."

"You owe me twenty dollars for two weeks' pay."

Art Langley stirred in his seat. "You can continue to live in the schoolhouse until the beginning of September. The rent is twenty dollars. That will make us even."

"But the influence on the children..." Miss Hayes started with vigor, but tapered into silence, moral outrage defeated by the prospect of parting with twenty dollars.

Gus Osborn banged a gavel against the tabletop to conclude the town council meeting. Charlotte found herself ushered out into the street, jobless and in disgrace. It had been wrong, so terribly wrong, what she had done. The list of people she'd hurt seemed endless.

She had six weeks until the beginning of September.

Six weeks to sort out the mess she had made of everything.

Thomas stood in forlorn silence at the edge of the cornfield. Water dripped from the brim of his hat and ran down his back inside the collar of his rain slicker. After a month of drought the skies had opened and not closed again. It never rained this hard in July. And it certainly never rained for three days solid.

The gunshot wound throbbed at the top of his arm. He'd worked from dawn to dusk, digging drainage channels, erecting stone walls to fortify the banks of the creek against flooding. It was no use. Even if he had the full use of both arms, it was too late to save the crops. The roots were rotting. The corn would die before it could ripen.

Bitter and defeated, Thomas walked up the muddy slope toward the cabin. He would lose the farm. He had borrowed money from the bank with the promise to pay it back in August. He had counted on making enough when he sold the crops to the stores in Flagstaff and Jerome, but he'd be lucky if he harvested enough to keep from starving until the bank evicted him.

Was there no end to his bad luck?

In the cabin, he lit a fire in the stove, put on a pot of coffee and sat at the table. He fought the urge to abandon the fields to their fate and ride into town, just to get a glimpse of Charlotte. He needed something good in his life, some tiny spark of joy, even if it was just looking at her from afar.

The anger that had flared in him after she revealed to the entire town that she had deceived him about her identity had evaporated, even before he reached home that day. Now he regretted his sharp words at her.

His eyes fell on the sheet of paper on the table. Of course, when he'd visited the post office just before he'd been shot, there hadn't been any letter for him from Michigan. He'd threatened to write every week until he received a reply. Last night, he had started another letter. Thomas pulled the piece of paper closer and stared at it.

Dear Mother

He'd never got beyond the first two words.

He heard shouts outside. The whinnying of a horse, wagon wheels creaking. What an odd time for someone to visit, on a rainy afternoon. He went to the door. The wagon had already turned around and was heading back up the slope. A small figure wearing a green skirt and jacket was hurrying out of the rain, up the porch steps.

Charlotte.

His heart gave a single hard thump. For a second, happiness at the sight of her enveloped him, so powerful his body shook with the emotion. Then Thomas considered their circumstances, and his pleasure faded. He'd lost everything. All he had left was his honor. He had to make her leave before he lost that, too.

At first, Charlotte rushed toward him with eager footsteps, almost making him believe that she was about to launch herself into his arms. Then she must have noticed his brooding scowl, for she halted beneath the porch canopy.

"Two prospectors were going by," she told him. "They gave me a ride in their wagon. I would have come earlier, but Dottie refused to let me have her horse. She said it's too dangerous to ride across the desert in the rain."

"You shouldn't have come." His tone was strained.

"I wanted to make sure you're all right."

"I am all right."

He returned to the table. Charlotte glanced around the cabin, went to the stove, opened the hatch and threw another stick of firewood into the flames. "I thought you might need help," she said lightly.

"I don't need help."

"I suspect you do." She peered into the milk jug, then into the stone jar where he stored fresh eggs. Both were empty. He'd not collected the eggs and, too exhausted to cook, he'd had nothing but milk for his breakfast, lunch and dinner, adding indigestion to his growing list of woes.

Charlotte marched to the door, paused to take his rain slicker from the peg on the wall and pulled it on. The garment swamped her.

"I won't be long," she said.

Unable to stop himself, Thomas followed her. She went to the barn. The rain had eased to a drizzle. He didn't feel the damp on his skin. He didn't seem to feel anything at all.

The chickens clucked with joy as Charlotte walked in. Polk danced around her feet. Harrison hurried to the wood stack, proudly leading her to a hidden egg.

Did chickens recognize people? Perhaps they did. Thomas watched Charlotte search, listened to her crooning and chattering to the hens, as if the creatures were beloved pets. When her basket was full, she handed it to him.

"Take these in. I'll be a moment longer."

He left her, assuming she wanted to visit the privy. Back in the cabin, he sat down at the table and stared at the unfinished letter.

Dear Mother

Words refused to come. When the door opened, it occurred to Thomas he'd lost track of time. Twilight was already falling, throwing shadows into the cabin.

Charlotte walked in with the milk pail, poured the contents into the jug.

"You don't know how to milk," Thomas said with a frown.

"I reached an understanding with Rosamund. If she gives up the milk, I'll stop bothering her."

Memories of their days together flooded over Thomas. It didn't matter that she lacked the skills of a farm wife. It hadn't mattered from the start. Her good humor, her pleasure in simple things more than made up for it.

"When will the wagon fetch you back?" he asked.

"It won't. You can take me back tomorrow."

"You can't stay here for the night."

"I've stayed before."

"Before, I thought you were my wife."

"I don't understand." She contemplated him, appearing genuinely puzzled. "Until Miss Hayes decided to stir up trouble, no one seemed to mind that I had lived here with you for two weeks, even though our marriage was later annulled. Why should it be any different from me living here now?"

Thomas tried to explain. It surprised him she didn't see it herself. Maybe people from big cities had a different moral code from small-town folks. "Marriage is a powerful shield to protect a woman's reputation. Before the annulment, you had the benefit of that shield, and then, the annulment was proof that the marriage had not been consummated. Now, if you stay here, you don't have that shield, and when you leave, you won't have that proof."

"I don't care."

"You should. You're a schoolteacher, with a reputation to protect."

"Not anymore."

Thomas listened to the tale of how she had been dismissed. Anger rose in him. "Miss Hayes," he muttered. "She's a professional spinster. No man ever wanted her. She resents the idea that men look at other women and find in them what she lacked."

"And what do you find, when you look at me, Thomas?"

Charlotte's hazel eyes searched his. His breath stalled. The words had sounded as if she was offering herself to him. *I see beauty and courage and joy and everything I ever wanted. Only now I have no home to offer to a woman.*

The loss of all his hopes and dreams crashed over Thomas. He stared at the letter in front of him and spoke in a low voice. "It doesn't matter what I see. You are an educated woman, fragile and tender, unused to hard work. You can't stay here. I can't take the risk that you'll be forced to tie yourself to me and find the life too hard and begin to hate me. I grew up being hated by everyone around me. I can't bear the thought of suffering the same fate again."

Thomas had been keeping his eyes on the unfinished letter while he spoke. Now he glanced up at Charlotte. Her expression reflected confusion and disbelief. The words, never spoken out loud, poured out of Thomas, harsh and bitter.

"I was born thirteen months after my father went off to join the gold rush at Comstock Lode. He came back three years later to find some other man's bastard in his house. I've heard people whisper that a drifter, a big man with fair hair, had been sleeping in the barn, helping with the farm chores. He spoke little English. Some say he was Russian, some say Polish. My mother has never told me if he took her by force but I assume he must have done."

"But Thomas…it wasn't your fault…"

"No," he said. "It wasn't my fault. But I bore the hate." He picked up the letter, crumpled it in his fist. No point in writing another one. "I know you're alone, and you have no one looking after you, and it might seem like a solution to come back to me, but you must not. It would be a mistake." He got up to his feet and headed for the door. "I'll go and sleep in the barn. In the morning, I'll take you back into town."

With those words, Thomas walked away. Walked away, clinging to the fear, to the sense of defeat, and to some vague idea of honor, instead of reaching for the happiness he had for a few short weeks believed could be his.

It was all going terribly wrong. She'd had a plan. First she would show Thomas her competence as a farm wife. Then she'd tell him that she loved him. Then he would forgive her for having deceived him. Then they would deal with the problem of his second bride.

Four steps, in the order she had decided might work best.

But now, she was bouncing on the wagon bench beside him, on her way back into town. In some odd way, the journey seemed identical to their original trip when he had fetched her from the Imperial Hotel, only they were going in the opposite direction, and at a much greater speed.

The same troubled silence.

The same emotion-filled glances.

He cared about her. She knew he did. But something had come between them. Something new. Something even worse than before. Charlotte had felt his rejection from the first moment she stepped into the cabin last night. The cold, hostile shield she'd felt around him had meant that although she'd made good progress with step number one—showing him she was a competent farm wife—she'd not had the courage to do anything about step number two—telling him that she loved him.

Thomas deposited her outside the schoolhouse. The earth was soft and slippery. The sun was out, but the smell of mud hung thick in the air. To start with, Charlotte thought he expected her to climb down on her own, but then he jumped down to the ground, circled the wagon and lifted her from the bench, a pair of strong hands curled about her waist.

She touched her fingertips to his cheek. "What's wrong, Thomas?"

He set her on her feet. "You should not do that. Miss Hayes is watching. I saw the curtains twitch in her window when we drove by." With that parting comment, he climbed back up to the wagon bench, gave a command to Trooper and rolled the wagon away along the muddy street.

Charlotte watched him pull up outside the mercantile. He didn't come out again. She waited. Ten minutes. Twenty. Eventually, she gave up the waiting and went into the schoolhouse, then came out again and resumed her waiting.

An hour later, Thomas finally strode out of the mercantile. He paused on the porch of the Imperial Hotel, tacked a poster to the wall, then did the same outside the railroad station.

Charlotte waited for him to climb up to the wagon and drive off. Then she hurried with careful steps along the muddy street to read the poster. It was a notice of a forthcoming auction. On August 31 Thomas would sell his farm.

It took no time for Charlotte to locate Gus Junior on the steps of the mercantile where he was sitting in the shade of the boardwalk canopy, writing out copies of the *Informer* on a wooden board balanced across his knees.

"The bank will foreclose on his farm in September," Gus Junior informed her. "Mr. Greenwood is going to try and sell the place before then. If he can make more money than he owes to the bank, he gets to keep the difference. It will give him a grubstake."

Gus Junior's voice seemed to have settled in its new, mature pitch, which he obviously enjoyed demonstrating, for he kept on talking. "Mr. Greenwood just picked up a letter that came from Michigan. I guess it's from his folks. Maybe instead of prospecting for gold he is planning to go back home." He ran a hand across his chin in a gesture that imitated rubbing the stubble of a beard. "I'm surprised he didn't read the letter right away. He never had a letter from Michigan before." His expression brightened. "Maybe he's ordered another bride."

"How many brides does one man need?" Charlotte muttered.

"There's a letter for you, too." Gus Junior jerked his thumb in the direction of the open entrance of the mercantile behind him. "From Boston."

Charlotte nodded her thanks to Gus Junior and darted inside. The envelope was addressed to Mrs. Maude Greenwood. Gus Osborn mentioned post office regulations, and mumbled something about identification, but in the end he gave the letter to her. Charlotte hurried back to the school-house and sat at a desk to read the message.

The letter wasn't from Miranda. It was from Annabel.

Dear Charlotte,

I have to write a letter, although I know it will take too long to arrive. I have no way of sending a telegram. I am a prisoner in the house and I have no money. I hope the servants will post this.

Miranda is on her way out to you. She will most likely arrive before this letter. Like you, she is traveling without funds. If she hasn't arrived, she may have been arrested for fare-dodging, or whatever is the correct term for someone caught traveling without a ticket.

Cousin Gareth became beastly to both of us after he brought home the body of that unknown lady and had it buried in the graveyard with great ceremony, claiming it was you. Of course we knew it wasn't you. You'll be glad to know we cried buckets anyway.

We knew it wasn't you right from the start, even before we got your Emily Bickerstaff letter. You see, after Cousin Gareth had reported you missing, a telegram came from the constables. He tossed it into the fireplace and took off with great haste, but

the fire was not lit and we were able to retrieve the crumpled-up telegram.

It said the body was a female in her early
twenties, around five and a half feet tall,
weighing one hundred and thirty pounds,
and she had straight light brown hair.

See? We knew it couldn't be you. But
Cousin Gareth brought her home anyway
and pretended. At first, we thought it was
a good thing you were declared dead, that
you'd be safe for a bit, but then Cousin Gareth got the lawyers to name Miranda as the
heiress to Papa's fortune, and he became
beastly, as I already mentioned above.

Miranda wanted to shoot him, but Cousin
Gareth must have guessed because he hid
all Papa's muskets and pistols. In the end
Miranda had no choice but to run away,
just as you did. She left at night, because I
couldn't create enough of a diversion on my
own to allow her to escape during the day.

Now I get to the most difficult part.

I think Cousin Gareth followed Miranda.
I saw Miranda's shadow slide across the
lawn, and then another shadow went after
her, and the next day Cousin Gareth was
gone but all the servants were still here.
That's why I'm able to write this letter. Once

I seal the envelope the servants won't open
it, and Gareth isn't here.

I don't know if Miranda knows she is
being followed, or if she managed to shake
Cousin Gareth off, or if Gareth has guessed
that you are in fact Miss Maude Jackson.
He probably has, and he knows you are in
Gold Crossing, Arizona Territory.

It may not matter, now that the lawyers
have named Miranda as the heiress. Or
maybe it does. If Cousin Gareth gets his
claws into Miranda and marries her, he may
try to kill you, because otherwise he will
have married the wrong sister. Am I making sense?

You must be careful. Please send money
so I can come, too. I'm not brave enough to
travel without a ticket.

Your loving sister,
Annabel

Charlotte folded the letter. A cold, sick feeling settled in the pit of her stomach. Miranda was
stranded somewhere between Boston and Gold
Crossing, maybe languishing in a jail or in the
clutches of Cousin Gareth. Annabel was alone
and frightened at Merlin's Leap. Thomas hated
her and was about to lose his land. Cousin Gareth
might be on his way to Gold Crossing, perhaps to

kill her or, if he had failed to force Miranda into marriage, to make another attempt at forcing her.

There was only one thing to do.

She had to marry and claim her inheritance.

Slowly, with an odd sense of calm flowing through her, Charlotte made her way to the Imperial Hotel. The sun was shining bright in the sky again, the heat scorching. The ground had stopped steaming. The drying mud had cracked to form pretty patterns, like the scales on alligator skin.

Her eyes took a moment to adjust as she stepped out of the sunshine into the shadowed lobby where the shutters were closed against the heat. Gus Junior was standing behind his newspaper stall. The latest headline on his banner said *Schoolteacher Dismissed in Disgrace*. He was also still displaying the special issue with *Gunshots and Mayhem—the Shock of Schoolteacher's Hidden Identity*.

The next headline to which she would give rise flashed through Charlotte's mind as she walked up to Art Langley. *Disgraced Schoolteacher's Surprise Wedding*.

"I need to talk to you." She glanced back to Gus Junior, who was shamelessly craning his neck to hear every word. "In private," she added.

Art scooped up his cards, stacked them on the counter and jerked his head toward the back.

Charlotte followed him into his private quarters. The living room was a surprise, with large, colorful oil paintings of Western landscapes hanging on the walls, and Native artifacts displayed in glass cabinets.

The furniture was elegant, feminine. It crossed her mind that Art Langley might once have had a wife. Charlotte wondered how he'd feel about getting another one. She sat down across him in a padded, bowlegged chair and said, "I have a business proposition for you."

Chapter Seventeen

Thomas sat at the kitchen table and stared at the letter that had arrived from Michigan. He recognized his mother's handwriting on the envelope. He'd been sitting there, hat propped on his head, mud caked on his boots, his coat still buttoned up, ever since he returned from taking Charlotte back into town.

All his life, he'd wanted to know.

And now he was afraid to open the letter.

A horse cantered up outside, hoof beats drumming. It was becoming quite a traffic junction, his isolated homestead. Thomas felt his stomach clench as he waited for someone to burst in through the door with some further calamity. Instead, he heard a polite, calm knock.

"Mr. Greenwood?"

He recognized the new, masculine voice of Gus Junior. "Come in."

Gus Junior entered. He was starting to look

quite grown-up. Short and squat like his father, his shoulders had padded out and his arms thickened with muscle.

"Mr. Langley sent this for you. Says it's very urgent." Gus Junior handed him a folded piece of paper.

Thomas took it. The letter was not sealed. It appeared to be a page hastily torn from a pad of hotel receipts. He unfolded the paper, scanned the few words scrawled on it and lifted his gaze to Gus Junior. "Did you read it?"

A smile drifted across the boy's face, rueful and amused at the same time. "I'm a newspaper man. Can't let a scoop pass by."

"Will you print it?"

Gus Junior hesitated. His expression softened in an oddly understanding look for someone so young. "I'll only print it if you turn up. Otherwise I'll just write up something about the wedding. Mr. Langley is inviting everyone in town for a reception at the hotel. The newspaper is supposed to comment on what kind of dresses the ladies wear and what kind of food is served. And to say that the bride looked radiant."

Thomas nodded. His mind filled with the image of Charlotte, how she had looked when she stood beside him on the porch of the Imperial Hotel, her body trembling with fear, her eyes wide with terror as she spoke her wedding vows in front of the preacher. She'd been beautiful then. The most beautiful thing he'd ever seen.

He gave Gus Junior a drink of water, helped the boy to draw a bucketful of water from the well for his mustang. Such a beautiful horse, Thomas thought as he watched the animal bend its head and drink. Charlotte would like something similar. It would be good for her to have a horse of her own.

When the thud of hooves had faded after the departing messenger, Thomas sat back down at the table. His eyes lingered on Art Langley's note.

Charlotte Fairfax needs a husband. I've agreed to a marriage of convenience. Strictly a business arrangement. If you want to claim your bride, come to the church at one o'clock tomorrow afternoon.

In his mind, Thomas listed every objection.

Charlotte was all wrong. Small and fragile and unused to hard work.

No, his heart shouted. *She is learning.* She'd made friends with the chickens. She'd even milked the cow. She had helped him tend the crops. She could produce edible meals. No one was born to a role in life. Everyone had to learn and adapt.

Charlotte would suffocate in the heat. She'd

get lonely and bored. She'd grow old before her time with hard toil and childbirth. She'd lose her health and her will to live, and die of exhaustion.

No reason for it to happen, his heart protested. The doc's wife was small, and she liked living in an isolated desert town. Dottie Timmerman had borne six children and it had caused her no harm. She'd worked hard all her life, not just as a mother, but as a nurse. During the boomtown days, she'd helped the doc set broken bones and take out bullets and patch up bodies bloodied in saloon fights and mine accidents.

Charlotte would be dissatisfied with him. He'd have no home to offer her. He'd have to take to the road, find a job. She'd learn to hate him. Hate was his destiny. He was born from hate and would carry the burden of it until he died.

Thomas found no strength in his heart to dispute the final argument. He reached for the letter on the table. He weighed the envelope in his hand, lifted it to his face. He recognized the scent of rose water, preserved in the thick paper, even after a week in the mail satchel. His heart seemed to cease beating as he tore open the flap.

There were two sheets, crammed with writing. The first page had a greeting on top.

Dear Thomas

Was it the first time those words had been addressed to him? His eyes skimmed the lines of text. Family news. Weddings. Children born. It was signed off "Your mother Evelyn."

The second sheet had no greeting. The ink was faded, as if the words had been written long ago. He guessed his mother had written the first page, had shown it to her husband and then slipped the second page in before sealing the envelope.

Your father was from Russia. His name was Grigory. I never knew his last name. He came one day, asked to sleep in the barn. He stayed for two weeks, working in the fields against his keep. Then he moved on. I told him to leave. I was too afraid to let him stay.

You were born nine months later. When your father returned from the goldfields you were already knee-high. It was clear that you couldn't be his son. Not just the timing, but the way you looked. We are both small, with dark hair and brown eyes. You were big for your age even then, and you had fair hair and blue eyes. When you got older, your eyes became more gray than blue.

My husband was furious to find you in the house. I feared for my life. So I lied. I lied that I had been taken by force one night by the Russian after he got drunk and caught me on my way across the yard in the darkness. I said that was the reason he'd gone away, for fear of being *hanged* for his crime.

I had not allowed for my husband's dark, brooding temper. He would not let the matter be. He spoke to people who'd known Grigory, got them to describe him in detail, and he went off looking for him. He was away for two months. When he came back, he seemed calmer, and he let me keep you.

I believe he killed your father. Because I was a coward, too afraid to tell the truth, an innocent man was killed. The man I loved. For I loved your father. I loved him from the moment I first saw him. And he died because of me.

The guilt has consumed me ever since. I love you, Thomas, my son, my child. I know that I've never shown you my love. Partly it is because I could never look at you without being reminded of my guilt. Partly it is because I was afraid of my husband's rage if I showed you any affection.

He knew, Thomas. He knew that I'd lied. And yet he took his revenge out on Grigory. He wanted to punish me, not just for my adultery, but for the feelings I had for another man. He might have wielded the knife, but I was the murderer. I killed your father by loving him and then not admitting to the truth.

I hope that one day you will forgive me.

I hope that one day you will be loved.

For you deserve so much love, Thomas. You deserve all the love I left you without by making you into an outcast in our family. For my own protection I pretended that you were an unwanted child, born of violence and hatred, not a true child of mine, not a true brother to your brothers, worthy of being loved.

But you are, Thomas. You are worthy of being loved.

And I love you, my son. I love you more than I can put into words.

There was no signature. The paper had two small dark circles on it Thomas took as marks from teardrops. He blinked, added a few similar marks of his own. He folded the faded letter, went to the bookshelf in the corner of the room and slipped the single sheet inside his Bible.

A child had to take what was given to him.

A grown man could make his own decisions.

If he had the courage, he could choose to love.

And hope and pray that he'd be loved in return.

* * *

A crowd had gathered outside the church. Orphans were kicking pebbles along the dusty ground. Adults stood talking in clusters. Charlotte avoided meeting anyone's eyes as she walked past them on Art Langley's arm. He'd come by the schoolhouse to fetch her. She wore what she always wore out in public on important occasions—her green skirt and her white blouse, but today both were freshly laundered.

Someone had decorated the church with colored streamers. Doc Timmerman, tall and elegant in a gray suit, sat in the front pew beside his wife. Dottie wore a lemon yellow gown and a straw hat which appeared to have a bird's nest complete with eggs perched upon it.

Behind the altar, Reverend Eldridge was leafing through the parish register and looking puzzled. When he saw her approach with Art, the preacher stepped forward. Unlike her first wedding, when he'd worn denim trousers, he was dressed all in black. Or mostly in black, for his feet were encased in thick red socks. Charlotte peeked past him. She could see no sign of the missing shoes.

"Would you like to invite the people inside?" Art asked her.

She shook her head. "I'd rather keep it private while we speak our vows." She gestured at

Dottie and her husband. "Expect, of course, the witnesses."

The preacher picked up his prayer book and adjusted his spectacles. They took their positions, and the preacher launched into a long sermon in a sonorous voice. How different her first wedding had been! She'd been full of fear, facing an unknown future with a stranger. Now a single-minded purpose ruled her thoughts.

Reverend Eldridge lowered his book. He studied her, a benign smile on his wrinkled face. "You remind me of another bride I wedded recently." Appearing flustered, he searched for something in his pockets. "I seem to have lost the card with your details."

Art Langley cleared his throat. "My mistake. I forgot to bring the card." He leaned closer to the reverend. "Would you have a blank one?"

The preacher shuffled in his red socks around the altar, searched beneath cloth and came back with a blank card. He lifted it to Art's face and ran his finger along the empty lines. "You write the bride's name here, and the groom's name here."

Art glanced back at the Timmermans. "Anyone have a pencil?"

A knot formed in Charlotte's stomach. She recalled observing her father deal with business associates. Those kind of delaying tactics usually meant one intended to renegotiate the terms.

Art strode off to the entrance. "Anyone have a pencil?"

Gentlemen searched in their pockets. Ladies peered into their reticules. Eventually, Timothy Perkins was dispatched to fetch one from Gus Osborn at the mercantile. Gus had refused to leave the telegraph unmanned during office hours. Only one or two telegrams came to Gold Crossing each week, but he took his duties seriously.

Timothy returned with a pencil. Art took his time filling in the card.

The reverend took the completed card and smiled at Charlotte. "You resemble another bride I wedded recently." He studied the card. "Do you, Arthur Langley—"

Art burst into a racking cough. "It's the dust," he wheezed. "I need air." He hurried back to the entrance, coughed looked around and coughed again. Finally he came back. There was a worried frown on his face.

Reverend Eldridge picked up the card. "Do you, Arthur Langley…" His face crumpled, making him look like a distraught child. "Did I already ask…?" Appearing lost, he darted his gaze between the few occupants of the small church, and then he fastened his attention on the entrance.

"Come in," he called out, waving a hand. "Don't be shy."

Charlotte turned. A big blond man stood framed in the sunlight, hat in his hand, the Sunday suit with a mended sleeve straining across his wide shoulders. He set into motion with slow, deliberate steps.

Behind him, the crowd filed in and settled into the pews. Art Langley stepped out of the way. Thomas handed his hat to Doc Timmerman and took his place beside Charlotte. Like a skilled pickpocket, Art swiped one card from the preacher's fingers and slipped another one in its place.

The reverend smiled. "You remind me of another couple I married recently." He lifted up the card, peered at it through his spectacles and said, "Do you, Thomas Greenwood, take this woman, Charlotte Fairfax, to be your lawfully wedded wife?"

"I do."

"But what about the other bride?" she whispered to Thomas.

He looked startled. "What other bride?"

"Gus Junior said you sent for another mail-order bride."

His gray eyes narrowed, then sparkled with amusement. "You should know better than to believe everything you read in that scandal sheet." He leaned closer to her. "I sent for your sister."

"My sister? Oh, Thomas." She flung her arms around his neck.

"Not yet," the reverend said. "I must ask you first. Do you, Charlotte Fairfax, take this man, Thomas Greenwood, to be your lawfully wedded husband?"

Not releasing her hold around his neck, Charlotte smiled up at Thomas. "I do."

"You may kiss the bride."

Strong arms closed around her. Then Thomas dipped his blond head and his warm, hungry lips settled over hers. It seemed forever ago that he had kissed her, when she first arrived in his valley. That kiss had been only a light touching of their lips. Now he kept the kiss going, his mouth slanting across hers, lips parted, the heat of his mouth burning against hers, the pressure of it causing an odd tingling sensation low in her belly.

It felt so right. It felt like coming home.

When Thomas lifted his head again, Charlotte was standing on tiptoe, her hands on his shoulders, her face tipped up toward him. He spoke softly, his eyes searching hers.

"I'll lose the farm. I can't offer you a home. It will be a hard life with me." His hands slid down to her waist, eased her closer against him again. "But I promise to love you."

At first, Charlotte could only focus on the happiness that filled her as she heard his promise to love her. Then the rest of what he had said penetrated her mind.

"Lose your farm?" she said with a frown. "What on earth are you talking about?"

"You've seen the notices. I borrowed money from the bank against the crops but the harvest is ruined. I can't pay back the mortgage. The bank will foreclose."

She eased out of his embrace and clasped her hands together in front of her, scowling at him with a mix of frustration and triumph. "Thomas, why do you think Cousin Gareth tried to force me into marriage? Because he is madly in love with me?" She made a disparaging sound to dismiss the suggestion. "Because I have lots of money and he wants it. But he can't have it, because now it's yours."

Even if she hadn't loved Thomas, it would have been worth marrying him for the expression of utter incredulity that now flashed across his features. His lips moved. Then he said in a hoarse voice, "There aren't any more secrets you've forgotten to tell me, are there?"

"No, Thomas. I think that was the last. But there's work for us to do." She ticked with her fingers. "We must take a train to San Francisco. Engage a lawyer and prove that I'm not dead. Get the family lawyer in Boston to transfer us some money. Employ detectives to find Miranda. She

is probably in jail. And we have to send money
for Annabel to travel out to Gold Crossing."

Gus Junior burst in. "Telegram for you."

Charlotte took the sheet. It was another Maude
Greenwood message, so it had to be from Miranda or Annabel. She unfolded the slip and read
the text out loud. *"'Money arrived from Thomas
Greenwood. Miranda already on her way so I
will travel. See you soon. Annabel.'"*

She launched into his arms again. "Oh,
Thomas, I do love you."

Behind her, the bemused preacher said, "You
may kiss the bride."

The cart rattled through the desert in the late-
afternoon sunshine. Charlotte curled her hands
around the wooden bench to control the bouncing. A sparrow darted in the scrub, but by now
she'd learned the birds didn't sing during the day,
only at dawn and dusk.

She turned to her husband. Art Langley had
offered them a free night at the Imperial Hotel as
a wedding present but she had told Thomas she
wanted to go home. She wanted to re-create the
evening of their first wedding, but this time she
would do everything right.

"Do you notice I'm wearing a plain cotton
dress?" she asked.

Before they set off after the reception at the

Imperial Hotel, she'd gone back to the school-house to change into the olive green four-dollar dress she had bought at the mercantile.

Thomas glanced at her. "You look lovely in anything."

"Just you wait and see," Charlotte muttered under her breath.

When at the end of the journey Thomas took a sharp left and urged Trooper into a canter to clear the brow of the hill, Charlotte craned her neck to take in the view that spread in front of her.

"What a pretty valley!" she cried out. "And you have a lake!"

Thomas shot her a frowning glance, as if he couldn't quite figure out her remarks. Charlotte tried not to smile. He'd soon catch on.

When the cart rolled to a halt in the small clearing at the top of the path, she waited for Thomas to apply the brake and dismount. He circled the cart and reached up with his arms to lift her down. Just like before, Charlotte rested her hands on his shoulders for support, but this time she didn't release her hold when her feet touched the ground.

She tipped her face up toward him. "You are supposed to kiss me now."

Thomas smiled down at her, lowered his head and covered her mouth with his. Slowly, he deepened the kiss, his lips sliding over hers, tasting, tempting. His arms came around her, anchoring her to his chest. On and on the kiss went, and once again Charlotte felt that strange coil of excitement low in her belly.

"My," she whispered when Thomas lifted his head. "That certainly was an improvement."

Thomas raised his eyebrows in question. She gave him a little shove. "You should charge ahead now, as if the devil is chasing at your heels. I'll follow."

With a baffled shake of his head, Thomas turned on a sturdy boot heel and strode down the path toward the cabin. Charlotte suppressed a grin as she hurried after him. Her normally clever husband appeared a bit slow-witted today, but it was understandable. A man did not think clearly on his wedding day.

He was waiting for her by the porch steps. The sun was sinking below the hills and a cool breeze blew in from the lake. Leaves rustled in the tall cottonwoods. The pair of blue jays she remembered from that first day hopped around on the ground, screeching and flapping their wings.

"Now you have to show me the cabin," she prompted him.

Thomas led the way and threw the door open. Charlotte clattered up the steps and entered the cabin, sweeping her gaze around the familiar room, the kitchen cabinets, the big window at the back, the floor where the setting sun threw dappled shadows on the smooth timber boards.

"What a beautiful home." She strolled over to the hand-carved love seats, ran her fingertips over the scalloped edge of the back of one. "It must take a lot of skill to make something like this."

She spun around and rushed up to the stove. "And a brand-new cookstove, with an oven compartment. How wonderful." She gave the green enamel front a pat with her hand. "I'm going to call it Vertie. It's for *vert*, the French word for green."

Finally, Thomas was catching on. The humor she loved so much sparked in his eyes.

"I'd best go and see to the animals," he said. "You can fetch water and make coffee."

She beamed him a smile. "I was just going to suggest the same. You might also like to fetch my bag from the wagon and put it in the bedroom."

She waited for Thomas to go, and then she picked up the steel bucket from the kitchen counter and set off toward the well behind the cabin.

Outside, rodents rustled in the grass, and the distant splash of a beaver tail came from the creek. Frogs croaked in a pond, and the inquisitive pair of blue jays chased after her. *Nature's rush hour,* Charlotte thought with a contented sigh as she hung the bucket on the well spigot.

Caution slowing her motions, she cranked the pump handle and achieved a steady flow of water that hardly splashed at all. She gave a tiny shriek, just in case Thomas was expecting it. As if on cue, he charged out of the woods.

He gave her a long glance full of regret. "I was looking forward to seeing you in a soaked dress and your hair hanging all disheveled."

"There are limits to the lengths one is prepared to go for authenticity," she said primly, and handed him the bucket. "You carry this. I'll go and change into my nightgown in the privacy of the bedroom."

Her heartbeat quickened as she darted back up the path toward the cabin. She wanted to give Thomas a perfect evening, a perfect wedding night, but how could one make something perfect when it was something one had never done before?

In the light of the setting sun that slanted into the bedroom, Charlotte opened the leather traveling bag Thomas had fetched from the wagon. She took out a nightgown of old silk and lace, the color of faded roses, hand embroidered with tiny seed pearls around the neckline.

It was the most beautiful garment she had ever seen, and of all people it had been Mrs. Duckworth who'd given it to her. On the morning of the wedding, the thin, sour-looking widow had knocked on the schoolhouse door with a parcel in her hands.

I'll never have an occasion to wear this again, she'd said with a touch of sadness. *But I'd like to see it put to use.* She had lowered her voice and went on, a blush heating her cheeks. *It has seen many happy nights. I hope it will see some more.*

With a wistful thought of how she had misjudged the lonely widow, Charlotte slipped out of her green cotton dress and into the silk nightgown. For a second, she stood still and took a deep breath, one hand pressed to her chest. Then she gathered her courage, coaxed her feet into motion and returned to the parlor.

Thomas was seated at the table. She could feel his eyes on her, bold and possessive and perhaps a little impatient. "You look..." He paused, searching for the right words.

"Like a bride on her wedding night?" Charlotte supplied.

Thomas nodded. For another minute, he simply stared at her. Then he started, like an actor remembering his lines. "Are you hungry?" he asked. "Would you like supper?"

"No," she said. "I'll make coffee."

She went to the kitchen counter and bustled about, measuring the coffee, filling the pot with water, lighting the stove. Through it all, she could feel Thomas watching her, and a new seductiveness entered her movements. She could never have imagined she possessed such boldness.

Thomas didn't mention eating again, although that last time he had set out bread and cheese. Neither did he offer to give her the shawl his mother had made. Charlotte knew he was saving his gift until morning, the way it should have been.

"See?" she told him when the coffee was brewing. "Not a grain scattered on the ground." She sat down opposite him. "Now we should talk and get to know each other while the water is boiling."

Thomas contemplated her. "I already know everything I need to know, but there is something I'm curious about. You said you want to go to San Francisco and engage a lawyer to draw money from your inheritance. How are you going to claim your fortune if everyone thinks you're dead? You can't telegraph your sisters to confirm who you are because you don't know where they are right now. Isn't it best to wait until they get here?"

"No," Charlotte said firmly. "I want some money quickly, in case Miranda and Annabel are in trouble and I need to bail them out. And we'll need money to pay back the mortgage on your farm."

She got up to check on the coffee and spoke from the stove. "And it won't be a problem to prove who I am. I told you, Papa was a sea captain, and he often brought business associates to Merlin's Leap. Shipping agents, ship owners, sailors, merchants. San Francisco has a big seafaring community. We'll be able to find someone who recognizes me and can confirm my identity. And I had another meeting with Mr. Wakefield before he left town. He has signed an affidavit to confirm that the woman buried at Merlin's Leap is his fiancée, Maude Jackson, and that there was a mix-up with our identities because we had exchanged gifts."

Using a cloth to protect her hands from the heat, Charlotte picked up the coffeepot, carried it to the table and poured into the cups waiting there. Before she lowered the pot, she slid a slate pot holder beneath it to protect the tabletop.

Thomas took a sip. "Good coffee. Just right."

Charlotte nodded, took a mouthful. It was perfect.

Outside, the darkness was thickening. Thomas got to his feet. "I'll light the lamps. And I'll have to go out again, to check on the animals."

Charlotte watched as he lit two lamps, a storm lantern for him to carry when he went out to take care of the chores, and an oil lamp to leave burning on the parlor table. Nerves twisted in her belly. She hated to waste such good coffee, but her throat seemed to have closed up.

"I'll get into bed and wait for you." Her voice revealed her tension.

Thomas gave her a long look, then merely nodded and turned to go. She noticed that he too had left most of his coffee. At the door Thomas turned back. "It will be all right, Charlotte," he said. "There's no need to be nervous."

But nervous she was. She carried the lamp through to the bedroom with unsteady hands and settled in the big feather bed beneath the patchwork quilt. As an afterthought, she jumped out again and crouched to peer beneath the bed where Thomas usually stored the bundle board. There was no sign of the wooden divider. A thought crossed Charlotte's mind: Thomas had probably burned it.

She slipped back under the covers. It seemed only seconds had passed when she heard footsteps thudding up the porch steps, and then their trail traversed the parlor, and Thomas entered, his presence filling the room.

He didn't say anything, merely ran his heated gaze over her reclining shape beneath the covers. And then he began to undress. One by one, he shed his articles of clothing. Charlotte saw lamplight play on the magnificent lines of his chest and shoulders, shadows leaping and dancing as his muscles flexed with the movements.

He bent to slide the long johns down his legs,

and she admired the powerful arch of his back, the lean line of his waist. Straightening, he tossed the undergarment on the back of the chair and turned to face her, fully naked, not a stitch on him.

"I thought you wear pajama bottoms," she said on an intake of breath.

"I lied. I sleep naked, but I didn't want to offend your delicate sensibilities."

With the urgency of purpose in his step, he strode up to the bed and lifted the edge of the patchwork quilt. "But now," he said in a husky murmur, "offending your delicate sensibilities is my duty as your husband." And with that, he jumped into bed and bundled her into his arms.

Love welled up in Charlotte as she nestled against his warmth. He always knew how to protect her, how to reassure her, and now he was using humor to ease her anxieties.

A few moments later, she felt the pressure of his arms ease around her as Thomas drew their bodies apart. "Shall we take this off you?" he said, tugging at her nightgown. "It would be a shame to ruin it."

Not waiting for a reply, Thomas slid one hand along her body, down to her knees, and gathered the flimsy silk in his fingers. Slowly, he edged the garment upward along her body and over her head. Charlotte helped, lifting her hips, raising her shoulders, holding her arms high.

Thomas let the nightgown drop to the floor by the bedside. "There," he said. "That's better." Bracing his weight on one elbow, he pulled the patchwork quilt aside and studied her. Charlotte could see his eyes flickering over her, and there was heat in his gaze—heat and hunger and longing.

"It's all right," she told him. "I'm not scared. You can do anything you want."

Thomas laid his hand flat on her belly and held it there. He had big hands, and the weight of that simple touch reminded her of his strength.

"I want to make a baby," he said. "That's what I want."

For a while, they lay in silence, his hand heavy on her belly. Outside, the wind rustled in the trees. An owl hooted in the darkness. One of the windows stood ajar, and through it came the faint scent of flowers from the lakeshore.

Thomas spoke quietly. "I had a letter from my mother. She told me about my father. He was that big fair-haired drifter I mentioned before, but he didn't rape her. She loved him. But she felt guilty about betraying her husband, so she lied about it."

Charlotte stared up at him. "How could she—"

Thomas shook his head to silence her questions. "We'll talk more about it some other time. You can read my mother's letter. But tonight is not about the past. Tonight is about you and me, and the future."

His eyes held hers. "I only mentioned it because I wanted you to know before we might make a baby that I wasn't born of violence. I was born of love, just as any child of ours will be."

Charlotte touched his cheek with her fingertips, the way she had done on the day they first met. "I'm glad you found out the truth," she told him. "But even if you had been born of violence, it is clear to me there is no cruelty in you. Whatever hardships you may have suffered while you were growing up, they didn't poison your mind. They did the opposite. No man could be gentler or kinder. You'll make a wonderful father to any child we may have."

Thomas accepted her comment with a wordless nod. His hand on her belly began to move around in a slow, lazy circle.

Charlotte lay languid on the soft feather mattress. All her senses seemed heightened. She could feel the slight abrasion from the callused skin on Thomas's palm, could feel the quivering in his muscles and knew he was restraining himself, forcing himself not to hurry, to give her time.

Little by little, his hand edged up to her breast, cupping it gently. "It fits perfectly," he said, cradling the weight in his palm. His thumb brushed across the nipple and Charlotte gave a moan of pleasure.

"You like that?" Thomas said.

"Yes. Oh, yes."

He repeated the caress, then let his hand slide downward, below her belly. Charlotte made another frantic, inarticulate sound and arched her back on the bed.

"Yes, oh, yes."

A fire burned within her now. New, daunting sensations caught her and swept her along with them, like the ocean waves at Merlin's Leap. Thomas leaned over her and kissed her, a deep, probing kiss that made the knot in her belly tighten until she thought she could bear it no longer.

He lifted his head and looked into her face.

"Ready to make a baby?"

Her gaze swept along the curve of his shoulder, saw the healing scar there, and the puckered ridge where the bullet had skimmed his arm, and a new curiosity sparked in her.

"Can I touch you, the way you touch me?"

Thomas smiled. He rolled onto his back and crossed his forearms beneath his head. "You can touch me anywhere you like."

A little shy now, Charlotte rose to a kneeling position on the bed and studied his body in the soft glow of the lamplight.

"Have you always been so big and strong?" she asked.

"I was big even as a boy, but I only developed the strength when I worked the mines, and then on the farm. Hard labor makes muscles grow."

Tentatively, she ran her hand over the padded contours of his chest. When she brushed past a flat brown nipple, Thomas flinched, so she did it again. "I love your size and strength, because you use it to protect those who are vulnerable."

"And I love your courage and determination." He reached out for her, tucked her into the curve of his body and rolled over, until he lay above her, his weight braced on his elbows, his legs sliding between hers. "And now you need to show some of that courage and determination, because I expect this will hurt."

"You bore a knife wound and a bullet without complaint."

There was a rueful tone to his voice. "I hope this won't be quite as bad."

He lined his body with hers and slowly entered her. It *did* hurt. Charlotte gasped with the pain. Thomas kissed her—deep, comforting kisses—and between the kisses he whispered soothing words to her while his powerful body moved above her with the gentleness that was so much a part of him.

And then the pain eased, and in its place came

a new sensation, like a temptation that called for something more. Charlotte moved with him, her hands clutching his shoulders, seeking to meet the rhythm of his thrusts.

Would it always be like this? This amazing sense of togetherness, of discovery, of belonging? Tension gathered deep inside her, and then it broke into an avalanche of pleasure. She wrapped her legs around Thomas's waist and clung tight, holding him close, holding him to her, and felt the same waves of release roll through his body that had just buffeted her own.

As Thomas sank beside her, she could hear his harsh breathing, could feel the trembling in his limbs, and realized they mirrored her own. He hauled her into his arms and held her close, her head tucked in the crook of his neck where she could feel the frantic thrumming of his pulse.

Later, when their heated bodies had cooled and their swift heartbeats calmed, Thomas pushed up on one elbow and looked into her face. "Welcome home, Mrs. Greenwood," he said. "I forgot to say that when I lifted you down from the cart." His eyes searched hers. "I love you, and now that you truly belong to me, I trust you will never try to leave me again."

Thomas yawned and stretched his limbs on the big four-poster bed at the Palace Hotel in San

Francisco. Beside him, a breakfast tray from the room service sat upon a marble-topped nightstand. A streetcar clattered by outside. Dawn light rimmed the thick curtains that blocked out the view over the city.

Charlotte was already up, sitting on a plush velvet sofa. A cream satin nightgown hugged her feminine curves. She adjusted his mother's shawl on her shoulders and leaned down to pick up another document from the low table in front of her. Turning over the page, she studied the text in the light of the electric lamp on a stand beside her.

"Come back to bed," Thomas called out to her.

His wife glanced over at him and smiled. "In a bit."

His whole body tingled with love and contentment. He couldn't decide which part of marriage he liked the best. To sleep beside his wife all night, with her curled up against him, just as she had on their first night together, when he had tried to stay awake to enjoy every moment of it. Or to join their bodies in the act of love and bring pleasure to each other, with greedy touches and fevered kisses as their passion rose. Or to simply watch her in idle moments, just as this.

To talk. To share. To cherish.

To love and be loved.

Charlotte rose and walked over to him, her

steps soundless on the thick carpet, the satin gown rippling against her slender frame. Thomas let desire flood over him. He'd been right to believe God had been just in his creation, giving men and women an equal capacity to enjoy the physical side of marriage. His fragile wife had proved anything but fragile when it came to satisfying his needs and her own.

"I need you to sign this." She held out a parchment deed and a pen.

Thomas scooted up on the bed. "Is it important to you?"

"It is."

He nodded, took the document that would transfer his land into their joint names. Warmth filled him at the thought that despite all her wealth it mattered to Charlotte that they would share the ownership of his valley. At first, he'd been alarmed to find out he'd married a rich woman. He'd worried she might want him to go and live in some fancy mansion in the East

His relief had been great when he learned that the only home she wanted was his sheltered valley. His fears allayed, he had learned there were benefits to having money. Room service and satin nightgowns. Lavender soap and bathtubs big enough for two. Generators ordered from Edison Machine Works.

They had engaged Pinkerton detectives to

track down Charlotte's sisters. So far, there had been no news, but it was early days. He could tell Charlotte was worried. He loved to hear her reminiscing about the feisty Miranda and the young, sensitive Annabel. His sisters-in-law. Thomas looked forward to welcoming them, having a warm, loving family, something he'd missed all his life.

He glanced at the deed in his hand. There was a blank line after the description to identify the parcel of land. He looked up at his wife. "It says nothing where the name should be." Charlotte had told him she wanted to name the place. He'd always just called it "The Valley" or "The Farm." Others might say "Greenwood's place."

"Sign the document first," she told him.

He carefully wrote out his name.

"Aren't you going to read it first?" his wife asked.

Thomas smiled, a little rueful. "I trust you'll not lie to me again, ever. You learned your lesson the hard way. I hope you learned it well."

"I did," she said, a little shamefaced. And rightly so.

He handed the deed back to her. "What's the name?"

She lifted the document to her face and blew on it to dry the ink, lips pursed into a circle that made him want to reach up and kiss her. Satisfied that his signature wouldn't smudge, Charlotte clutched the deed to her breast, raised her eyes to him and said, "Paradise. The name of our valley is Paradise."

* * * * *

If you enjoyed this story, make sure you check out these short, sexy reads from Tatiana March

*THE VIRGIN'S DEBT
SUBMIT TO THE WARRIOR
SURRENDER TO THE KNIGHT
THE DRIFTER'S BRIDE*

MILLS & BOON®

HISTORICAL

AWAKEN THE ROMANCE OF THE PAST

0317/04

MILLS & BOON®

EXCLUSIVE EXTRACT

The Earl of Penford knows his passion for Lorene
Summerfield is scandalous, but when he's accused of
her husband's murder, he must clear his name—and
win her hand!

Read on for a sneak preview of
BOUND BY THEIR SECRET PASSION

Her old romantic dreams burst forth. Why hold back?
Dell's kiss was even more than she could have imagined.
Why not give herself to it?

She pulled off her bonnet and threw her arms around
his neck, answering the press of his lips with eagerness.
He urged her mouth open and she readily complied,
surprised and delighted that his warm tongue touched
hers.

He tasted wonderful.

She plunged her fingers into his hair, loving its soft-
ness and its curls. She liked his hair best when it looked
tousled by a breeze. Or mussed by her hands.

He pressed her body against his and the thrill intensified. How marvelous to feel his muscles, so firm against
her. And more. One hand slid down from his hair to his
arm to his hip. How wanton was that?

But she was a widow, was she not? Was not everyone
telling her she had license to do as she pleased? It pleased
her to touch him. Although she was not quite brazen

enough to touch that hard part of him that thrilled her most of all.

'Lorene,' he groaned as his hands pressed against her derriere, intensifying the sensations in all sorts of ways. 'We should stop.'

She did not want to stop. 'Why?' She kissed his neck. 'I am a widow. Are not widows permitted?'

'Do not tempt me,' he said, though his hands caressed her.

She moved away, just enough that he could see her face. 'If you do not want this, then, yes, we should stop, but I do desire it, Dell.'

For a long time, she realized. Since she first met him. He was the man she had dreamed about in her youth, a good man, kind, honorable, handsome. But something more, something that made her want to bed him.

Don't miss
BOUND BY THEIR SECRET PASSION
By Diane Gaston

Available April 2017
www.millsandboon.co.uk

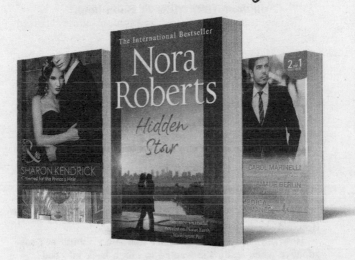

MILLS & BOON®

Congratulations
Carol Marinelli
on your 100th Mills & Boon book!

Read on for an exclusive extract

How did she walk away? Lydia wondered.

How did she go over and kiss that sulky mouth and say goodbye when really she wanted to climb back into bed?

But rather than reveal her thoughts she flicked that internal default switch which had been permanently set to 'polite'.

'Thank you so much for last night.'

'I haven't finished being your tour guide yet.'

He stretched out his arm and held out his hand but Lydia didn't go over. She did not want to let in hope, so she just stood there as Raul spoke.

'It would be remiss of me to let you go home without seeing Venice as it should be seen.'

'Venice?'

'I'm heading there today. Why don't you come with me? Fly home tomorrow instead.'

There was another night between now and then, and Lydia knew that even while he offered her an extension he made it clear there was a cut-off.

Time added on for good behaviour.

And Raul's version of 'good behaviour' was that there would